SEER

Lola Docksey

Front cover artwork by Amanda Lindupp of
Sacred Path Art
etsy.com/uk/shop/sacredpathart

The historians among you may observe that the Norse raven (or eagle) marking each new chapter has nothing to do with the Oseberg ship.

This raven was a fibula found in Denmark, dating from the early ninth century. It was also used as the logo of the business I ran with my husband, Nick Docksey, and it is for him that I put it here.

Without Nick's encouragement and absolute belief in me I would never have started these books. Tragically, he died of cancer before the first was completed.

He was the best, the wisest and bravest man I have ever known. A warrior in the truest sense.

These books are for him.

You will find Nick (and a few of his friends) between these pages. He always wanted to be a Saxon warlord. I'm glad I could make that happen for him, if only in fiction.

This book, and all that follow, are for you, my darling man. Thanks for giving me such a beautiful life.

Love always.

SVALA

KINGDOM OF AGDER. September 771AD.

Svala paused a moment to catch her breath, leaning on a heavy, wooden staff. It was elaborately carved with runes and sigils and, together with the blue, woolen cloak on the ground beside her, identified her as a Völva, a practitioner of sorcery and prophecy. The sun was bright, and although the autumn air had seemed chill when Svala left home, the long climb up the mountainside warmed her muscles so she now felt uncomfortably hot. She put down her willow basket and dabbed at her face with the hem of her apron.

Svala ran a critical eye over the contents of the basket.

She had harvested plenty of fruits, herbs and berries today. There was no shame in turning back now, she told herself. Besides, she could always come again tomorrow if more was needed. She placed a hand on her swollen belly, smiling at the thought of the little life growing within. The moon was just starting to wane in its cycle – by the time it reached fullness again her child would be born.

She turned to look back down the path to where her five-year-old daughter, Kadlin, was loudly battling imaginary foes with a large stick. Svala shook her head and smiled. Kadlin's clothes were always dirty within moments of being worn. Her face, with its big, blue eyes and small, snub nose, was more often streaked with dirt than not. Her beautiful, tawny hair resembled a bird's nest by the end of each day, tangled with twigs, feathers, and other accumulated detritus. The child was bright and studied hard – having surpassed even her mother's learning at such a young age – yet there was a wildness in Kadlin that Svala feared. The girl had a raw talent for the occult, but her passion was for more adventurous pursuits.

'Kadlin,' Svala called. The girl dropped her stick and obediently ran to her mother's side. 'What are these?' Svala pointed at a clump of low shrubs bearing scarlet berries.

'Cowberries,' Kadlin replied confidently, 'for pissing pains.'

Svala bent down and retrieved an apple from her basket. 'And this?'

'An apple!' The child giggled at such a simple question. She grabbed the fruit from her mother's hand and took a bite, grinning gratefully as her stomach growled. Svala began collecting the cowberries while her daughter ate. Just these last few and then they would return home.

The pain hit without warning. It was deep and sharp, and Svala was shocked by its intensity. She cried out, dropping her staff and knocking over the basket as she fell to her knees. Red berries bounced and scattered before her.

'Mamma!' Kadlin watched, terrified, as her mother's skirts bloomed with blood. Svala wanted to comfort her, but the overwhelming pain robbed her of speech. Rolling onto her back, she fumbled her skirts up to her thighs and spread her knees wide. The baby was coming, and its passage into this world was heralded by a tide of blood. A scream was torn from Svala's throat as the earth reddened beneath her. She felt Kadlin grab her hand and heard the frightened girl sob. *Frigga,* Svala prayed, *help me!* She had attended enough births to know that the prayer was wasted. There were tears on her cheeks as she forced herself to control her breathing.

★

Svala's cries were weaker and less frequent by the time

the first stars appeared in the darkening sky. She was cold now, and glad of the cloak that her daughter had covered her with. Kadlin still crouched beside her, gripping her hand as the light faded. She heard her daughter gasp in fright and felt the small hand slide from hers.

Svala opened her eyes, and her heart froze.

Beneath a tree, not twelve paces from where Svala lay, stood a woman. She was startlingly beautiful, with long, silken hair, and eyes that sparkled despite the shadows. Her fine clothes, richly embroidered with coloured thread, seemed to age and decay from her waist down, becoming mouldering rags by the time the fabric reached her bare feet.

Hel's body – for there was no mistaking the goddess of the dead – was also rotting below her waist. The legs and feet visible as she shuffled slowly toward them were bloated and putrefied. In places, the flesh peeled away from her bones, revealing puffy white maggots which wriggled and fell, leaving a festering trail of decomposition behind her.

Kadlin scrambled for the stick she had abandoned earlier. Trembling, she stood protectively beside her mother, holding the stick with brave determination. Hel chuckled, a sound like an old man's wheezing cough and the wind through autumn leaves.

A cold sweat ran down Svala's spine as she realised her

daughter could also see the apparition. Was the goddess here to claim them both? *Frigga, goddess of hearth and home, All-mother, protector of children, put your arms around my daughter now, I beg you,* she prayed. *Thor, wielder of Mjollnir, defender of Asgard, protector of the weak, stand before my daughter and keep her safe, I implore you.*

As the final pains ripped through her body, Svala heard a rustling voice inside her head. 'Do not fear me, Svala, daughter of Yrsa, daughter of Gudrun. I have no interest in the living.' Hel extended an elegant hand toward her and smiled kindly. 'I ease pain. I end suffering. I care only for the dead.'

Svala gave a grunting roar as the strong arms of the goddess slid beneath her and gently lifted her and her newborn son. She watched as her body slumped on the ground below her, as limp and lifeless as the child she had delivered.

YRSA

Yrsa felt the death of her daughter and grandson as the great wolf, Hati, chased the last of Sól's golden rays from an indigo sky. His mournful howl echoed the cry of her own broken heart as she sensed their passing.

As a Völva, she had never married, but this did not preclude her from bearing children. Her sons had been left with their respective fathers as was the custom, but her daughter, Svala, she raised and trained as one of the Völur. Being a Völva afforded a woman certain privileges; she was highly regarded by everyone from peasants to kings, and her skills and counsel were ever in demand. The Völur commanded power and respect. They were treated with the utmost reverence but were also feared, and this fear inevitably resulted in isolation. A Völva lived alone, outside the main town, unless she were old and skilled enough to take on female apprentices who would live with her throughout their training.

Yrsa had four such apprentices, including her daughter and granddaughter. The others, twenty-one-year-old Aud, and fourteen-year-old Jofrið, accompanied her in silence now as they followed Svala's route up the mountainside. Each of the three wore a blue cloak and carried a wooden staff in one hand and a flaming torch in the other. Yrsa strode ahead, never turning to check if the others still followed. She was a confident, formidable woman with the accumulated wisdom of forty-three years ingrained on her face, but tonight her eyes betrayed the desolation she felt inside, so she kept her hood up and her face forward.

A leader never shows weakness. To lead, you must always be seen to be strong. A leader stands boldly between her people and the enemy. She is their shield. If she gives them cause to doubt the strength of that shield, they will cease to stand behind her.

Yrsa had said these words to Svala a thousand times during her training. Now, as she blinked away unshed tears, she felt their weight.

She sensed Kadlin before she saw her; a wall of grief so thick it seemed impenetrable, so loud, in its silence, that it deafened. Yrsa felt it like a punch, and it momentarily winded her. She stopped and raised her torch. Its light glinted on the inlaid copper spirals of her staff and created shadows in the runes and symbols she had carved into it, making them appear deeper and more pronounced.

'Kadlin?'

The little girl raised her head, squinting in the unaccustomed light. She was shivering with cold and gripped a large stick in one hand like a weapon. Yrsa smiled reassuringly and crouched beside her, taking off her cloak and wrapping it around her frozen granddaughter. Yrsa welcomed the biting pain of the cold, night air as she looked upon her own dead child and smoothed the hair from Svala's face.

'Travel well, daughter,' she murmured. 'Be at peace for you are well loved and will long be remembered.' She looked at the tiny, blue body on the blood-soaked ground between Svala's thighs. A boy. The purple rope of the umbilical cord still twisted its way back inside his mother. Yrsa took a sharp knife from her belt and severed the cord. She picked up the tiny form and held him for a moment, lightly kissing his brow before placing him in his mother's arms.

Jofrið gathered Kadlin to her, crooning to the child in soothing tones as she tried to massage some semblance of warmth back into her little hands and feet. Aud helped Yrsa to lay out Svala's cloak on the earth, and curl both mother and babe upon it as if in sleep. They folded the hood and sides of the cloak over the bodies, and between them managed the slow and careful process of bringing Svala and her children home.

ULFRIK

BRAMSVIK. KINGDOM OF AGDER. May 781AD.
(Ten years later.)

After twelve weeks at sea, Ulfrik Varinsson was glad to finally be back in his hometown of Bramsvik. The last frosts of winter had still been upon them when he and his crew set off to trade in the great marketplace, Birka, on the Baltic coast. Now, the days were longer, and the banks of the rivers they travelled on their return were lush and green. The air was sweet with the fragrance of Spring and the meadows alive with the sounds and colours of new life. Ulfrik wanted nothing more than the comfort of his own hearth and to greet his wife and children, but first he must supervise the unloading of his cargo.

There were only two other boats in the small harbour when they arrived, and Ulfrik managed to secure a decent mooring with easy access for the horses and carts he required to transport his goods. His ship, 'The Ox', was a knarr; a merchant's vessel built for capacity rather than speed. At fifty-four feet she was shorter and slower than a longship, with a wider and deeper hull, and could be operated by a smaller crew. From a business point of view, the trip had been a good one. Ulfrik had not only managed to offload all the merchandise they had set off with but had also turned a handsome profit. The Ox was now riding low beneath the weight of new cargo; furs and leather from the Reindeer People, wool and dyed cloth, amber beads, walrus ivory, axe heads and carved axe handles, and luxury sundries.

There was also the 'other' cargo.

Ulfrik's bowels turned to ice water at the thought of what was hidden in the stern. He closed his eyes a moment, summoning rational thought to chase away the fear that washed over him. It had not been his fault. He had made the best decision he could under the circumstances. The only decision. Jarl Erik would understand.

'Ulfrik!' He flinched as Thorvald One-Eye, the jarl's righthand man, clamped a hand on his shoulder. 'Jarl Erik is pleased to hear of your return,' the man boomed, jovially. 'No-one else gives a shit, but the jarl is pleased. How was Birka? Profitable, I hope?' Thorvald grinned.

The large scar that had robbed him of his right eye, running from his temple to his cheek, pulled at Thorvald's mouth and twisted the smile into a grimace.

'The gods were kind,' Ulfrik replied, 'as is the jarl.'

'Kind? No. He expects a wondrous return on his investment.'

'He will not be disappointed.' Ulfrik forced a smile.

'He anticipates your presence as soon as you've finished unloading. I don't advise you to keep him waiting long. The jarl is keen to discuss the other matter.' The two men exchanged a meaningful look.

Ulfrik nodded, reluctantly. 'I must call on Hilde, first,' he said.

'Not if you wish to continue breathing.' Thorvald warned.

'Perhaps you have not noticed, friend, that Gunnar is not with us,' Ulfrik continued, calmly. 'There was… an incident… at Birka, while we were carrying out the jarl's business. I need to inform Gunnar's widow that her husband died bravely, and with honour, defending his crew mates. She should hear it from me before news reaches her from less compassionate mouths.'

One-Eye frowned. He nodded curtly. 'Be brief.' He stood for a moment, watching the crew of eighteen men and women carry wooden crates, chests, sacks and bundles of furs to the waiting carts that Ulfrik had hired on the dock. His remaining eye spotted one person in particular. 'And our dear Asbjorn? Did he come back 'a man'?'

Ulfrik sighed as he watched the jarl's son pick up a small crate of walrus tusks. Asbjorn was eighteen, still unmarried, and the apple of every young maiden's eye. His clothes were noticeably finer than those of his shipmates, his hair and beard more elaborately braided, and he wore more jewellery than any of the women onboard. 'He's still a peacock,' Ulfrik replied, 'but a hard-working and more well-travelled peacock. Go on. Take him.'

Thorvald laughed aloud and clapped Ulfrik on the back. 'The gods themselves smile to see you safe and well, Asbjorn,' he called. 'Your father is waiting. Come! Leave that to lesser folk.' Asbjorn did not hesitate. He dumped the crate he was carrying into the hands of the nearest crew member and vaulted flamboyantly over the side of the knarr onto the dock. 'It's good to be back, Thorvald,' he said enthusiastically, embracing the older man. 'There is a woman I would see first, though, before I visit my father. It's been a long journey.'

'You mistake me, Lord,' One-Eye responded, respectful yet firm. 'Jarl Erik does not ask. He commands it. Your cock can wait.' Asbjorn scowled. For a moment it seemed that he would argue but he thought better of it. He noticed a skinny, eleven-year old boy struggling to lift a sack onto one of the carts and called out to him. 'Alfgeir! I was just speaking of your sister! Does she know I'm returned?'

'If so, Lord, she would be here,' the young boy replied. 'She has not stopped wailing for you these past two months. Truly, Lord, my parents will be even happier than Ragnfrið to hear you are home! She has petitioned the gods for your safety so many times, and made so many offerings, I think we should have nothing left had you taken much longer.'

Asbjorn grinned. 'Tell her to find me at the Hall.'

Ulfrik watched Thorvald and Asbjorn leave, then climbed back aboard The Ox. He headed for the stern, where he moved aside the cloak he had covered the three barrels with. Reaching down behind them, he felt around until his fingers found a small package the size of his palm, wrapped in cloth. With shaking hands, he tucked the parcel inside his clothing, re-covering the barrels again with the cloak.

'Ingvar!' Ulfrik shouted as he strode back along the deck. Ingvar was the eldest of three children born to him by the Völva, Svala. Their daughter, Kadlin, had been raised and trained by Svala's mother, Yrsa, and was a Völva herself now. Their third child, a boy, was stillborn, and his mother had loved him so much she had journeyed with him to Helheim rather than see him go alone. This is how Yrsa had explained it to him at the time, when she had sent Jofrið, sobbing, to his door with the news in the middle of the night. Ulfrik had married another woman three years later. She was a good woman. A fine woman. She was skilled with a bow, kept a clean home, and had given him two more healthy children. But Ulfrik's heart would always belong to Svala. Ingvar reminded him of her. He had Svala's green eyes and generous smile, her sensible nature and steadfastness. He was eighteen years old – the same age as Asbjorn – yet where Asbjorn was still a pup in so many ways, Ingvar was already a man with a family and responsibilities of his own.

'I need to see Hilde before word gets around,' Ulfrik said to his son. 'She should hear it from me. Find Gunnar's chest and load it on a horse.' Ingvar nodded. He turned to go but Ulfrik caught his arm. 'Jarl Erik wants to see me. It will not go well if I keep him waiting. I know how much you want to get home, but can I leave you to oversee the unloading of the ship?'

'Of course, Father,' Ingvar replied. 'Go.'

Ulfrik lowered his voice. 'The three barrels beneath my cloak.' He gestured toward the stern. 'Magnus knows of them. Have him bring them to the Hall but tell him not to go in until I arrive. He will know why. And son,' he put a hand on Ingvar's shoulder. 'Trust them to no-one else.' Ingvar nodded solemnly.

Ulfrik headed back toward the gangplank, but found his way blocked by a small boy. Alfgeir smiled confidently and drew his scrawny frame up to its full height. 'I have been helping to unload your ship with no thought of reward, Ulfrik,' the boy said. 'That is the kind of person I am. A generous person. And strong! Look!' He flexed a small bicep.

'What are you doing here, boy,' Ulfrik growled, fearful that this child had been going through his cargo unchallenged. A woman hauling a bundle of furs onto her back turned and, in the narrow gangway, almost knocked Alfgeir flat. He leapt out of her way into the path of Ingvar, who nearly dropped Gunnar's weighty sea chest.

'I could be useful on your next voyage,' the boy continued, seemingly oblivious to the trouble he was causing. Herdis, a broad, loud woman who had crewed with Ulfrik for many years, laughed at him. 'Such a boy could be useful indeed,' she mocked. 'He is skinny as a worm. We could use him as bait to catch our supper.' This prompted an outburst of laughter from the crew.

'Bait?' Alfgeir shouted, offended. 'The only creature brave enough to eat me is Jormungand himself! And then where would you be, if you hooked him? Dead! That is where.' More laughter. Alfgeir glared, angry and humiliated. Ulfrik sighed. He did not have time for this and talk of being eaten by Jormungand, the great World Serpent who dwelled in the ocean depths, was not improving his mood. He picked the boy up, slung him over his shoulder and carried him onto the dock. 'Stay off my ship,' he warned as he put Alfgeir down. The wounded expression on the child's face stabbed at Ulfrik's heart. He had once been young and eager as this and the boy had shown spirit and willing, but, Ulfrik reminded himself, he may never get to travel the Whale Road again. There was every chance Jarl Erik would kill him when he found out what he had done.

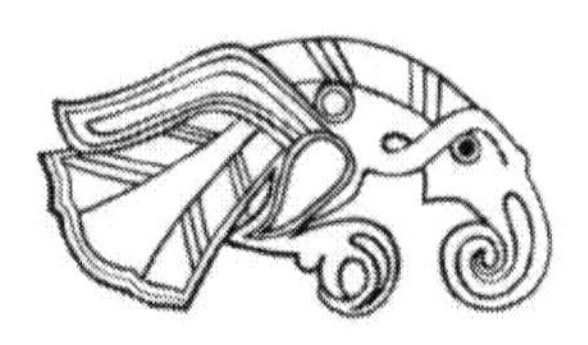

KADLIN

It had been a long ride and Kadlin's muscles were aching by the time she reached the farmhouse. She was fifteen now - a woman - with a calmness and confidence that made her seem older. A small knife in a leather sheath and several herb pouches hung from her girdle, and a long staff carved with runes and sigils of power was strapped to her back. Her blue cloak lay bundled neatly behind the saddle of her grey mare.

The small, remote farmstead consisted of a timber framed house, a barn and a stable. Five cattle and a handful of sheep could be seen grazing in the paddock beyond. The apple trees beside the house were laden with fragrant Spring blossom, and Kadlin joyfully inhaled their scent as she rode closer. A large dog lazed in the shade beneath one of the trees, tongue lolling and eyes half closed in blissful repose. It reluctantly roused itself at her approach and barked an alarm.

A plain, anxious woman, who Kadlin took to be the farmer's wife, hurried out to meet her. She carried a boy of about fifteen months on her hip. She settled the dog and seemed tense as she nervously appraised their visitor. 'I'm sorry to bring you so far out of your way, Lady,' she said, by way of greeting. A thrall hastened out from the barn to hold the bridle of Kadlin's horse while she dismounted.

'You are the wife of Gorm Einarsson,' Kadlin inquired, as she untied the staff from her back and leaned it against the wall. The woman nodded and tried to smile, but her face was still pinched with concern. 'I am Hallveig,' she said.

'I am Kadlin, daughter of Svala, daughter of Yrsa,' Kadlin replied. 'And who is this?' She smiled warmly at the toddler and stroked his cheek with a finger. He grinned at her. Hallveig's demeanour changed and she beamed with motherly pride as she showed off her son. 'This is my Ingvar.'

'Ingvar? I have a brother by the same name. Hello, Ingvar.'

The little boy nuzzled his face bashfully into his mother's neck. As he did so, the cloth of his breeks raised slightly, revealing fresh, harsh bruising on his leg. Hallveig's expression sobered again, and she shifted her stance to recover his skin.

'Is there anything you need, Lady,' she asked, avoiding Kadlin's gaze. 'Food? Drink?'

'A drink would be welcome,' Kadlin replied, pleasantly, 'but first I'll see your husband.' The woman nodded obediently and, eyes still firmly staring at the floor, led the way inside.

The interior of the farmhouse was modest but comfortable. They found the farmer, Gorm Einarsson, sprawled in a cosy chair beside the unlit hearth, with his right leg elevated on a stool. He was a large, muscular man, with an arrogant face and an air of superiority. Kadlin disliked him on sight and the feeling was clearly mutual, as Gorm made no attempt to disguise a disappointment that bordered on rage when he saw her. 'The invitation was for your grandmother,' he snarled. 'I need Yrsa. I need the best.'

'Be grateful she sent me instead,' Kadlin responded politely. 'Had you stayed on your arse when Yrsa entered this room, she'd have cut your throat.' She smiled sweetly and shrugged. 'I am less easily offended.'

Gorm scowled, unused to being chastised by a woman. 'I travelled a long way to consult the Völur yesterday,' he began.

'The same distance, no doubt, that I have travelled to see you today,' Kadlin pointed out. 'Perhaps you could explain why?'

'I am cursed,' the man grumbled. 'Unexplained trips and falls. My dog bit me last week for no good reason, nor bad reason either. Poor luck and ill health have plagued me these last few weeks. I sought out the Seer and asked her to break this curse before it kills me, but she sent me away and said she would call on me today. On the journey home, my bastard horse - which has been a good horse until now - reared as if seeing a snake and threw me to the ground. So, you see, in truth it is your grandmother's fault that you find me on my arse. Had she removed the curse when I asked, I would not have fallen and broken my leg.' He winced in pain, and Kadlin noticed that his ankle was swollen and red.

'The gods do love irony,' she said, crouching down to examine his leg.

'A weaker man than I would have died by now under my wife's care,' Gorm continued bitterly, glaring at Hallveig. 'She is tender and loving as a troll, this one, and just as fair to look upon!' The man was not endearing himself to Kadlin, and she was not surprised in the slightest that someone wanted him cursed. Still, she had accepted the job of lifting it from him and was now honour bound to do so. She moved her attention from his ankle to his calf, and then up further to his thigh. The leg seemed sound and she detected no broken bones.

As she crouched beside him, Kadlin noticed something tangled in the webbing beneath Gorm's chair. She looked closer, and saw it was a small talisman fashioned from twigs and thorns. There was hair woven into it, and Kadlin had no doubt that it came from the man himself. It was a curse, then, and not the product of paranoia or sheer bad luck as so many of these things turned out to be. She hesitated a moment before reaching for it.

'Odin's balls,' Gorm exclaimed impatiently. 'If I'd wanted to be stroked I'd have summoned a whore, not a witch!'

Kadlin realised that her hand was still on his thigh. She released it, instantly, and stood, slipping the talisman carefully into her pocket as she did so. She looked at him sharply. 'Only gods and kings can summon me, and you are neither,' she admonished icily. 'Remember to whom you speak, Gorm, son of Einar.'

Gorm turned white, realising his mistake. 'Forgive me, Lady. I meant no offence. The pain...'

'Your leg is not broken,' Kadlin interrupted. 'The ankle is merely sprained. That is all. It will soon heal.' She turned to Hallveig, who was cowering in the doorway. 'I'll take that drink now, if you please.' Wide-eyed, the anxious woman nodded and led her from the room.

The farmhouse kitchen was clean and basic. Hallveig

handed little Ingvar into the care of a female thrall and poured two cups of watery ale from a pottery jug. She held one out to Kaldin, and as she did so Kadlin noticed a patchwork of bruises on her outstretched arm. They ranged in colour from older yellows and browns, through reds and purples, to the black and blue bruises of the last few hours. Hallveig hastily pulled her sleeve down to cover them, saying cheerily 'When I was a child, I used to wish to be a Seer. I envy you, Lady. It must be such a wonderful life!' Kadlin choked on a mouthful of ale, shocked that anyone could want the life that had been thrust on her. 'To be respected,' the farmer's wife continued, wistfully. 'To have a purpose. To have power! I should like to be such a woman.'

Kadlin studied her for a moment, unsure how to reply. There seemed to be no gall in Hallveig's words, nor any attempt at mockery. It was a perspective that surprised and momentarily stunned Kadlin. She would rather have friends and be a part of the community than live outside it and have their reverence and respect. The people feared her, and her connection to the gods. You do not invite the things you fear into your home and seat them by your hearth - not unless you want something from them. You do not laugh and share stories with them. Respect was a cold offering and no substitute for the bonds of friendship. She had purpose, true, but it was not a purpose of her own choosing and therefore weighed on her as a duty. She knew she should feel honoured to have been chosen by the Norns. She tried very hard to see their gifts as a blessing, but it felt like a weight around her shoulders, anchoring her to Bramsvik, and to a life of privileged servitude. She wanted to travel and see the world, to be a mighty shieldmaiden and win victories in battle! As to power, Kadlin did not feel she had much of that, either. She was strong in the Sight, and in divination and prophecy. She could see things that others could not, and her charms and spells were potent with the strength of her will. But this was not power. It was a burden. Just one more thing that set her apart from other girls and made her different.

'When I was a child,' she eventually responded in a low voice, 'I wanted more than anything to be a Valkyrie and to fight beside the All-Father, Odin.' It was Hallveig's turn to look taken aback, and she raised an eyebrow. Kadlin smiled. 'The opportunity has yet to present itself,' she added wryly.

Once they had finished their drinks, Kadlin asked to see the horse Gorm had ridden the previous day. Hallveig led her to a barn which currently housed three horses and a tethered goat. One of the horses was Kadlin's own mare, Mathilda, and was being groomed by the thrall who had taken her bridle earlier.

In the far corner of the barn stood a low, wooden table with meagre offerings upon it. There was a bowl of oatmeal, a half cup of ale, and a simple garland of meadow flowers that looked to have been freshly picked and woven that day. Kadlin studied them without touching.

'You have a farmstead gnome.'

The other woman nodded. 'I believe so. Yes. It likes the horses. That one there is often found with braids in her mane.' She pointed to a chestnut mare. Kadlin ran her fingers through the horse's mane and quickly found them tangled in the tiny, matted plaits known as gnome braids. 'So I see,' she said. 'Is this the one your husband was riding yesterday, when he fell?'

Hallveig nodded, and Kadlin continued her gentle inspection of the animal. She ran her fingers lightly over its head, lifted its mane to look beneath, and checked its belly. She found what she was looking for behind the horse's right ear. A small, black symbol had been painted in the crease, hidden from view unless you were looking for it. The animal flicked its ear, irritated at the intrusion. Kadlin rubbed the mark with her thumb, erasing it, and looked accusingly at Hallveig.

'Leave that,' Hallveig snapped at the thrall. 'Go help with the meal.' The man fled, leaving the two women alone in the barn.

Kadlin reached into the pocket of her dress and pulled out the small talisman made of twigs. It had three, sharp, blackthorn spikes hanging from it, which she took care to avoid. Hallveig went white at the sight of it and her lip began to tremble.

'I removed this from beneath your husband's chair,' Kaldin explained. 'But you know this as you put it there.'

Hallveig's voice was no more than a whisper as she replied, 'I have to protect my son.' Kadlin pursed her lips. It was as she suspected. 'Put it back, Lady,' Hallveig continued, desperately. 'I beg you. You don't know what kind of man he is.'

Kadlin struggled with her conscience as she looked at the talisman. She recognised the craftsmanship and strongly suspected who Hallveig had purchased it from. This was a powerful charm. If she left it undisturbed, Gorm would likely be dead before the next new moon. He was a bully and a violent man, and no doubt a blight on the lives of his family, but he had petitioned the Völur for help and they had responded. Kadlin was honour bound to free him from this curse if it was within her power to do so. The Norns were watching, and they could not be cheated. Reluctantly, she opened one of the larger pouches that hung from her girdle and took out a small clay dish, a candle stub, some dried sage and grass, and a flint. She balled up the grass, set it in the dish, and struck the flint until it caught light. She added the sage, filling the air with its pungent aroma.

'I agreed to help,' she said by way of justification. 'It would be dishonourable to let him die.' Kadlin cautiously removed the thorns from the talisman. One by one, she held them in the flame until they were alight, muttering words to counter the curse, then dropping the thorns into the dish so that they burned.

'Your honour will not let Gorm die, but it will allow him to kill me? Or Ingvar? Because that is what will happen if you leave us defenceless.' Hallveig's words stung her morality, but Kadlin knew where her duty lay. She took what remained of the talisman and held it in the flame for as long as she could, before dropping it into the dish to be consumed by the flame. She crushed the remains to powder with the hilt of her knife, then reached out and briefly clasped the other woman's hand.

'I have fulfilled my obligation to your husband. The curse is gone. If someone else were to ask for my help now, I am free to give it.' She filled the words with meaning and saw a light of hope flicker in Hallveig's eyes.

'Then help us. Please.'

Kadlin spit into the ashen contents of the clay dish and mixed it to a paste. There was just enough to coat her palm. 'Master Longbeard,' she called, softly and reverently, looking directly at the creature who sat cross-legged beneath the offering table, watching them. 'Do I have your permission?'

The farmstead gnome, unseen by any other than herself, slowly bobbed his head. He had been paying close attention to the exchange between the two women, and well understood what was being asked of him. From the length of his beard, Kadlin estimated his age at around three centuries. A powerful ally indeed for a woman and child in fear for their lives.

Kadlin pressed her hand firmly against the wall, pushing her will and energy deep into the wood of the old barn. She felt it burn as the re-formed curse left her palm and imprinted there.

'The wights of this place are watching him,' she explained to Hallveig. 'If Gorm treats you kindly all will be well, but if they witness him mistreating you or your son, they will release what I have placed here, and he will die through some misfortune.'

'Don't tell him, Lady,' Hallveig begged, taking her hand. 'Don't warn him. He will kill you for this.'

'I am Völva,' Kadlin replied, reassuringly. 'He would not dare.'

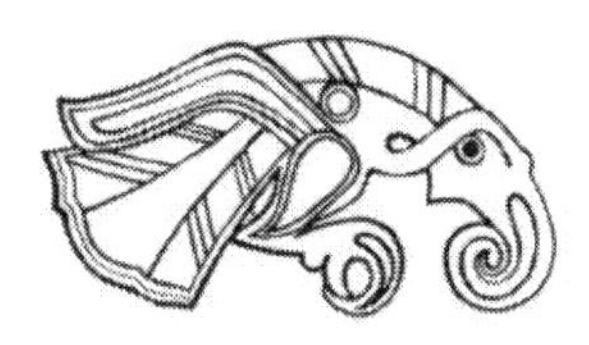

ULFRIK

The sky was darkening by the time Ulfrik arrived back at the town of Bramsvik. Gunnar and Hilde lived a short distance outside the main town, a journey which – were he not leading a second horse laden with Gunnar's possessions – would have taken ten minutes of hard riding. As it was, being slowed to a painfully laborious pace, it had taken Ulfrik the better part of an hour to reach their hof.

Hilde had guessed, of course, as soon as she and the children saw his solitary approach. The little ones were too young to comprehend at first and asked constantly for their father during his visit. Hilde took the bad tidings hard and, despite the urgent need for brevity, Ulfrik felt unable to simply leave after giving her the news of her husband's death. He was angry that Jarl Erik had involved them in something that was not their affair. He was even angrier that he now had to lie to the widow of a friend about it. Gunnar had been a good man, and his family deserved better than falsehoods. Ulfrik gave Hilde twice the wages her husband had earned and resolved to see that she and the children were comfortable in the coming year. It was easy to put on a brave face in the warmer months, but in winter when food was scarce and your children cried from hunger, when the chill winds invaded your bones and the frosts bit hard at your hands and face; that was the time when sorrows magnified, and life lost its appeal. He would keep an eye on Gunnar's family and see they were well.

Magnus was waiting outside the mead hall when Ulfrik finally returned. He and his son, Brodi, were waiting in the shadows beside a horse and cart. 'He can be trusted,' Magnus said, noting Ulfrik's look of concern. 'He knows nothing save these barrels are the property of the jarl and need protecting. I thought two men were safer than one until you arrived.'

Ulfrik nodded, seeing the sense in this. He didn't tell Magnus he strongly suspected anyone with knowledge of this cargo may be dead soon. There was a reason he had left his own son out of it. Jarl Erik Thorsson was a strong leader, but he was not a trustworthy man. 'Send him home, Magnus,' he advised. His eyes conveyed the unspoken danger his words could not.

Magnus read his expression. 'Go on home, Son,' he said to Brodi. 'But first give me your oath that you will speak of this to no-one. Not anyone.' Brodi looked confused. At fourteen he was eager to prove himself a man but, although he had proven adept with a knife and spear, he did not yet have the wit and wisdom to think with his head rather than his ego. 'Whatever you need me to do, I'm ready,' he said defiantly, looking at Ulfrik. 'I will not let you down, Ulfrik. Give me a chance.'

Ulfrik put a hand on the boy's shoulder. 'Of all the men your father could have trusted with this, he asked you. Be proud of that. I send you home because you are no longer needed, not because you don't have my trust. Now give Magnus your oath, and we shall know that we can trust you again in the future.' He forced himself to smile and saw relief on the boy's face.

'I swear before Var, goddess of oaths. May she strike me down if I speak a word of this to anyone,' Brodi said, earnestly.

'Good man. Now run home. You must be hungry,' Magnus said, adding 'What will you tell your mother if she asks where you've been?'

Brodi grinned at having permission to lie to his mother. 'I shall say you were telling me of your voyage, and I didn't realise how late it had become.'

'No.' Magnus shook his great head. 'You were nowhere near me or Ulfrik tonight.'

'You've been at sea for three moons, Magnus,' Ulfrik pointed out. 'No-one will believe the boy did not come and find you.' His merchant's brain, well used to spinning tales to make his wares more appealing, was already working on a story. 'You saw your father earlier,' he said to Brodi. 'He told you he was busy but said he would meet you outside the Hall and to wait for him there. You waited until it got dark and then figured he must have gone home without you. You did not see him again after you left the dock.'

'Why not say he was fishing by the river? Why say he was here?' Magnus did not like the new version of events.

'Then where are his fish? What if others were by the river and he does not mention seeing them?' Ulfrik turned to Brodi. 'Who has entered the Hall since you've been waiting here?'

Brodi thought a moment. 'Thorfrida, Olvir and Egil from The Ox are here. Ragnfrið arrived not long after us. She has probably come to have sex with Asbjorn. Atli Half-Leg didn't stay very long. I think he had a fight with Kettil as I heard them shouting at one another...'

'So,' Ulfrik interrupted, 'if anyone asks who you saw or what you observed while you were waiting for your father, you can truthfully tell them all of this. It is not good to lie, but when you need to, keep it as close to the truth as you can. Besides,' he added with a smile, 'this way it is Magnus's fault that you are late, and no-one will be in trouble with your mother except him.'

Brodi laughed. 'Don't worry, Father,' he said as he jumped down from the cart. 'She will forgive you.'

'What did you tell Hilde,' Magnus asked soberly, when his son had gone.

'That her husband died bravely, saving us from thieves.'

'And what will you tell the jarl?'

Ulfrik sighed heavily. 'The truth.'

★

The mead hall was as hot and stifling as Muspellheim, realm of the fire giants. Ulfrik would not have been surprised to see their colossal king, Surt, seated at the end of the hall instead of Jarl Erik. A feast was underway, celebrating the safe return of the jarl's only son. Two tables ran the length of the room, and it seemed half the town had turned out to share in their jarl's generosity and good humour. Three pigs had been slaughtered and were roasting on spits over the central fire-pit, and several thralls hastened to refill the guests' tankards with ale.

Jarl Erik and his wife, Ingrid, sat on wooden chairs on a raised dais at the far end of the hall. The jarl was around forty years old, with broad shoulders and a physique that spoke of the warrior he had once been. He had hawkish eyes - keen but cold - and his long, red hair was white at the temples. His hair and beard were braided and decorated with ornate silver beads that glinted orange in the firelight. Ingrid, his wife, had once been beautiful, but years of watching her husband warm their bed with younger women had hardened her looks. There was a bitterness in her face that could not be softened by fine jewellery and fancy clothes.

The jarl spotted Ulfrik as soon as he entered and sent Thorvald to intercept him. 'You're late,' One-Eye growled. 'Don't be surprised to find your own carcass spitted over a flame by the end of the night.' He gestured toward the pigs. Ulfrik's belly rumbled. He had not eaten since yesterday and the smell of food made his hunger hard to bear.

'I got here as soon as I was able,' he replied. 'Magnus is guarding three barrels outside. He will need help to bring them in.'

Thorvald instructed a couple of thralls to fetch the barrels and bring them, discretely, to the jarl's private chamber. Ulfrik saw fear in their eyes as they hastened to obey. They knew, as he did, that when a thrall is entrusted with a secret, he is usually butchered to protect that secret. Ulfrik doubted that these two would be seen again after this night.

'Come,' Thorvald said, taking a torch from the wall and leading him away from the heat and the food. He pulled aside a cloth covering the entrance to the private rooms and took Ulfrik into a secluded chamber at the back. Thorvald used the torch to light a lantern, illuminating a richly decorated room that managed to be grand yet intimate. There was a small table in the centre, but no place to sit. The last time Ulfrik had been in this room he had been bullied into a deal that may now cost him his life, and which had already cost the life of one of his crew.

'Ulfrik!' Jarl Erik beamed as he entered the room but there was no warmth in his eyes. 'My son informs me you collected the tribute without incident. Three barrels, he says. I knew I could count on you. You've done well, my friend. Very well.' He took the lantern from Thorvald One-Eye and placed it on the table beside a large map inked on animal skin.

Ulfrik frowned. 'Without incident, Lord? We met with Sitric at Birka, as planned, and took three barrels of silver from him, but did Asbjorn not tell you that we were then ambushed by Franks? They knew of our meeting and were waiting for us.'

'They took the silver?' All pretence at joviality was wiped from the jarl's face.

'No, Lord! No. We escaped with every piece of it thanks to Gunnar. He gave his life defending us. We would all have been killed but for…'

'They were Franks?' Jarl Erik interrupted. 'You are sure?'

Ulfrik bit back a retort about how Gunnar's sacrifice deserved recognition. Instead, he said 'I know their language, Lord. They were expecting us and knew our business.'

Thorvald looked uneasy. 'Then we are betrayed.'

'I fear so.'

At that moment the door at the other end of the room opened and the two thralls rolled in one of the large barrels. Jarl Erik froze at the sight of it. 'What is this?'

'They know our faces now, Lord, as well as our intentions,' Ulfrik explained hastily as the thralls left again to collect the other barrels. 'Had we tried to deliver the tribute in Haithabyr as planned we would all have died, and the silver been lost. I thought it safest to…'

'Safe?' The jarl was purple with rage. He snatched a leather pouch from a shelf and shook its contents - hack silver - onto the map where Birka was marked. 'Sitric raised this from loyal jarls like me. I made an agreement to deliver it to King Sigfrid's men at Haithabyr.' He swept the pile of silver neatly down the coast to the Danish market town as if to demonstrate the ease of the task. 'What do you imagine he will think now you've failed to do so? I will tell you. He will think that you…

that I… have stolen it. We are far from safe. Your incompetence, Ulfrik, may have put us at war with the Danes!'

Ulfrik said nothing. He had not been told why King Sigfrid was raising funds in secrecy and in a hurry, but given the Frankish intervention, he could speculate. Ulfrik's trade brought him into contact with merchants from all over the known world, so he heard regular updates on news from other countries and kingdoms.

He knew that King Charlemagne of Frankia (sole ruler since the suspicious death of his co-regent brother a decade before) was on a mission to expand the Frankish Empire and bring his Christian god to its people. For the past few years Charlemagne's troops had been invading Saxony and forcing the defeated Saxons to renounce their gods through Christian baptism. Until recently, a Saxon noble known as Widukind had led a successful rebellion against the Frankish invaders, but after a spectacular defeat two years ago Widukind had fled to the land of the Danes, seeking the protection of his wife's brother, King Sigfrid. If Sigfrid was raising funds on the quiet, it could only mean one thing; Widukind was planning a return to Saxony to liberate his people.

'Who is your contact in Haithabyr,' Jarl Erik asked. Ulfrik fumbled in his clothing for the small package he had brought from The Ox. He handed it to his jarl.

'Whoever bears the other half, Lord. Sitric named a

tavern for us to meet.'

Jarl Erik unwrapped the palm-sized, intricately carved piece of whalebone. It was clearly one half of a larger whole which, when placed together, would form a complete design. He rewrapped it and handed it back to Ulfrik. 'You will take these barrels and deliver them to your contact in Haithabyr. Let us hope that King Sigfrid is a patient man. Be ready to leave again tomorrow.'

'But, Lord, the Franks will be waiting for us! They know my face and those of my crew. It would be suicide to...'

'Then make peace with the gods before you go, Ulfrik. Either you make the delivery as planned, or I have someone else deliver the silver along with your cowardly head and those of your family and crew. I expect you gone by midday.'

KADLIN

As his wife predicted, Gorm Einarsson had not been thrilled at news that the curse - although broken - would return to claim his life should he ever harm his family again. He had been equally unimpressed with Kadlin's insistence that she still be paid in full (three hams, a bladder of milk and a sack of wool) for her services. She had declined Hallveig's offer of a meal and a room for the night and insisted on riding home the same evening. For any other woman the prospect of travelling alone would be unthinkable, but no-one was foolish enough to attack a sorceress, even at night.

Now, as daylight faded, she regretted her decision. It was Spring, and night fell quickly. The sun took with it any vestiges of warmth, and Kadlin hugged her cloak tightly around her against the chill air. The waning moon was in its final quarter, providing meagre light, so she gave Mathilda free reign and trusted the horse to find her way home. The rhythmic beat of Mathilda's hooves, and the gentle roll of her back as she meandered along the path, lulled Kadlin into a dreamy daze. She allowed her mind to drift toward sleep.

Yrsa's hof was constructed away from the main town, high on a hill just before it steepened to mountainside. A small homestead beside a stream, it consisted of a house, chicken coup, grain store, and a small barn, enclosed within a low fence. It would be the simplest of tasks to climb over the fence, yet none would ever dare. Instead, all visitors entered through the tall gate at the north end of the property. Either side of the gate were two imposing poles adorned with sun-bleached animal skulls, antlers and bones. A partially decomposed rodent was nailed to the gate, and a warding sigil, stained with blood, carved into the wood. It was designed to impress and intimidate would-be visitors. It worked. You did not want to fuck with whoever lived here.

It was beside this gate (or, more accurately, standing several feet away from it) that Kadlin encountered the man. Drowsy as she was, Kadlin probably wouldn't have noticed him had his horse not whinnied and drawn her attention. The man's eyes were fixed on the skulls and bones, rendered even more sinister by moonlight, and he was nervously fingering a Thor's hammer at his throat.

'You must be troubled indeed, friend, to call on the Völur at such a late hour,' Kadlin called.

The man reacted as if a *draugr*, the living dead, had lumbered into view. Startled, he cried out and stumbled backward, tripping over himself and ending up on the ground. Kadlin dismounted and held Mathilda's bridle while the man regained his dignity and scrambled to his feet.

'Forgive me, Lady, I didn't see you,' he said. 'I have an urgent message for Yrsa Gudrunsdaughter.' He fumbled in his pocket for something and held it out to her. Kadlin glanced at it but made no attempt to take it from him.

'You must be cold,' she said, simply. 'Come inside.'

YRSA

Her bones were aching. Yrsa shifted uncomfortably in her seat and tried to pad more of the blanket around her hips. It was no use. The pain burrowed into her very marrow and there was nothing she could use to dull it. Nothing that would leave her wits intact, anyway, she thought, unconsciously stroking a leather pouch of dried hemp leaves that sat in her lap. She would need her wits tonight. The runes had told her so.

She rarely slept anymore. Not for more than a few hours at a time. At fifty-four she was one of the oldest women in the kingdom of Agder - certainly the oldest in Bramsvik - and she felt every day of it. The loss of her daughter ten years ago had wounded Yrsa more deeply than she let on. A piece of herself died with Svala, and in the hole where that piece had once been there now lived a dragon who gnawed at her bones and devoured her flesh from the inside. His fiery breath burned cold as ice, searing her joints and sending her muscles into spasm. The constant pain weakened her spirit as well as her body.

She had felt a sense of urgency these past few weeks. Something was coming and Kadlin needed to be ready. Ready for what, Yrsa couldn't tell, but she felt that time was running out somehow. Whatever it was, this nameless doom that stalked her, it would be set in motion tonight. She would need her brain and so she would put up with the pain a little longer.

She was finally drifting off to sleep when the sound of hushed voices disturbed her. The door to the hof opened slowly and two hooded figures slipped inside.

'Grandmother? Are you awake?' It was Kadlin's voice.

'There's a candle on the table,' Yrsa replied. Kadlin stoked the embers in the hearth, lit a reed from their low flame and brought it carefully to the table. She lit the candle, illuminating the room with a flickering glow. Yrsa squinted as she studied the stranger. He was in his mid-twenties - Jofrið's age - but displayed none of her confidence or vitality. He wore the same anxious expression that most people had when they crossed Yrsa's threshold, as if he believed these moments may be his last.

He kept his eyes cast down at the floor and clutched something small in his right hand.

A man risked his life disturbing the Völur at this hour of night. It took great courage, or great fear, to do such a thing. Their visitor had not had the nerve to look her in the eye since he walked through the door, so it wasn't courage that brought him here. Fear then. Who could a man fear more than her? Only a god or a king. King Harald Redbeard had sent him here, and he was more afraid to fail his king than he was to wake Yrsa.

'I will leave to visit King Redbeard in the morning,' she said, relishing the look of awe that now crossed the man's face.

'H-how…' he stammered.

She held out her hand and the man reluctantly approached, handing her a beautifully ornate gold ring set with a large, blood red garnet. It was an expensive piece of jewellery. As Yrsa studied it, the garnet seemed to melt, becoming liquid and bleeding onto her palm. She screwed her eyes shut and when she opened them again the ring was whole.

'Queen Gunnhild was delivered of a daughter three nights ago,' the messenger said. 'King Harald asks that you come at once to give the child blessings and tell her future. He asks that *all* the Völur attend and would hear you all speak. He assures you will be well compensated.'

Yrsa wondered why the king wanted all the Völur. This was highly unusual, if not a little offensive. 'I've given you my reply,' she responded. 'We will leave in the morning. You may rest yourself in the barn.'

The man swallowed. He would clearly rather pluck out his own eyes than speak these next words. 'He said for you to come immediately, Lady. During the birth… They say there was a sign… The king needs answers. He said it was urgent.'

'But not urgent enough, it seems, that the king would visit me himself,' she snapped. 'Instead he thinks he can summon me like a thrall. I am old and there are very few things would tempt me from my home on a cold night. Don't make me give you my response a third time.' She closed her eyes and sank back against the pillows on the chair. Ice needles shot through her shoulders and down her spine. She grunted in pain, barely aware that he was speaking again. He repeated something over and over in a low voice as Kadlin ushered him outside. An apology, Yrsa thought, dully. It was usually an apology. A few moments later she heard the door open and close once more and felt Kadlin's hand on hers.

'Can I fetch you something,' her granddaughter asked, crouching beside her. 'Another blanket? Or something to drink?'

Yrsa opened her eyes and smiled wearily. Gratefully. She shook her head. 'Tell me of your day,' she said. 'How did you find Gorm Einarrson?'

Kadlin stood and walked over to the hearth, adding a log to the dwindling fire. 'I found him cursed, as you well know. I recognised your handiwork.' She blew on it, encouraging the flame, before coming back to sit beside her. 'No wonder you would not go yourself,' she added accusingly.

Yrsa cackled. 'I could hardly take payment to undo something I had already been paid to do!'

'You put me in a difficult situation,' Kadlin chided. 'You could have told me, at least.' There was a hint of criticism in Kadlin's words. The sting of deceit.

Yrsa's tone sobered as she replied 'If you set a truth before a person, they gain knowledge. Nothing more. If you wish them to learn wisdom, let them discover the truth for themselves and see what they do with it.'

'You think I lack wisdom?'

In fact, Yrsa's granddaughter was one of the wisest people she knew. She showed good judgement and balanced reason most of the time, combined with a genuine compassion for the people she served. However, the natural arrogance of her youth often led her to be over-confident in her own opinions. She took a stand when more seasoned Völvas knew to be cautious and to listen.

'No, I don't think you lack wisdom,' Yrsa replied,

truthfully. 'I think you sometimes lack the experience and perspective to apply it effectively.' She felt Kadlin's ego take a beating from those words.

'I will try to do better,' the young woman murmured with sincerity. 'If you don't mind it's been a long ride and I'm tired.'

Yrsa reached for her hand as Kadlin stood. 'So, what did you do with it? With the truth that you learned today?'

Kadlin sighed. 'Thanks to you I was honour bound to break the curse, but I couldn't leave Hallveig and little Ingvar unprotected. I reformed it and set conditions. It will kill him if he harms them again.' She paused, then added defiantly, 'I didn't charge her for that.'

Yrsa grinned to herself as her granddaughter pulled her hand free and went to bed. 'Good night, dear girl,' she whispered, amused, as she closed her eyes. 'You truly are the best of us.'

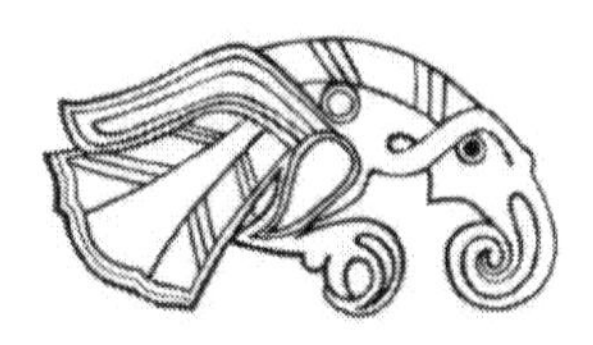

AUD

Aud was seven years old when her parents gave her to Yrsa. It was an honour, they told her, to be accepted by the great seer. One day she, too, would command such respect and make her family proud. Despite their words, Aud had known they were grateful to be rid of her. She unsettled them and their friends with her impossible insights into their lives. Ever since she could talk, she had spoken of secrets she had never been privy to; had been able to see behind the mask of a person when everyone else was duped by a smile or honeyed words. She spoke with a child's honesty and had no concept of adult discretion. Friends and family stopped visiting. Her father beat her, but she didn't understand what she had done wrong. It was no surprise to her, then, when her mother approached the Völva about having her daughter trained. For all their talk of family and pride, Aud knew it was selfishness and shame that prompted their actions. They brought her to Yrsa's hof in the autumn of her eighth year when all around was beginning its cycle of decay, and they never returned.

Aud fell in love with Yrsa the moment they first met. She was powerful and strong, with eyes that could see beyond the façade of human skin and bone. She was beautiful and magnificent, and Aud adored her. It was an innocent love at first, developing over the years into something deeper and more meaningful. Unfortunately for Aud, it was unrequited. Yrsa liked men, and men liked her. She had affairs and had borne children. Her daughter, Svala, was a year older than Aud, and Yrsa would only ever see her as a second daughter. A slightly less talented and much less beloved daughter.

Now, at thirty-one years of age, Aud was the eldest of Yrsa's apprentices and the most experienced. The majority of Völvas her age would have left their teacher long ago, possibly taking on apprentices of their own, but Aud was fiercely loyal to her mentor and had no interest in being her own mistress. She was plump and dour-faced and wore her hair in two long braids which fell either side of her large bosom. She was belligerent and often volatile in nature, and this morning, as with most mornings, she was complaining.

'I don't see why we had to bring them, too,' she said for the tenth time since leaving the hof. She was riding in the front of the wagon with Yrsa, while Jofrið and Kadlin sat on fur pelts in the back, trying to pretend they could not hear her. The furs offered little protection from the bumps and jolts of the journey, but they were better than bare wooden boards. The two, broad backed oxen who pulled the wagon – Earth Churner and Sour Nose - trundled along the path at a pace that should see them reach Bramsvik by mid-morning.

Truth be told, Aud didn't really care if Jofrið accompanied them or not. Her ire was directed, as always, at Kadlin. To her mind, Kadlin had stolen the love that Yrsa could have shown to her. After Svala's death, Kadlin was treated with loving kindness that Aud had never known in her life. Each kiss, each embrace, each tender word Yrsa spoke to her granddaughter pushed the blade of resentment deeper into Aud's heart. She left the wound untreated and allowed it to fester.

'It's an insult,' she muttered, indignantly, slapping the reigns in irritation.

As the most senior of the Völur, it was usual for Yrsa to attend the King or Queen alone. On occasion - when illness had weakened her, or if she felt the circumstances warranted it - Yrsa had been known to take Aud with her on such visits. Jofrið and Kadlin were both powerful seers, but the hierarchy of their group dictated that Aud was above them due to her age and experience. King Harald had requested all four of the Völur attend the celebration of his daughter's birth, and that implied (or seemed to imply) that he did not trust the skill of the two highest ranking Völvas.

'Did you expect me to refuse a king,' Yrsa demanded, losing her patience.

'You did last night,' Aud retaliated, stung by Yrsa's tone of voice. 'You could have refused him this, too, if you wished, but then Kadlin would miss her big chance to impress royalty.'

Yrsa waved a hand dismissively, turning away from her. 'You sound like a jealous fool. I give Kadlin no favours, as you well know. This was out of my hands.'

King Redbeard's messenger (whom they now knew as Arni, son of Andvett) slowed his horse to ride alongside them. He had been fidgety all morning, having risen before the dawn and been ready to leave by cock crow. Their careful preparations had pained him, eager as he was to return to his master. He had paced the barn while they packed their bags, muttered to the sky as they dressed their hair and cleansed their bodies, yet Aud noted he was not in such a hurry when offered a seat at the table to share in their breakfast.

'A fine ship waits at Bramsvik to transport us to Tromø,' Arni said now, directing his comments to Yrsa. 'You will travel in comfort, Lady. Given fair weather and a good wind we should reach the King's shore by midday tomorrow.' He was happier and more relaxed now they were finally underway.

Tromø was a large island to the east of Bramsvik, close enough to the coast to be easily visible from the mainland. Here, King Harald Redbeard had constructed his fortified homestead. Aud had been there only twice, the last being nine years ago. She noticed that her mentor seemed uneasy about their current visit and wondered why. Yrsa hadn't said as much, but Aud could sense it.

'We won't be needing your ship,' Yrsa said. She offered no further explanation but Aud felt the truth of it as soon as the words were spoken. 'Ride on ahead, Arni Andvettson,' Yrsa continued. 'Tell King Redbeard to prepare a feast for tomorrow eve. We shall join you there. May Njörð grant you safe passage.'

Arni swallowed nervously, unwilling to disobey a Völva but clearly fearful of returning to his lord empty-handed. 'Lady, I…' he began.

'Must I say everything more than once? Go, before I plague your journey with sea monsters.'

Arni blanched. He bowed his head curtly, kicked his heels and urged his horse to a gallop. Aud smirked as she watched him ride away.

'You had no cause to be so mean to him,' Kadlin chided her grandmother. 'He was only trying to serve his king.'

'As am I,' Yrsa snapped back. 'But I will do so at my own pace! I have no desire to travel all the way to Tromø with some young know-nothing telling me how, and when, and why!'

Aud could tell Yrsa was in pain. She always barked at those around her when she was hurting. Being bumped along a track in an oxen cart was the last thing her tortured limbs needed. Aud yearned to take her home and make her comfortable beneath the shade of the linden tree. Let the king sort his own affairs! It wasn't right to expect an old woman to undertake such a long journey. That was one of the problems of being a Völva, she mused; people assumed you to be above such mundane things as human pain and misery.

It was more than pain that troubled Yrsa, though, Aud thought to herself. There was a lightning storm of anguish encircling her old friend; a dark, brooding cloud that lashed out at anyone foolish enough to attempt to penetrate its core. Aud had been stung several times on the journey whilst trying to discover its cause. She shuddered. What awaited them at the home of King Redbeard? What dark future had Yrsa seen? The last time Aud had seen her mentor like this was the day Svala and her baby died.

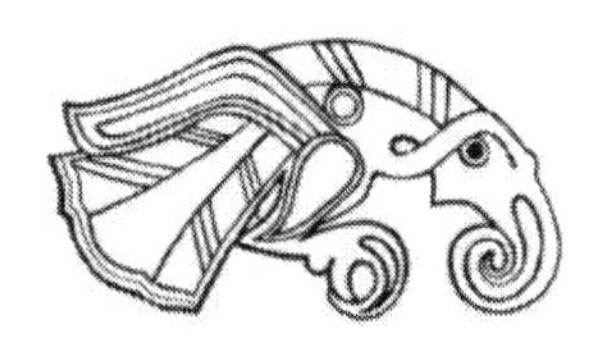

ULFRIK

Ulfrik bid a tearful goodbye to his wife at daybreak. He had arrived home, famished and exhausted, long after sunset on the previous day, having spent most of the evening riding from hof to hof to inform his crew of Jarl Erik's orders. When he finally arrived home, joyful celebrations quickly turned to shock and disbelief when he explained he was only there for one night. Despite the awful hunger gnawing at his guts, he found himself unable to eat much of the hearty meal Astrid cooked for him. He was too tired and soul-weary to do more than hold her that night, despite everything he had dreamed of doing these past long, lonely months. Instead, his wife had fallen asleep wrapped in his embrace, and Ulfrik had closed his eyes and inhaled the sweet smell of her until he drifted off.

Their two small children were still asleep when he left the next day. Astrid wanted to wake them, but Ulfrik couldn't bear to see their tears again. Instead, he kissed their brows while they slept, whispered soft words of love to them, and slipped outside. He left Astrid with as much wealth as he could possibly travel without and told her where he'd buried an urn filled with hack silver. 'You're frightening me, Ulfrik,' she said, when he insisted she repeat the directions back to him. 'What's wrong?'

'Nothing,' he lied. 'I just don't know how long this journey will take, and I want to be certain you and Lief and Greta are provided for while I'm away.'

Ulfrik gave Ingvar the task of organising provisions for the voyage. Jarl Erik had not allowed them enough time to plan sufficiently, but they could stop at any port along the way and restock their supplies. As long as Ingvar could find them enough food and water for two or three days they would manage.

By the time Sól's fiery face rose full in the sky, The Ox was once again heavy with cargo. The crew, despite their anger at having to leave again so soon, had arrived early and laboured hard to reload the knarr. Ulfrik was surprised to see a grim-faced Asbjorn among them. He had assumed Jarl Erik would keep his only son in Bramsvik, safe from Frankish assassins and the possible wrath of the Danish king.

'I am part of this crew. Let him try,' was all Asbjorn said when pressed on the matter. Ulfrik was impressed by the young man's loyalty to his shipmates. It was a side of the jarl's son he'd never witnessed before. Asbjorn was known as a braggard, a bully and a womaniser. He spent more time preening himself than a Frisian whore. When Jarl Erik had invested in their last voyage on the condition that his son join the crew, Ulfrik had baulked at the suggestion.

'Teach him to trade,' the jarl had said, as if it were the simplest of requests. 'If he does well, I'll get him a ship of his own. Or perhaps I will purchase half of yours and make you his partner. What would you think of that?'

Ulfrik had smiled, not trusting himself with a verbal response to that question. Jarl Erik made it sound as though he were bestowing a great honour rather than risking Ulfrik's livelihood, not to mention undermining the rights of his own eldest son, Ingvar. There had been worse to come, though, when the jarl entrusted him with a covert errand.

'You're a clever man. A trustworthy man. You know how and when to hold your tongue, and you're not easily outwitted. I need you to meet someone at Birka. A man named Sitric. He has cargo you are to collect.'

'Cargo, Lord?' Ulfrik had panicked. He had spent the

autumn trading in the West. Now that the winter storms were over, and the passage East was not so perilous, The Ox sat low in the water beneath the weight of goods to be traded at the main marketplaces of Birka and Haithabyr. It would be hard enough to turn a profit while baby-sitting the jarl's son. To reserve precious space for someone else's goods on the return journey could mean financial ruin.

In the end, he'd been given no choice. Ulfrik had not been deceived by the jarl's assurance that this would be an easy matter, and that all of Bramsvik would ultimately benefit from prime trading in the future. He had seen it for what it was – a chance for Erik to earn the favour of a great king. What he had not foreseen was just how much this was going to cost him personally. First, Gunnar, cut down by Frankish spies after they collected the silver from Sitric. Then his chance of greater profit as they had fled back to Agder without stopping at Haithabyr. And now the lives of his entire crew, including his son, were being placed at risk. His sacrifice to Njörð, god of the sea and of all merchants who travelled the Whale Road, must be great this time. The usual rabbit or hare would not be enough to buy the blessing of the gods for such a voyage. This time he had instructed Ingvar to purchase a ram.

'Ulfrik Varinsson, we must speak.' The familiar voice raised the fine hairs on the back of his neck. Yrsa, oldest and most highly regarded of the Völur, and grandmother to two of his children, stood behind him. He must have truly angered one of the gods to have such a day!

'I would be honoured, Lady,' he began, forcing a smile and turning to face her. The rest of the sentence was forgotten as he saw his daughter, Kadlin, alighting from the back of a cart along with Jofrið. His relationship with Kadlin was a difficult one. He loved her as much as he loved any of his children, but as the daughter of a Völva she had been kept from him; raised outside the town by her mother and, later, her grandmother, and trained in arts the likes of which he couldn't conceive. It was challenging to know how to treat her on the rare occasions when they met. As a daughter she had his love, but as a practitioner of magic she had his reverence, and – he had to admit – he feared her, as he did all the Völur. They were powerful, and unpredictable, and the sight of all four of them climbing down from an ox-drawn cart with travel bags in their hands sent his heart into nervous spasm.

'We need passage to Tromø,' Yrsa explained. 'Today. And you need something from me.'

Ulfrik panicked. 'There's no room,' he said, truthfully. 'The ship is full.'

'We shall see,' Yrsa replied, looking over his shoulder at the approach of Jarl Erik and his man, Thorvald One-Eye.

The jarl, as Ulfrik suspected, had come to insist that

Asbjorn remain in Bramsvik. No doubt he was also checking that Ulfrik left in good time, but his main concern seemed to be his son, and the perils awaiting them at Haithabyr. Asbjorn stood his ground, insisting he should be allowed to make his own decisions.

'You made a deal with Ulfrik that I should be a part of this crew,' he growled. 'I had no say in it. You made the decision for me and now I'm bound by it.'

The jarl glared at Ulfrik as if this was his fault. 'For one voyage only,' he replied, heatedly. 'That journey is done.'

'Is it, Father? Then why are you sending The Ox out again? I have heard nothing from these people for the last few weeks except how much they were looking forward to seeing their families again and returning home. I don't believe any one of them would be leaving so soon if you had not insisted on it. You want me to be an honourable man, so let me do what is honourable. I am part of this crew until we return from Haithabyr.'

Had such words been spoken in private, Jarl Erik may have worn his son down. Here on the docks, in front of the crew, the Völur, and several passers-by, he had no choice but to accede or risk losing face.

'Then Thorvald shall go with you,' he said, simply.

A full crew. A full cargo. And now he was being pushed to find space for five more people! It was impossible. 'My

Lord, the ship will sink if we overload it. We are already at maximum capacity, to make room for…'

'One more will make little difference,' the jarl retorted, heatedly.

'But five will.'

It was Yrsa who had spoken. A hush fell over the dock as Yrsa, the only person there with more authority than the jarl himself, hobbled forward. Her movements were stiff and graceless, and she was clearly in some pain.

'I have already made arrangements with Ulfrik,' she lied. 'He takes us as far as Tromø. No further. We will not be a burden for more than a day.'

Ulfrik stepped back a little, hoping the jarl would not ask him to confirm her words. He would rather do battle with the Fenris wolf than oppose Yrsa when she was hurting.

'To add yet another would endanger lives, including my own,' she continued, pointedly.

'It is for the safety of all on board that I add him, Lady,' Jarl Erik said.

'Then you must subtract one, also,' Yrsa retorted. 'It's common sense.' She gestured to something by her feet. A stone. Aud bent to pick it up and handed it to the old woman, and Yrsa tossed it, seemingly at random, toward the knarr. It landed with a smack on the nose of the ram that Ingvar was leading back to the ship. The animal bleated and bucked, catching Ingvar by surprise and pulling free of his grip. It butted him in the guts, sending him sprawling at the feet of the jarl, where he lay gasping for breath.

'It seems the gods have chosen this one,' Yrsa said, without the hint of a smile.

Ulfrik didn't know how Yrsa knew of their peril given that the crew were ignorant of it themselves, or how she had managed to save his son and make it seem like the divine will of the gods, but she had given him Ingvar's life and for that he could have kissed her.

He would take the Völur to Tromø.

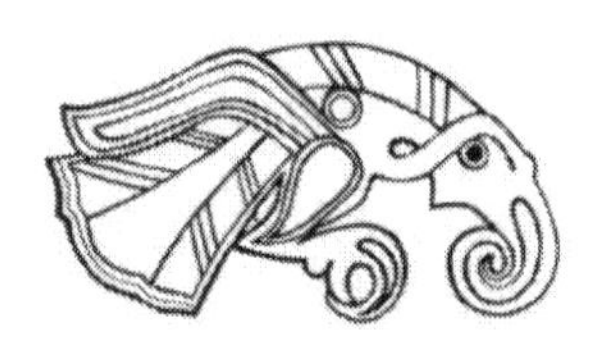

KADLIN

Even though her father was a merchant, and regularly travelled to far off places, Kadlin had never been to sea. She recalled once, as a small child, her mother had brought her to visit Ulfrik and he had taken her to see the boats moored at the dock.

'One day I'll have a ship of my own,' he had promised, 'and I'll take you anywhere you want to go.' He had told her tales of the merfolk, and of gargantuan fish that could swallow a longship whole. He talked of lands where the people were brown as the earth, and of marketplaces so vast that the whole of Bramsvik could fit in one corner. She had longed to travel with him and see the world and all its many marvels, but her favourite stories had been those her mother told her; tales of the gods and goddesses, of giants and Valkyries and eight-legged horses.

Now that she was here aboard her father's ship and setting sail to visit a king, Kadlin felt over-whelmed. The knarr was designed to transport goods, with a wide, deep hull which held the cargo and helped to balance the ship at sea. Above this was the main deck where the crew ate, slept, worked and - when necessary - rowed. There was not much space with a crew of eighteen men and women, one goat (to provide fresh milk and possibly meat on their journey), five crated hens, a full cargo and the four Völur. Surprisingly, though, she did not feel too cramped. Having nothing but the sky above her, and water all around, gave the illusion of spaciousness.

The first thing Kadlin did when she boarded the knarr was seek out the ship's gnome and make herself known to it. Not every vessel had a wight, but this one did. A ship with a wight was a very precious thing indeed, as the gnome took great pride in his abode and would keep it free from woodworm and rot. He would not keep rats away (for that you needed a cat) as they were no danger to his home, only to the cargo, and ship gnomes did not concern themselves with such human things. Nor did he particularly care for the lives of those on board. Protection for the voyage must be sought directly from the gods by means of a sacrifice. But if you kept the deck clean, maintained a good humour, and now and then left a small offering for the ship's gnome, he would ensure that the boat itself was in good condition and sailed true.

Kadlin found him at the front of the The Ox, sitting with his legs dangling over the side of the knarr and one arm draped around the crude, carved head of the prowbeast. He was a little under two feet tall, with arms and legs which would have seemed disproportionately long on a human, but which were perfect for climbing the rigging of a ship. His nose, too, seemed overly lengthy, with a sharp bridge and pointed tip. His hands were thick and muscular with knuckles like knotted rope. His eyes were the deep, blueish green of the ocean, and his long, shaggy blonde hair was bleached almost white by the sun. He was unseen by the crew and completely disinterested in them, but he noticed Kadlin. He turned to look at her, and she saw that his braided beard barely reached his waist. A young one, then, probably no more than eighty years old. She had brought a small pot of curd as an offering, which she placed on the freshly scrubbed, wooden planks of the deck.

'You have a fine ship, Master Gnome,' she began. It was a matter of courtesy to start the conversation with a compliment. 'I am Kadlin, daughter of Svala, daughter of Yrsa, and this will be my first time at sea. I'll only be on board until tomorrow, so I wanted to introduce myself and thank you for your hospitality.' She waited a few moments, but the gnome said nothing. He climbed down, picked up the pot of curd and sniffed it suspiciously. He pushed a large finger into the pot, swirled it around and then sucked it. Apparently pleased with her offering, he climbed back up to where he'd been sitting before, turned his back on her, and proceeded to eat noisily. Considering herself dismissed, Kadlin left him to his meal.

When all was packed and stowed on board, and the crew had said their final goodbyes to friends and loved ones on the dock, they assembled for the sacrifice and the blessing of the voyage. Ulfrik approached Yrsa, leading the ram that had butted Ingvar earlier.

'It took a while to catch,' he said, grinning. 'Would you honour us, Lady?'

As captain, Kadlin's father usually performed the sacrifice and blessing rite, but to do so when there was a Völva in the group would have been disrespectful and improper.

'We'll need something greater than this, Ulfrik Varinsson,' Yrsa replied, flatly. Then to Jofrið she said, 'Fetch Sour Nose.'

Kadlin caught her breath. Sour Nose was one of the oxen who had pulled their cart to Bramsvik today. The offering of a ram seemed overly extravagant for a merchant, but to sacrifice a beast as large, powerful and costly as an ox was unusual to say the least. What could be so perilous about this voyage that Yrsa would suggest such an offering? Others in their assembly were obviously wondering the same as a low murmur went around the group.

'I've no wish to offend the gods, but a ram is the best I can afford.' Ulfrik said, sweating.

'Did I ask for payment? I will bear the cost. Bring me the ox,' her grandmother replied.

'Yrsa…' Jofrið began.

'Bring me the ox,' Yrsa commanded. For a moment Kadlin thought she saw sadness on Yrsa's face before it was replaced with her usual stoic expression.

Jofrið hastened to do as she was told. She unhitched Sour Nose from the cart and led the beast, snorting and lowing, over to Yrsa. Kadlin remembered the birth of the ox, who had earned her name by being born with lesions on her nose. The wounds had oozed a foul-smelling mucus which formed a crust around the nostrils of the little calf, making it hard for her to breathe and feed at the same time. Her mother had contracted the disease while pregnant, and she'd been infected while still in the womb. The cow had died after giving birth, and Kadlin – only six at the time and not long having lost her own mother – had been distraught. Yrsa had given permission for her and Jofrið to try to save the calf, and they had slept in the barn with Sour Nose while they patiently nursed her back to health. She was more than a beast of burden to them, and Kadlin was sad to see her die, but if there was one thing she had been taught over the years it was that duty, honour and the will of the gods came before all other concerns. If her grandmother said this sacrifice was necessary, then it was her sacred duty to assist. She was keenly aware that the lives of all on board depended on this. If the sacrifice failed to please the gods, the ship could be lost and the crew with it. Her affection for Sour Nose could not be allowed to eclipse that.

Kadlin fetched a large bowl from their belongings and a switch of pine they had cut earlier on their trek to the town. Aud and Jofrið stood either side of Sour Nose, holding the rope of her halter while Ulfrik tied the ring through her nose to a hefty post on the dock. It took five men to hobble the ox and hold her down, and Kadlin held the bowl as close as she could beneath Sour Nose's head.

Ulfrik handed Yrsa his knife. She raised the dagger high and spoke loudly and clearly.

'Mighty Njörð, god of the sea and dweller in Nóatún, we offer you this sacrifice and ask that you accept it.' Yrsa sliced the large artery on the side of the animal's neck. The blade was sharp, and she was well practiced. It was a relatively small cut, but blood gushed in torrents, filling the bowl almost instantly and splattering Kadlin's arms. Sour Nose began to thrash, trying to stand despite the ropes hobbling her legs. Three more of the crew threw their weight into holding her down.

'Great Njörð,' Yrsa continued, 'accept our sacrifice and grant this ship safe passage across the sea. This is a good ox. A strong ox. She has a true heart and a sweet nature.

Accept her life and consecrate her blood.'

The blood still poured but no longer pumped from the stricken animal as she gradually weakened and slumped. It drenched the dock and ran as a red river into the sea. Kadlin stood and lifted the bowl while the crew formed a tight circle around them. Yrsa dipped the pine switch in the bowl and flicked it so that the lifeblood of the ox fell as crimson rain on those assembled.

'Bless this crew as they ride the waves to Haithabyr. Protect them from the cravings of Rán's daughters. Keep them safe while they are at sea and bring them home to their families.'

Finally, Kadlin carried the bowl over to the knarr to bless the ship. She should have been excited at the prospect of her first journey at sea, spending time with her father, and the chance to read for royalty, but as she approached the ship Kadlin felt an overwhelming sense of sadness and loss. So strong was the feeling that she almost lost her balance and dropped the bowl. She steadied herself, but as she did so a single tear rolled down her cheek and splashed into the blood, contaminating the blessing. The enormity of what she had done froze her to the spot, and in that moment Yrsa took the bowl from Kadlin's hands…

'Wait!' Kadlin cried, but it was too late. She watched in horror as her grandmother emptied the contents over the prow of the knarr, soaking it not only with the consecrated blood of Sour Nose, but also with a powerful sense of sorrow and loss. Kadlin's vision shifted, and it seemed that she was witnessing two events at the same time. On the one hand she could see the crew, newly blessed and celebrating the completion of the ritual, but she could also hear them screaming and see them dying as crackling flames leapt high around them.

From the deck, the ship's gnome watched her with growing interest.

★

Kadlin would have liked to have spoken to her brother before they set sail, but after what happened with the sacrifice she couldn't bring herself to do so. Ingvar had been raised by their father, and she by their mother and grandmother, and so the two rarely had occasion to meet or catch up on events in each other's lives. She had attended his handfasting the previous summer, when he wed his childhood sweetheart, Gytha, and since then Kadlin had heard that Gytha was pregnant with their first child. She would have liked to talk to Ingvar about his impending fatherhood and share her excitement at the prospect of becoming an aunt. Instead, she found herself a space at The Ox's stern, curled up on the floor with her travel bag as a pillow, and pretended to sleep. She didn't raise her head when the ship cast off, nor when the crew shared evening meal. The stars were bright in an inky sky before she felt able to face the others. It was Yrsa who roused her.

'You're missing it,' she said, softly, looking out over the black water. 'I thought you'd be excited for your first voyage at sea.' She held out a plate of dried fish and bread.

'Thank you,' Kadlin replied, taking the food. 'I'm sorry. I was tired.'

Yrsa sighed heavily and sat down on the deck with as much grace as her aching bones allowed, leaning her back against the hull of the ship. 'When you were small, and you thought you had done something wrong, you would not sulk, or cry, or blame it on someone else like other children. Instead you would curl up in a corner and pretend to sleep. A whole day you did this, once, when you spilled a pail after Aud milked the goat. Now, true, it was you who spilled it, but Aud knew you were too weak to carry that heavy pail. Yet still she asked you, and you tried because you wanted to prove yourself useful. Should I have punished you? No. The fault lay with Aud. But you blamed yourself and pretended to sleep from dawn 'til dusk. Always try to judge people by their intentions, rather than the outcome of their actions. The gods are wiser than us. They understand this.'

Kadlin's stomach growled. She took a small bite of the fish and chewed it, feeling awkward that Yrsa had seen through her subterfuge.

'You're not a child any more Kadlin, and I didn't raise you to be weak. When we make mistakes, we stand and take the consequences. We do not hide from them. This is how we learn, and how we grow, and how we become stronger.'

The shame threatened to overwhelm her but Kadlin knew her grandmother was right.

'I've put everyone at risk,' she began. 'I felt suddenly overcome with sadness earlier, as if I had lost something very dear, or as if…' She paused, trying to form her feelings into words. 'It was as if I was leaving you behind and would never see you again. It only lasted a moment, but I shed a tear and it fell in the bowl. You blessed the ship with tainted blood, and I had a vision of death.'

It seemed an eternity before Yrsa responded. The old woman sighed.

'Oh, my dear, the Norns wove a dark and dangerous path for this crew moons ago. I have felt the warp and weft of it coming together in recent days, and I fear its resolution. I sacrificed Sour Nose in the hope of preventing something that I know cannot be prevented! Whether Njörð accepts or rejects our offering, the path remains the same.'

'The Norns create opportunities,' Kadlin said. 'You taught me that. They offer choices and judge us by the decisions we make. No fate is set in stone.'

Yrsa considered for a moment. 'No fate is certain. That is true. The Norns don't move us around like puppets. What they do is provide opportunities for us to reach our full potential. Imagine your life as a piece of cloth. The warp,' she held up one hand with the fingers splayed, each pointing upward, 'is the chances for greatness the Norns provide for you. The thread of your life – the weft – is dictated by you, and you alone. The choices you make at each of these moments in your life influence which direction your life thread moves next.' Yrsa wove a finger from her other hand in between the fingers of the first. 'If you act with courage and honour, they take you to an even greater challenge and a better chance to prove your worth to the gods. If your choices are unwise, or your actions shameful, then certain opportunities that would have been yours are no longer in your future. It all comes down to choices in life, Granddaughter, and what you do with them.'

'Then I am right. We can still change this doom that you've foreseen.'

Yrsa laughed. 'Oh, to be your age and have such confidence. No, my dear, you are forgetting the effect of other people's choices on our lives. There are more players than the two of us at work here. I fear there are two decisions yet that will have a monumental impact on the threads of all our lives.' She paused. 'One remains hidden from me.'

‘And the other?’ Kadlin felt suddenly chilled and pulled her cloak a little tighter.

‘The other must be guided by their own heart. I can only influence so much.’

YRSA

It was long after everyone else had gone to sleep that Ulfrik sought her out. Other than Thorfrida, who was on watch at the prow, they were the only two still awake. She felt the awkwardness of him - his hesitancy and fear - and it irritated her.

'Are we not beyond this,' she asked, keeping her voice low so as not to wake the crew who slumbered around them. 'We've shared a family for twenty years, yet still you approach me as if I were a dragon. Or a bear. Do you think I will bite?'

'Forgive me, Lady,' he said, smiling.

'Stop doing it and then we'll talk of forgiveness. And you

can drop the formalities.'

Ulfrik chuckled and she sensed the tension melt from him. 'How are you, Yrsa,' he asked, warmly, coming to stand beside her and staring out at the vast, black water that surrounded them. They were following the coastline to Tromø, and by daylight would still have been able to see land on their port side, but on such a night - with clouds covering the stars and only a waning, crescent moon to light their way - The Ox seemed to float in liquid darkness.

'Old,' Yrsa said, in response to his question, 'and without the patience to waste time on idle pleasantries.' She turned to face him. 'You didn't wait until all were sleeping to enquire after my health. Ask your question or leave me to my thoughts.'

Ulfrik glanced at the dozing crew, afraid of being overheard. There was no privacy to be found aboard a ship, nor any place to speak in secrecy. He lowered his voice to a barely audible whisper and brought his face closer to her ear.

'We do not travel to Haithabyr by my own choice, and neither do we go on my own business.' He hesitated, as if concerned that he was breaking some sacred oath. Finally, he sighed and said 'I trust you, Yrsa, and will speak plainly. We carry a cargo from Jarl Erik to be delivered at the market. I fear, when we do, it'll be the death of my crew and me. The jarl knows the risk yet sends us anyway. I suspect you already know something of this as you made him remove Ingvar from the ship. For that you have my gratitude.'

'I did no such thing,' Yrsa retorted. 'I merely interpreted the will of the gods.'

'Well,' Ulfrik continued, 'I wanted to ask if you would interpret their will for me.'

Very little surprised Yrsa anymore, but this request did. She had known Ulfrik for most of his life. Her own mother had helped bring him into the world. She knew him to be a good man who honoured the gods and loved his family. She also knew that his father, Varin, had drowned as the result of a curse when Ulfrik was seven years old. It had left the young boy with a healthy fear of all things magical and occult, and not once in all the years she'd known him had Ulfrik Varinsson ever sought a reading from her or any other. Not even during the years he spent with her daughter, Svala. She hid her surprise and nodded her agreement. He looked relieved.

'And the price,' he asked.

'We've yet to discuss our fare to visit King Redbeard,' she replied. 'This will make us even.'

'Your passage to Tromø was paid in full when you saved my son,' Ulfrik responded. 'I'm a merchant, Yrsa. I believe in fair trade. What is your price?'

She thought for a moment. 'A favour,' she said, eventually.

'Name it.'

'I'm not certain yet,' she told him, honestly, 'but I will ask something of you before you leave for Haithabyr, and you will not deny me. No matter what.'

She could see this troubled Ulfrik, but he agreed.

★

Yrsa told Ulfrik to wait until first light, explaining that a reading at the start of a journey would align more acutely with the energies of the dawn, and therefore allow her to give a more accurate interpretation of the gods' response. In truth, she'd simply been tired, and her eyes were no longer sharp enough to read runes by moonlight. Vanity had not allowed her to admit this and ask for a lantern. Age had brought her wisdom and experience, but she did not regard it as a friend. Little by little it was stripping her of her dignity and independence. She was damned if she was going to let it take her pride and reputation, too.

Yrsa always carried her rune staves with her. They were a part of her everyday dress, like putting on her shift or hangerock, and she would have felt naked without them. She managed to get a few, restless hours sleep and was ready for Ulfrik when the first rays of light peered over the horizon. Olvir, a young man of sixteen, and a recent addition to the crew, was on watch at the time and observed her with interest as she cleared a small space on the deck and spread out a clean, square piece of cloth. He turned his back, quickly, when Ulfrik clipped him round the ear and told him to mind his own business.

'Ask your question,' Yrsa instructed, quietly, when Ulfrik came to sit beside her.

'Can the gods tell me anything of this journey,' he whispered urgently, aware of the crew members stirring around them. 'Is there a way to safely deliver the silver?' He looked up sharply, realising he had let something slip. Yrsa pocketed the information but didn't react to it. 'Most importantly,' he continued, 'will we ever return home?'

Yrsa picked up the soft, doeskin pouch in which she kept her rune staves. It was old, with many repairs to the stitching, and was shiny in places where it had been handled over the decades. The staves themselves she had cut from an ash tree the year she had her first bleed. She had carved the symbols deep into the wood, and over time they had darkened to a rich, deep, earthy brown. She had other rune staves, but these were her favourite. She gently tipped them from the pouch and held them a moment in her cupped hands.

'Urðr, guide my hands,' she murmured, addressing the Norns by name. 'Let my casting be true. Show me what brought us to this moment. Verðandi, guide my thoughts.

Let me interpret your meaning clearly. Show me what actions need to be taken. Skuld, guide my words. Let me speak truthfully, without bias. Show me the price to be paid.'

Yrsa closed her eyes a moment in silent prayer, then held her hands above the cloth and let the runes fall. She gathered up every stave that had fallen outside the cloth, or was face down, and put them back in the leather pouch. Of the twenty-four staves, only nine remained. An auspicious number. Nine was the number of Yggdrasil, the World Tree, and of Oðin, the All-father. Nine was the number of worlds within the branches and roots of Yggdrasil. As she studied them, she began to see a pattern emerging, as if a tale was unfolding before her eyes.

'I see deceit,' she warned. 'Trust none but those you hold most dear. There is someone aboard who will betray you.'

'These are my crew,' Ulfrik protested. 'I trust any one of them with my life.'

'Then you are a fool and you will die,' Yrsa said, bluntly. She gestured at the runes. 'There is blood and fire in your future, Ulfrik. Listen to what the gods are telling you. Trust none but those closest to you.'

'Why? Why would anyone here wish me harm?' Ulfrik asked, incredulous.

'This is not about you,' she replied. 'This is about someone else's secret. The cargo you mentioned; the sooner you deliver it the better.'

She saw his eyes flick nervously toward the stern.

'It will be delivered, then,' he enquired.

'Perhaps.' Yrsa studied the staves closely. The rune *dagr* caught her attention. *Dagr*, the rune of transformation, and of opposites becoming one. 'You must disguise it,' she advised him. 'Disguise it so well that even if someone were to hold it in their hands, they would not see the truth of what it is. It must be concealed yet not hidden.'

'How is that possible,' Ulfrik asked.

'The gods only reveal so much,' she replied. 'Some of the work you must do yourself. What I can tell you for certain is this; there is someone on board who will kill to prevent that silver reaching Haithabyr. Your only hope is to transform it into something else before you get there. It must be concealed but kept in plain sight. The more you try to hide it, the less your chance of success.'

'How…' he began again, but Yrsa held up a finger to shush him. More than one of the crew was awake now, and with every person who stirred came the chance of their whispered conversation being overheard. She must let him know what she had seen and there was no time to soften the blow.

'Death will plague you every step of this journey until you are rid of that silver, Ulfrik. I'm sorry. Deliver it as soon as you can. The longer it's in your possession, the more people are going to die.'

ULFRIK

Ulfrik felt empty the rest of that morning, as if his insides had been washed and scoured, and there was nothing left but a shell. He couldn't think. Couldn't feel. He was numb. A part of him wished he had never asked Yrsa for a reading, but that was the weak part; the part of him that wanted to hide. He'd hoped Yrsa would have some words of comfort for him, or at least sage advice, but instead she had confirmed his worst fears – death was coming for him and his crew, and there was every chance he would never see his family again.

Ulfrik looked at Kadlin standing beside the prowbeast. There was little of her mother in her, and he could see even less of himself. He loved her, but he didn't know her anymore. All the fond memories he had of time spent with his daughter were from before her mother died, when Kadlin was small. It was difficult to reconcile that boisterous and feisty little girl with the respectable young woman he saw today. She'd always been bruised, with scrapes on her knees and twigs in her hair and would tell him proudly of her adventures. One day she'd be battling trolls, the next it was giants or bears.

He recalled one summer day when he and Svala had taken the children fishing. He'd been sat on the riverbank with Ingvar, who was six at the time, teaching the boy how to bait a hook and how to keep quiet so as not to scare the fish away. Ingvar, who had been hoping to catch some plaice or maybe a dab, spent ages sitting still as a rock patiently waiting for one to bite. Suddenly, Kadlin had barrelled past them into the river brandishing a stick, yelling that the World Serpent was hiding in the water and that she would save them! The frightened fish had scattered, and poor, patient Ingvar had burst into tears. Kadlin had been devastated to realise she was the cause. Later, when Ingvar had calmed down and it was time to return home, she'd run back to the river and persuaded the water nymphs to give her a fish for her brother.

It was the first time Ulfrik ever remembered being afraid of her.

Her mother, Svala, never used her gifts around him. It was an unspoken rule with them, and one of the things he loved most about her. He had not - would never - ask her to be anything but herself, yet she instinctively knew that part of her unnerved and frightened him. Those closest to him, who knew of his father and understood his distrust of magic, found it strange that he had fallen for a Völva. She was, they reasoned, the very opposite of what he needed. What did they know? Her beauty, her grace, her gentleness, her kind nature and easy smile, these were the things that Ulfrik loved about his Svala. And he loved the way she loved him. Even though they couldn't live together, and could never be wed, Ulfrik would gladly have given her the rest of his life. The powerful sorceress who spoke with the gods, cast curses and spells and could see into the future - this was not the Svala he knew.

Ulfrik sighed, wishing he could ask her about his current predicament. She had been wise beyond measure and would surely have had some advice for him. He looked once again at their daughter, standing by the prowbeast with the wind whipping her hair. He should speak to her. Svala would have been ashamed to see him now, fearing the company of their own child. His chest tightened at the prospect, but he made himself walk over and address her.

'I should have spoken to you sooner, Lady,' he said, using the proper greeting. 'What do you think of The Ox?'

She turned, and for a moment he saw his little girl in her eyes, full of wonder and excitement. Then, in an instant, the look was gone, replaced with the practiced, sedate expression she normally wore.

'Hello, Father,' she greeted him, politely.

Ulfrik searched his brain for a topic of conversation but drew a blank. It really shouldn't be this difficult to talk to your own daughter, he thought. He couldn't think of a single thing to say that might interest her, and it grieved him to realise how little he knew of her now.

'I wanted…' he began. 'How are you, Kadlin?'

She seemed startled by the use of her name, and he panicked a moment, wondering if he should have been more proper and had caused offence. Then she smiled. 'Truthfully, I'm nervous,' she replied, with an honesty and vulnerability that surprised him.

'It's your first time at sea. There's no shame in being nervous,' he said. 'Don't worry, The Ox is a sturdy ship and she's never sunk yet! Tromø is not much farther. You'll be back on dry land soon.'

She laughed, and he marvelled at how her face transformed; like the sun coming out from behind a cloud. She did not have her mother's delicate, elfin features, but she was beautiful. 'I'm not worried about the sea,' she said. 'I love it out here. It feels like… freedom.'

'Then what?'

'Have you ever met King Redbeard,' she asked, and a small frown furrowed her brow.

'A few times.' Ulfrik replied. 'We often trade there.'

'What is he like? I think I remember seeing him once when I was small, but I'm not certain.'

'Is that what you're worried about,' Ulfrik asked. 'Meeting royalty?'

Kadlin nodded. Ulfrik was stunned. How could a Völva, someone whom most people would be terrified to even look at, let alone speak to, be afraid of meeting anyone?

'He's just a man,' he said, incredulously. 'Don't tell him I called him that, as I like my head upon my shoulders! But seriously, daughter, a king is just a man who has gained power over other men. Whereas you… you speak to the gods! You walk in worlds that most men fear to think about, and you control forces that would make warriors piss themselves. Don't ever be afraid of a king, Kadlin. The thought of your grandmother, alone, is enough to make most men soil their breeks. I promise you King Redbeard is shitting himself at the prospect of meeting all four of you!'

She laughed at that, and he felt a rekindling of the bond that once existed between them.

'It has taken a whole day for the two of you to finally speak to each other,' Yrsa said from behind him, wiping the smile from his face instantly. 'What can you have said to your daughter, I wonder, that is so amusing?'

'Father was just explaining that women like us make men lose control of their bowels,' Kadlin replied, straight-faced. Yrsa glared at him sternly.

'Was he now? Well, just because women have always had that effect on you, Ulfrik Varinsson, does not mean it's normal.'

'I… I…' he stammered.

'Close your mouth, man,' Yrsa instructed. 'You'll catch a fish.'

★

King Harald Redbeard lived on Tromø in a fortified farm on the southern side of the island. The port was much larger than the tiny dock at Bramsvik, with ample space for seven or eight ships. Ulfrik had been here many times before and knew there would be a levy to pay before any of the passengers or crew were permitted to disembark. He was surprised, therefore, to be greeted by a messenger of the king, a retinue of guards and a carriage, instead of the usual grubby, tax collector.

'Arni,' Jofrið shouted, waving at the messenger. The young man blushed and raised his hand, stopping short of waving. Ulfrik had Asbjorn and Olvir take the ladies' bags to the carriage and escorted the women to the dock himself. He said farewell to Kadlin, who assured him she was less nervous after their chat.

'The blacksmith here is very good,' Yrsa murmured as he helped her into the carriage. He looked at her, confused as to her meaning, but she did not elaborate. It was after they had left, while he was pondering the question of how to disguise the silver, that he understood what she meant.

The crew were pleased when Ulfrik gave them leave to get a decent meal in town, and they didn't question it. They were used to stopping at ports on the way and building relationships with locals along their trade route. It was not uncommon to trade at several villages, and stock up on supplies, before reaching the main markets. He told them to be back onboard by midnight as they would be setting sail at dawn. Ulfrik sent Egil to hire a horse and cart, and then had Magnus and Bjarni load the three barrels of silver onto it, along with six wooden crates of axe handles, three chests of axe heads and a cask of mead. Bjarni was the strongest of The Ox's crew, having earned him the name Bjarni Arm-Strong, and was an obvious choice for the task.

'Where do you think you're taking that,' Thorvald One-Eye asked, when most of the crew had already dispersed. Only he, Asbjorn, Magnus and Ulfrik knew the barrels contained hack silver bound for the Danish king. Ulfrik scowled. Thorvald may be the jarl's righthand man back in Bramsvik, but out here he was just another deck hand.

'This port is guarded day and night,' Ulfrik said, 'so theoretically it's safe to leave your cargo unattended. But if you think I'm letting these barrels out of my sight, you are a fool. Where I go, they go. I need to get these axe heads affixed to the handles, and the blacksmith here is good at his job, so the barrels and Magnus are coming with me. Now why don't you go run after your precious peacock and leave me to my business.'

'Hel's tits! I never thought to hear you stand up to One-Eye like that,' Magnus grinned, once they were alone. 'Now what the fuck are we really doing with all of this?'

Trust none but those closest to you, Yrsa had said. In the absence of his son, Ulfrik told Magnus his plan and took him to visit the blacksmith.

KADLIN

The king's carriage was much more comfortable than anything else Kadlin had ever ridden in. It had actual seats with some sort of padding, and the sides of the carriage were strung with garlands of fragrant herbs to scent the air as they rode along. Jofrið had wanted to share Arni Andvettson's horse and ride with him on the short journey to King Redbeard's home, but Yrsa forbade it.

'Stay together tonight,' she cautioned, with uncharacteristic concern. 'And beware of your words. Reading for a king is not like reading for anyone else. Men think themselves gods when they gain a little power, and act as such. They think they are beyond consequences. I have yet to meet a king whose mind is not warped by pride and paranoia.'

'I don't understand,' Kadlin said. 'Are you saying we shouldn't speak the truth?' Throughout her whole life she had been taught the importance of honesty, so Yrsa's words confused her. The Völur were emissaries for the Norns and lying about what they revealed came at a price.

'Always speak truthfully,' Yrsa replied. 'Always. Better to anger royalty than the gods. But how much or how little of the truth you reveal... that's for you to judge. Kings and Queens are not like normal people. They value flattery above candour.'

The armed guards sent to greet them had clearly been for show rather than necessity as they encountered no hostility. Rather, they were shown great reverence by the locals they passed along the path. King Harald Herbrandsson, also known as King Redbeard due to his vibrant facial hair, lived on a farm only a short ride from the port. A large, wooden fortification ran around the boundary of the farm, with sentries positioned at the gate. Arni led the carriage to a comfortable hof within the grounds.

'My lord welcomes you to Tromø and thanks the Völur for making the journey,' he said, pleasantly. 'A feast is being prepared as you instructed. Rest and cleanse yourselves, Ladies, and I'll return shortly to escort you to the king.'

'Why is that boy always telling me what to do?' Yrsa griped, after Arni had gone.

'He was being polite,' Jofrið replied, 'as well you know. I think he's nice.'

Aud rolled her eyes. 'You don't think he's nice. You just want his cock,' she corrected.

'And perhaps if you had one every now and then you'd be less foul,' Jofrið countered. Aud took off a shoe and threw it at Jofrið, who squealed and threw one back. The two proceeded to chase each other around the hof, hurling insults and footwear.

Kadlin took her grandmother's arm and led her away from their squabbling companions. There was a chair beside the hearth, and Yrsa gratefully sank into it. As she did so there was a knock at the door. Kadlin sighed. It was the first time the four of them had been alone together since leaving home - their first chance for privacy - and she had been looking forward to speaking with her grandmother. She opened the door to find two thralls standing outside, one holding a jug of weak mead and some cups, and the other a bowl of warm water and cloths. Kadlin smiled.

It felt good to wash the salt from her body. She hadn't realised how much sea spray clung to her skin until she began to clean it off. When the four of them were properly cleansed and had quenched their thirst they braided their hair, adding such beads and charms as they felt appropriate. Aud always added feathers to her hair. She had a great affinity to the element of air, and to birds of all kinds, and collected feathers daily on her walks. The best of these she strung on thin lengths of leather with which she bound her long braids. Jofrið wove narrow strips of fabric into her hair. She had once bragged to Kadlin that she tore a piece of cloth from the clothing of each of her lovers, and that the remembrance of their nights of passion fuelled her magic, but Kadlin didn't know if this was true. Jofrið also added three bronze charms to her hair. One was shaped like a cat in honour of the goddess Freya, another was a serpent - as long as a finger - that curled its way around a thick braid, and the third was a tiny bell that jingled pleasantly as she moved. Yrsa's hair was ornamented with many different things that she had collected over her lifetime. There were little stones with holes in, glass beads, beads of amber and jet, twigs and bones that she had carved with runes or sigils, the skulls of a raven and a frog, and falcon feathers. Every item with which the Völur adorned themselves was meaningful and strong in magic, to aid their work.

Kadlin herself wore only one item woven into her braids - a blue, glass bead that had belonged to her mother and complimented the colour of Kadlin's eyes. Her father had brought it back from one of his voyages and Kadlin remembered being entranced by it as a child. The craftsman who made it had added small dots of glass at random around the bead, creating raised bumps that a child's fingers could not resist. She wore it in remembrance of her mother, and to encourage Svala's spirit to assist her magical workings.

'Here,' Yrsa said quietly, holding something out to her. 'Wear this.' She handed Kadlin the magnificent ring that Arni Andvettson had given her as a token from the king. It was exquisitely crafted from gold with a large, blood red garnet in the centre, and intricate gold knotwork either side of the stone. Kadlin had never seen such a fine piece of jewellery. She tried it on, finding it fit the middle finger on her right hand perfectly.

'It's beautiful,' she breathed, 'but I can't wear it. I'll be far too afraid of losing it.' She removed the ring and tried to hand it back, but her grandmother wouldn't accept it.

'It's a gift,' the old woman said with a smile.

'You could buy a small farm with this!' Kadlin exclaimed. She owned nothing much of any real value, and to be offered such an expensive and extravagant present made her panic a little. 'Thank you for the gesture but what would I do with such a ring?' She tried again to place it back in Yrsa's hand.

'Wear it,' her grandmother insisted, closing Kadlin's fingers around the ring and patting her hand gently. 'It's all I have to give.'

Kadlin wasn't sure why it was necessary for Yrsa to give her anything, but she knew it would cause offence if she continued to refuse the offering. She replaced the ring on her finger and hugged Yrsa.

'Thank you,' she said, awkwardly. The words felt inadequate for such generosity. She caught Aud scowling at her from the doorway and realised she would pay for this later.

★

King Harald's mead hall was the most impressive building Kadlin had ever seen. The double front doors were nine feet tall, each richly carved with scenes of intertwined serpents and battling dragons. Jarl Erik's mead hall could have fit inside it twice with room to spare. Wind-holes were cut into the walls at intervals to let in light and air, and Kadlin noted each had shutters that slid into place to keep out the rain, or to keep in the warmth on cold nights. Approximately one hundred candles and a central firepit added extra heat and light, not that any was needed on such a fine Spring afternoon. Six substantial trestle tables ran the length of the room, three either side, each bedecked with fragrant garlands of herbs and flowers like those that had adorned their carriage. The whole room smelled wonderfully fresh and aromatic. On a raised dais at the far end of the room were two immense, wooden thrones. As Kadlin drew nearer she could see each was engraved with countless fish of every size and shape.

Arni led them through a doorway at the back of the hall, leading to the royal family's private rooms. The walls were hung with fine tapestries in coloured threads, and Kadlin wished she could linger a while and appreciate their beauty. One of them, she was sure, depicted the story of Brynhildr and Sigurd, but she could not place the characters and scenes so intricately woven on the others.

King Harald and his wife, Queen Gunnhild, were seated by the hearth. It was plain to see how the king came by his name of Redbeard, as the flaming, wiry hair on his face was at striking odds with the nut-brown mane on his head. King Harald's beard was parted into three, with each kept separate by a thick, gold bead the size of a finger bone. His hair was woven on one side, like a basket, and had been set with the aid of pungent, pine resin which made his hair shine. The hair on the other side of his head hung loose except for one, thin braid. He was not as tall, nor as large as Kadlin recalled from her childhood. Although an impressive and regal figure, she did not find him as intimidating as she'd expected.

Queen Gunnhild was quite a bit younger than her husband. She looked weary, which was only to be expected so soon after giving birth, but Kadlin sensed there was more to it than that. The queen was scared. Whether she feared her husband, or meeting the Völur, or the supposed bad omens seen while she was giving birth, Kadlin couldn't tell. Despite the dark circles under her eyes, Queen Gunnhild was clearly a handsome woman. She reminded Kadlin of Sif, wife to Thor and goddess of the harvest, with her long, golden hair and rosy complexion. A small boy of around a year old was playing by her feet with a wooden, toy longship. He hurried to his mother's side as they entered the room and peered out at them from behind her skirts. The queen stayed seated, but the king rose to greet them. His many gold and silver arm rings clinked as he extended a hand to Yrsa.

'Welcome to Tromø, my Ladies. I hope your journey was a pleasant one.'

Kadlin heard Aud snort and hoped the king hadn't heard her. King Harald took each of their hands in turn and kissed them.

'Congratulations on the birth of your daughter,' Yrsa replied. The tension in the room instantly magnified. With one innocuous sentence, she had confirmed the source of their fear. Both King Harald and his wife were terrified of the portents and what they might mean.

'Thank you,' Queen Gunnhild said softly. 'Forgive me for not rising to greet you properly. It was a difficult delivery.'

'I shall make you a balm to help with the discomfort, my Queen,' Yrsa said, comfortingly. She waved at the little boy, who grinned at her and held up his toy. 'This must be Gyrd. What a fine ship you have there! He is a strong, young lad, King Harald. May I introduce my granddaughter, Kadlin Svalasdaughter.'

Kadlin wasn't usually nervous when meeting new people, but then she was used to being the most influential person in the room and therefore had no cause to ever feel daunted. Meeting a king, however, particularly in these resplendent and ostentatious surroundings, put her on one foot. She remembered what her father had told her. *I promise you King Redbeard is shitting himself at the prospect of meeting all four of you!* The words put a smile on her face and chased away her concerns.

'It's an honour to meet you, Lady,' King Harald said, addressing her. 'You have formidable blood in your veins.'

'And you will remember Aud The Forthright,' Yrsa continued swiftly. Aud had refused to be known by the name of either parent from a young age. For a long time, in her youth, she had apparently been referred to as simply Aud Agðir, meaning Aud of the kingdom of Agder. Later, once her propensity for blunt and candid speaking became known, she was called Aud The Forthright. Kadlin had overheard people call her Aud The Tactless, but this was unfair. Aud spoke the truth, and could be brusque at times, but she was almost as skilled as Yrsa when it came to diplomacy.

'Of course,' King Harald replied, turning to Aud. 'If my advisors had half your wisdom and integrity, Lady, I would be a richer man.'

'And this is Jofrið Ingasdaughter, known to some as Jofrið Second-Sighted,' her grandmother continued. Kadlin had heard other names for Jofrið, too…

Once the introductions had been made, and formalities concluded, Yrsa asked to see the new princess and the Völur were taken through to a second chamber in which the royal children slept. Princess Asa was being cared for by a thrall. Despite being less than a week old, the tiny baby had silken tufts of strawberry blonde hair and her mother's radiant complexion. She was, Kadlin thought, a most beautiful child. Had she been told that Asa was an elf Kadlin would have believed it to be true.

'We were told that omens were seen when your daughter was born,' Aud said to King Harald. 'What omens? And how many witnesses?'

The king shifted uneasily, glancing back to the other room where they had left the queen.

'It was a challenging birth. Gunnhild… it was not this way with Gyrd,' he responded, awkwardly. 'It took too long. Almost two days. On the second day a sudden and ferocious storm struck the island. It appeared so swiftly that many of our fishermen were still at sea. Two ships were lost, and many men were drowned that day.' He paused, and Kadlin could see that the king mourned those who had died. Unlike Jarl Erik, this man seemed to truly care for his people. 'At the end,' King Harald continued, 'my wife was so weak she could no longer push, and the women said the baby would die inside her. Gunnhild summoned all her strength and made one last attempt. Asa was finally born, and as she took her first breath it began to rain blood from the sky.'

★

When the feast was concluded, and it was time for the Völur to enter the other realm, the trestles were cleared, and a high platform was swiftly constructed to one side of the mead hall. Four comfortable chairs were placed upon it, and the four women were assisted up on to the platform. Kadlin sat at the end, beside Aud, making her the last to give her reading.

Yrsa began by asking which of the women in the hall knew the songs to summon spirits. Those who did stood and, following her lead, they began to sing and dance. There had been a time, not so long ago, when every woman would have known the songs. In more recent times, when some were beginning to follow a Christian path, not every mother felt comfortable passing this knowledge on to her daughter. Kadlin was grateful that so many here knew what they were doing and could sing well. It was known that certain words, sung sweetly enough, could entice the ancestors and the wights of a place to come and listen.

Kadlin saw myriad wisps appearing at the upper edges of

the hall. As the women sang and danced, these shadows slowly took form and she was able to see the faces of the ancestors, and of the wights of Tromø. By the time the last note had been sung, the mead hall was filled with humans and spirits alike, and she could feel the veil that separates our world from the other pressing against her like a weight. She allowed her mind to push through it, feeling a fleeting sensation of cobwebs on her skin, and then she was in the other realm. She focused on the ring that her grandmother had given her and used it to anchor herself to this reality too, maintaining a fine balance so that she could walk in both worlds at once. Kadlin could sense the presence of Yrsa, Aud and Jofrið, and knew that they, too, had crossed the veil.

'Thank you.' Yrsa's voice sounded loud and clear as a hush fell over the room. 'You sung well, and you were heard. Many have joined us here tonight.' A low, excited murmur went around the hall. 'We have travelled from Bramsvik at the behest of King Harald. I am sure you all know why.'

According to the king, the blood rain had been witnessed by most of the town's inhabitants, and news had spread swiftly of it coinciding with Asa's birth. People feared its meaning, and some had even called for the baby's death. *The gods wept tears of blood,* they said. *Without a doubt, the child is evil and should be sacrificed!* King Harald believed a favourable, public interpretation of the omen was the only thing that could save his daughter's life.

There were perhaps a dozen others at the feast who had questions for the Völur. They were the usual thing. Will I find a husband? Is my wife faithful? Will the harvest be good this year? Such questions they took in turn, so that each of them answered three of the twelve. It was only when King Harald came to pose his questions that they all gave him a reply.

'Do the gods demand I kill my daughter?' One by one the seers answered no, and Kadlin saw the king relax a little. 'Is she evil?' Again, they responded in the negative. Finally, he asked 'Will she ever threaten the people of Tromø, or cause them harm?'

Yrsa was the first to seek answers for him. She rolled her eyes and slumped in her seat, and for a few moments was lost entirely to the other side. She returned a short while later with a great, shuddering gasp, and Kadlin was alarmed to notice fear on her grandmother's face. It was a fleeting expression, lasting no more than an instant, and then Yrsa composed herself.

'Great King, your wife has given birth to a child who will one day become a great Queen! Through her, your line will see a King of Kings who will rule over many lands.'

This seemed to please and appease King Harald, and a great cheer went up from all those assembled in the hall. Kadlin, though, felt nervous as Jofrið began her reply. *You deflected,* she thought, looking at Yrsa and wondering why. *You didn't answer his question.*

'Your daughter will love the kingdom of Agder, and be true to its people,' Jofrið said. Another cheer from the room, but Kadlin noticed she had talked of Agder, the kingdom, rather than the island of Tromø, as King Harald had asked. Aud also gave an evasive answer, telling their royal hosts that Asa would think fondly of Tromø and call it her home, even when she ruled in another land.

When Kadlin's turn came, she allowed herself to step deeper into the other world. She focused her mind on the tiny, beautiful baby she had seen in the crib. The answers came to her as feelings at first, and she understood why the others had been reticent to respond freely. Asa's life seemed filled with anger, and with pain. Anger directed mainly at her father. Kadlin pushed this aside and concentrated on the actual question. Would Asa ever threaten the people of Tromø, or cause them harm?

She found herself standing in the rain outside the mead hall as a dark storm thundered overhead. People screamed. Swords flashed. All around her was darkness and chaos. An arrow flew past her head, and as she followed its trajectory she saw a woman being dragged from the hall by three men. Kadlin recognised Asa immediately, even though she was now the same age as Aud. The scene changed - another land, another time - and Kadlin was racing toward a ship waiting by the riverbank. Asa ran beside her, cradling a crying child. As they reached the ship, Asa looked directly at Kadlin and said 'Tromø is my home. I will never let them take it.'

Kadlin gasped as she came back to her body. She took a moment to process all she had experienced. The silence in the hall pressed in around her and she knew the king was impatiently waiting. *Always speak truthfully.* Yrsa's words came back to her. *But how much or how little of the truth you reveal… that's for you to judge.*

'Your daughter will defend Tromø and its people always,' she replied, feeling the certainty of her words. 'She will never…' Kadlin faltered, remembering the battle she had witnessed. 'She will never intend them harm.'

'Thank you, Ladies,' King Harald said, smiling gratefully. 'May the gods give you blessings.'

Kadlin saw Yrsa close her eyes and give a prayer of thanks. She was about to stand when Queen Gunnhild raised her voice to ask a question.

'And will she find love,' the queen asked. 'Will her marriage be a happy one?'

Kadlin felt a chill as the question was asked, as if a shadow had covered the hall. She glanced at Yrsa and saw her grandmother looking at her with a terrible sadness in her eyes. Yrsa looked away before Kadlin could react, slipping once more into the other world.

'My queen, so strong will be her feelings for her husband that she will never marry again, even after his death.' Yrsa said, and Kadlin was struck by the ambivalence of those words. Strong feelings could mean love but could also mean hate. However, the queen seemed satisfied.

'She will be the most beautiful of women,' Jofrið added after a slight hesitation, when it was her turn. 'She will have more than fifty suitors yet marry only one.'

'The Princess Asa will lose her heart only once, and she will mourn his death greatly,' Aud said gently, showing more compassion than Kadlin would have thought possible.

Kadlin felt uneasy at the prospect of looking beyond the veil again. Her friends were giving very oblique answers to simple questions, and she was not used to having to edit her replies. It wasn't that anything they said seemed untrue, it was just that she could feel them holding back, suppressing something. It was with some trepidation that Kadlin once again crossed over into the spirit realm.

For a second time she found herself standing outside the mead hall while the storm raged around her. A fierce battle was underway, and Kadlin wove her way, unseen, between warriors as they fought. Once more, she saw Asa as an adult, being dragged from the hall by three men. The image changed. Same place. Same storm. But the forces of Tromø were now defeated and the battle was over. Foreign soldiers celebrated. Kadlin saw Asa on her knees in the mud and the rain, wet clothes clinging to her body and hair plastered to her face. A man was forced to his knees in front of her, facing Asa. He had his back to

Kadlin and she could see that his hands were bound. A fine-clothed man raised an axe and, with a single blow, decapitated the captive. Asa was splattered with his blood, as if the rain itself had turned scarlet. Kadlin looked down at the man's head, which had rolled to her feet. His beard was more white, now, than red, but she still recognised the king. She stepped away from the head and almost tripped over the lifeless bodies of Queen Gunnhild and their son, Gyrd.

A voice sounded loud and clear above the cheers and shouts of the men. For a moment Kadlin couldn't believe what she was hearing. She looked back at Asa and saw her still kneeling in the blood and rain, numb with shock, while a goði performed a marriage rite and wed her to her father's executioner.

Behind them stood the three Norns, the wise women who create the fate of all men. Verðandi, Norn of the here and now, creator of opportunities, looked directly at Kadlin.

'Choose, Kadlin, daughter of Svala, daughter of Yrsa. What will you do?'

There were tears in Kadlin's eyes when she clawed her way back to the human realm. She willed them not to fall. She knew it had only been moments since she crossed the veil, but it felt longer. Deliberately, she did not allow herself to look at those sat beside her. This was her decision. The fact that the Norns had appeared in her vision meant that this impacted her directly. It was a turning point in her life, and what she chose to do now would determine her future course.

How much or how little of the truth you reveal... that's for you to judge.

Kadlin looked at King Harald and Queen Gunnhild, and the little boy sat upon the queen's knee. Could she really allow this to happen to these good people without warning them?

Kadlin blinked her eyes and the tears fell, drawing intakes of breath from those close enough to see.

'No,' Yrsa murmured, sensing her granddaughter's choice, but it was too late.

'My Queen,' Kadlin said in a voice that quivered with emotion. 'I know the meaning of the red rain.' King Harald leaned closer on his throne, his face now tense as a bowstring. 'Your daughter's marriage will not be a happy one. I have seen a vision of the future, and on the day your daughter weds, death will come to Tromø.'

There were angry shouts from the people in the hall, but the king silenced them.

'Who,' he demanded. 'Who will die?'

Kadlin swallowed. 'Everyone.'

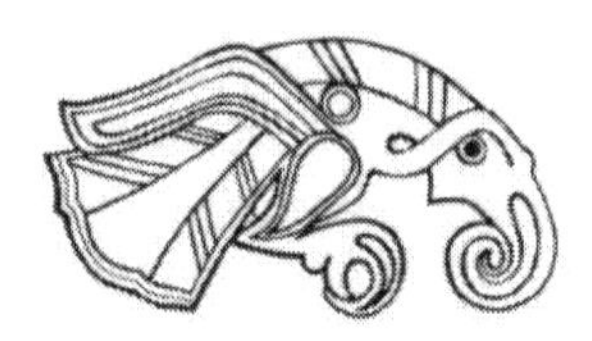

ULFRIK

Ulfrik and Magnus found the blacksmith easily enough. He was a wiry man, no larger than Ulfrik himself, though with half the belly. He laughed when Ulfrik showed him the axe heads and asked if he could recreate them from silver.

'If I had half a brain I may think to do so,' the man chuckled. 'Why would I want to do such a foolish thing? Silver may be shiny, my friend, and make pretty trinkets for your woman, but it will not do when making an axe. You stick to selling your wares and leave the metalwork to me. Silver axes! Would you like me to craft you some handles out of hay? They'd last just as long.'

'We don't need your sarcasm,' Magnus growled. 'Can

you do the job or not, you witless bastard?'

'Witless!' The blacksmith doubled over with laughter. 'Witless, he calls me - the man who wants axe heads made of silver.' He took a moment to compose himself, and wiped tears of mirth from his eyes. 'No, I think not. Good luck finding anyone foolish enough to put his name to that. Try to fell a tree with a silver axe and I'll tell you which will break first! And don't even think about taking one into battle. I'm serious. Don't.'

'Master Smith,' Ulfrik began, 'there has been a misunderstanding, and it is entirely my fault. I don't want silver axes - I am just trying to disguise this.' He prised open one of the barrels and invited the man to look inside. 'I'm told you are the best in all of Agder,' he lied, 'and I need the best. The port taxes alone on this shipment will cripple me before I even get to the market, but the taxes on weapons would be minimal. Help me disguise it and I shall make sure you're known as the greatest smith this side of Uppsala.'

'And how will you be paying me, exactly,' the blacksmith enquired, peering into the barrel.

'Not with any of that, you weasel,' Magnus replied, replacing the lid firmly.

'Friends,' Ulfrik said, lifting the cask of mead. 'Let's have a drink and discuss terms.'

It was agreed that the smith would melt the silver and cast the new axe heads for them. In return, he was to keep the three chests of real axe heads they had brought with them. Initially, he told them to come back in three days. He had other, more important jobs to do first, he insisted. But after a few more cups of mead he was persuaded that Ulfrik and Magnus - his new, good friends - really needed the axe heads by tonight and couldn't wait.

Fortunately, Ketil (for that was his name), already had moulds for weapons similar to theirs. Side by side you could tell a difference, but Ulfrik doubted anyone would notice a subtle change in the design. The sky was dark, and the moon was high by the time the work was finished. Ketil used twelve moulds at a time, carefully melting and pouring the silver expertly into shape. When each was done, and had been cooled, Magnus and Ulfrik removed the axe heads, cleaned the moulds, and lined them up again ready for Ketil to cast the next batch. By his own admission it was not the best work Ketil Smith had ever done, but they could either have speed or quality and they opted for haste.

'They'll never pass as steel,' Magnus lamented, turning one over in his hand. 'Steel does not gleam. Not like this. We've wasted our time.'

Ketil frowned. 'He's right. Unless you've a face like the All-Father you'll see through this in a moment.' The All-Father, Odin, was missing one eye. The joke made Ulfrik think of Thorvald, and he wondered if the jarl's man would be fooled. He doubted it.

Ketil walked over to a large brazier that he had used to heat the silver. There was a thick layer of soot and ash in the bottom, and he scooped this out into pan. Next, he rubbed the surface of one of the axe heads with a little lamp oil, and then with soot and ash. The transformation was miraculous! What had been but a shiny curio moments before now looked like a dull, metal axe. Elated, the three men continued to work this magic on the rest of their hoard. They emptied the chests of the real axe heads and filled them again with the silver ones.

'He'll never be able to keep quiet about this,' Magnus grumbled on their way back to port. 'By tomorrow night everyone on this island will know what we did. We should kill him.'

'By tomorrow night we shall be long gone,' Ulfrik replied, with a smile on his face. 'What does it matter? As far as Ketil knows I'm just a penny-pinching merchant who doesn't want to pay his taxes.'

They stopped at a river along the way and refilled the empty barrels with river rocks to give them weight. So far, apart from missing out on a meal, everything had gone to plan.

The guard at the port, recalling their faces from earlier, let them through without a fuss. It was hard going lifting three barrels of rocks, six crates of wooden handles, and three chests of silver axe heads onto the ship by themselves, and they were exhausted by the time the work was done.

'Fuck me, I could eat a whole boar,' Magnus exclaimed, helping himself to a strip of dried fish from their rations. Ulfrik joined him, eager to silence his nagging stomach.

The crew began to drift back to the ship in various states of insobriety. Warmth disappeared along with the light at this time of year, and they were keen to huddle beneath blankets before the chill seeped too far through their skin. It wasn't long before Ulfrik was snoring alongside them, content in the knowledge that Yrsa's advice had been heeded; the silver was transformed and could now be hidden in plain sight. It made him anxious to think of it laying in unlocked chests with the rest of the cargo, and he did wonder what would happen if Thorvald One-Eye decided to open the barrels and found them full of rocks, but fatigue overcame his worries and he was soon sound asleep.

In his dream, The Ox was being tossed on monstrous waves while a giant serpent called his name. He wakened to find Thorfrida shaking him roughly by the shoulders.

'Ulfrik! Ulfrik, wake up,' she hissed. She pointed to a commotion at the entrance to the port. 'They mentioned The Ox. We may have a problem.'

'Do we have a full crew,' he asked. Thorfrida glanced around, counting heads. She nodded. 'Then rouse them,' Ulfrik said, speaking softly. 'Do it quietly and have them prepare to leave.' He rubbed sleep from his eyes, climbed carefully past those few crew members who were still slumbering, and headed over to the gate. He could only think of one reason for there to be trouble at such an hour - Ketil Blacksmith had betrayed them.

The armed guard posted by the entrance was currently arguing with an old woman.

'Go home, Groa,' the sentry barked. 'You can deal with your business in the morning.'

'The morning will be too late,' he heard her cry. 'I won't be cheated because you let them sail away!' She looked up and saw Ulfrik. 'You! Hey, you! Are you from The Ox? I need to speak with the captain of The Ox.'

'I'm the captain,' he confirmed, relieved not to find the blacksmith and a band of thieves waiting at the gates. 'What's the problem here,' he asked the guard.

'This woman claims…' the man began.

'I claim nothing! I was promised payment to deliver a thrall to your ship. You owe me a goat.' A young woman wearing the shabby, threadbare cloak of a thrall was standing, unnoticed, behind her. The older lady shoved her toward him.

'No thrall is worth a goat,' Ulfrik said, pleasantly. 'Neither is there space on my ship for a thrall. You've been the victim of a prank. None of my crew have bought this girl.' He turned and began to walk sleepily back toward The Ox.

'One of your chickens, then! I will settle for a chicken.'

'Good night,' Ulfrik replied without looking back.

'An agreement was made,' the old woman shrieked angrily, swiping at the guard with her staff as he tried to move her on. 'A deal is a deal. As a merchant you should understand this, Ulfrik Varinsson.'

Ulfrik stopped. He turned back and peered at the woman. She had spoken of goats and chickens, both of which he had on board, and now she knew his name. What was he missing?

'Come on, now, Groa, enough of your shit,' the sentry grumbled. He shoved the younger woman. 'Where did you get a thrall from, anyhow?'

Ulfrik looked at the young girl in the shabby cloak. The hood was pulled down over her face, hiding her features, and she seemed reluctant to leave the dock.

'Take pity, my Lord,' Groa called, adding 'Some would consider this a favour.'

'He owes you no favours, old hag,' the guard shouted,

angrily. 'Go on, now. Leave!'

'Wait!' Ulfrik hurried back to the gate and took the thrall by the arm. 'I'm sure we can find some use for her. A chicken, you say? One moment.' He was fully awake now.

'May the gods bless you,' Groa said. 'One chicken. Yes. The fattest one.'

'I'm sorry it took me so long,' Ulfrik whispered to the hooded figure as he escorted her swiftly back to the safety of the ship. 'What in Thor's name happened?'

'The king wants me dead,' his daughter replied.

KADLIN

Ulfrik didn't question her that night, and for that she was grateful. Kadlin doubted she could have explained the events at the feast without breaking down in tears. They rowed The Ox away from the dock under cover of darkness, setting sail as soon as they were clear of Tromø. She slept fitfully, and her dreams were filled with blood and death.

The sun had only just crested the horizon when Kadlin woke, yet most of the crew were already busy about deck. With wakefulness came memory, and the recollection of the night's events caused a pain so raw that she wanted to scream with the agony of it. She remembered the fury of King Harald. The anguish of the queen. The terrified cries of the young Prince Gyrd. When she'd revealed that Asa's marriage would signal the demise of all at Tromø, the hall had erupted with frightened people calling for the death of the little princess. Believing himself betrayed by the Völur, the king, in his wrath, had yelled at the guards to seize Kadlin. Much after that was a blur. She recalled Yrsa shouting something to Aud, and Aud had grabbed Kadlin by the arm and dragged her from the platform. Men had tried to stop them as they fled the hall, but Aud spat a warning and they had fearfully retreated out of her way. Aud had taken her to Groa and paid the old woman to smuggle Kadlin to the dock.

'Take her to Ulfrik Varinsson, the captain of The Ox,' she'd instructed, as they exchanged Kadlin's blue, woollen cloak with that of a thrall. 'Tell him Yrsa is calling in her favour.'

Yrsa. What had happened to her? Kadlin's last memory of her grandmother was of Yrsa standing imperiously before the king, demanding to know by what right he dared treat the Völur so. Had her decision to warn King Harald gotten her grandmother killed? And what of Jofrið? And Aud?

'Saltfish,' said a voice beside her, waking her from her thoughts. Kadlin sat up and found herself face-to-face with the ship's gnome. She frowned at him, uncomprehending, and he sighed. 'You are Kadlin, daughter of Svala,' he said, slowly, as if conversing with an imbecile. 'I am Saltfish of The Ox.' He proudly patted his chest.

'I thought I was too unimportant to merit your attention,' she replied, recalling the brusque way he'd dismissed her last time they met. She was too upset to mind her manners.

'True. True. But that was before,' Saltfish answered, seemingly unconcerned by her rudeness. 'Something has happened since then.' He was dressed in a faded, red tunic stitched together from old sail cloth and belted with a piece of rope. His skin was tanned, and his feet were bare. He reached out and took her chin in his rough fingers, bringing her face in line with his. The wight stared deep into her eyes, and Kadlin had the unnerving feeling that he could see through them, into her brain, and was reading her thoughts. 'You are interesting now. Yes, you are,' he murmured, releasing her chin. 'Yes, indeed!' He studied her a moment longer, then climbed up onto the side of the ship and stared out to sea.

Kadlin looked out over the vast blue green waters. They were still following the coastline and she could just about make out a hint of land on their port side. The weather was cooler today, with a strong wind that whipped the waves to white foam. The thrall's cloak she wore was thin and meagre, and the sun was not yet high enough to lend any warmth. She shivered.

'Do you not get lonely, Master Gnome, out here all alone,' Kadlin asked, pulling the cloak tighter. Its coarse fabric scratched her skin and she pined for the soft, thick, woollen cloak she had left behind.

'Saltfish,' the gnome corrected her. 'And we're rarely alone.' He pointed to the white-tipped waves and Kadlin's pulse quickened as she noticed nine women just below the surface of the water, swimming effortlessly alongside them like sleek seals - Rán's daughters, offspring of the ocean goddess Rán and her husband, Ægir. What Kadlin had mistaken for white foam was the long, flowing hair of the sisters as it streamed and billowed behind them. Their silvery skin shimmered like a shoal of fish as they sped through the water before plunging once again beneath the waves.

Although seemingly benign, Kadlin knew Rán's daughters were the bane of ocean travellers and would often take a fancy to a craft or crew and drag them to the seabed. She fervently hoped their visit this morning was out of curiosity rather than craving.

'You are shining a light, today,' Saltfish marvelled. 'Everything wants to get a look at you. What have you done, I wonder, little seer, to light such a bright flame within yourself?' He studied her again. 'I like it,' he concluded.

Kadlin looked at her hands and arms but could see no difference. Even using the sight, she detected no change, though she knew what the gnome was speaking of and had seen it in other people. Those whose wyrd was strong, or who had a sudden sense of spiritual purpose, glowed with a light that spirits and fae creatures found irresistible.

'I don't see it,' she admitted, disappointed.

'Well, of course not! You can't see it in yourself,' Saltfish said, as if explaining an elementary truth to an infant. He squinted. 'But trust me when I say that you are dazzling as Sól today.'

'I shine that brightly?'

'Uncomfortably so,' he confirmed with a chuckle, adding 'Don't go getting any more interesting, little seer. Blaze any brighter and you'll burn the ship down!' This amused the gnome so much that he had a fit of laughter and fell overboard. Kadlin gasped and looked over the side. She was relieved to see Saltfish holding onto one of the ship's ropes, skiing along the surface of the sea on his oversized feet and cackling with glee. Despite her worries, Kadlin grinned.

'Beautiful, isn't it,' Ulfrik observed, making her jump. She hadn't heard him approach. She'd been so engrossed in her conversation with the ship's gnome, and with watching Rán's daughters, that she hadn't noticed the glorious sunrise beyond the bow. The purples and reds of moments ago had given way to oranges and golds, gilding the waves and making them glisten. She inhaled deeply, tasting the salt tang of the air, and allowed herself to relax a little.

'You must be cold, Lady,' her father continued. 'Here.' He took off his own, heavy cloak and wrapped it about her shoulders. The warmth was instant and Kadlin smiled gratefully. There was an awkwardness to him as he continued 'Do you want to talk about it?'

Kadlin tried to block out the joyful whoops and manic laughter of Saltfish as he surfed the ocean alongside The Ox. She knew that Ulfrik must be desperate to know what had happened at King Redbeard's hall. He had fled Tromø in the dead of night, possibly endangering his own life and almost certainly ruining his chances of ever trading there again, all to save her from a peril he could not name. For a moment, she was overcome with gratitude and emotion. She wanted to throw her arms around her father's neck and sob into his shoulder. She wanted to tell him that she had made a huge mistake, and that Yrsa, Aud and Jofrið may now be dead because of her. She wanted to tell him that she felt more alone and afraid now than at any other time in her life. But Kadlin had been trained well and she knew that she now ranked higher than Ulfrik in the eyes of the crew - if not in their hearts. In a crisis, they would look to the Völva before the Captain. They would look to her to lead. Although they did not yet know her, and certainly had no love for her, the crew of The Ox had already collectively yet subconsciously recognised her as the greater power.

A leader never shows weakness. To lead, you must always be seen to be strong. A leader stands boldly between her people and the enemy. She is their shield. If she gives them cause to doubt the strength of that shield, they will cease to stand behind her.

Her grandmother's words reminded her that she couldn't show weakness in front of these people. Not even her own father. Yrsa had foreseen a 'dark and dangerous path' for the crew of The Ox, and now the consequences of her own actions had set Kadlin on that path, too. Whatever awaited them, she would never give them cause to doubt her strength.

'Thank you. No,' she replied, ignoring the disappointment on her father's face.

He nodded. 'Forgive my intrusion,' he said, and left her to her thoughts.

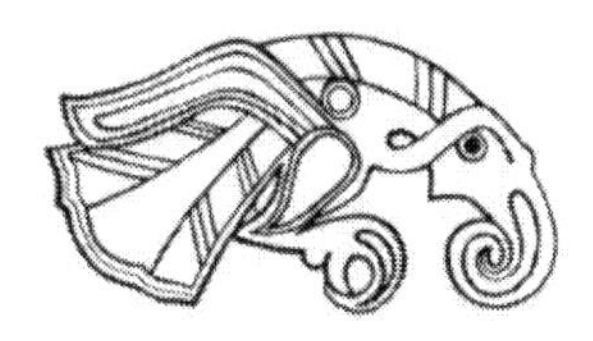

ALFGEIR

Alfgeir had gone to the docks that morning with the sole intent of challenging Asbjorn to Holmgang. He'd endured three wretched months of Ragnfrið crying and wailing over her boyfriend, petitioning the gods to keep him safe, and reciting ugly poetry about the strength of their beautiful love. The only thing that kept Alfgeir sane during this time was the knowledge that his sister would marry Asbjorn upon his return and would therefore be leaving their parents' hearth for a home of her own. Although there'd been no formal declaration of their betrothal, it was generally expected that the jarl's son would make the announcement as soon as he arrived back in Bramsvik.

Asbjorn had celebrated his homecoming with a night of feasting at the mead hall. He'd stepped aside for a private word with his father later in the evening, after which he had called for silence as he had an announcement to make. Everyone assumed he was about to ask Ragnfrið to be his wife but, instead of heralding his love, Asbjorn had declared that he and Ulfrik were setting sail for the land of the Danes once again come morning.

Ragnfrið had run home, shamed and sobbing, and Alfgeir had run out of patience. It was bad enough that Asbjorn had turned his sister into a lovesick cow, but to humiliate her and break her heart like that in front of the whole town was unpardonable. Their father was a weak and impotent man who could not be relied upon to defend his daughter's honour. If Ragnfrið was to be treated right, Alfgeir would have to make the challenge himself.

Asbjorn was eighteen and adept with axe and spear, whereas Alfgeir was eleven and the closest thing to a weapon he'd ever held was the knife he used to gut fish. However, he had valour and faith and he fervently trusted the gods to give him justice despite the odds. He would insist on his right to Holmgang - to fight Asbjorn in ritual combat - and he was confident the gods would grant him victory for the sake of his wronged sister.

So that morning Alfgeir had kissed the Thor's hammer that hung around his neck, whispered a prayer for strength and success, and strode into town with courage in his heart.

He'd been pleased to see Ulfrik's knarr, The Ox, still moored at the dock. Less pleasing was the sight of Asbjorn's father, Jarl Erik Thorsson, arguing with his son. Alfgeir's nerve had crumbled at the sight of the jarl. His heart had thundered in his scrawny chest as the enormity of what he was about to do overwhelmed him. He'd crouched behind a wagon, suddenly finding it hard to breathe, and wondered how he'd ever been foolish enough to think he could do this.

It was during the blessing rite that Alfgeir had an epiphany - perhaps the gods didn't want him to fight Asbjorn after all. Perhaps they meant for him to travel with Asbjorn and protect him, to ensure he returned to Ragnfrið safely once again. The more he thought about it, the more it made sense to him. He had always wanted to travel the Whale Road, and so, while the crew were distracted by the sacrifice, he snuck aboard The Ox and secreted himself amid the cargo beneath a bundle of furs to keep him warm.

He'd been woken just before dawn by a hushed conversation close to where he was concealed. Yrsa, eldest and most venerated of the Völur, was speaking to Ulfrik. Alfgeir heard every word they said yet understood little. His stomach had growled so loudly he was sure he would be discovered, but the captain and the Völva were so engrossed in their conversation they'd not noticed him.

When Yrsa warned Ulfrik of danger the hairs had raised on the back of Alfgeir's neck. If he had wanted confirmation from the gods, surely this was it! He'd heard it himself from Yrsa's mouth. There was a traitor aboard the ship, she said, and people were going to die! Now Alfgeir was certain he'd been put here to protect Asbjorn. He had smiled and closed his eyes, comforted to know that he had a purpose and that his gods believed in him.

*

Alfgeir had intended to make himself known once they were far enough from Bramsvik, but the whispered conversation he'd overheard made him hesitate. Yrsa said there was a traitor on board, but Ulfrik had insisted every member of his crew could be trusted. If they found him now, no-one could blame them for assuming Alfgeir himself was the spy, and so he remained hidden, nursing his hunger until they reached the island of Tromø.

As soon as the crew left the ship he'd crawled from beneath the furs, sighed with relief as he finally emptied his bursting bladder over the side, then ravenously raided the food supplies. He'd entertained himself for a while, poking around the ship and sneaking a peek in the sea chests of the crew. Each person brought their private belongings in a small, wooden chest which doubled as a seat, and it was a generally accepted rule that you didn't mess with the contents of someone else's chest, but Alfgeir was young and bored and he was unsupervised.

In one, he found a small seax with a patterned blade the length of his palm. It struck him as curious that the owner did not carry it with them. Like arm rings, weapons were worn about the body and were too precious to leave behind when the crew went ashore. Alfgeir amused himself by wielding it in battle against a troupe of imaginary trolls, before concealing the seax once again at the bottom of the sea chest.

Had he known how much trouble that blade was going to cause, he would have thrown it overboard and begged the gods for mercy.

THORFRIDA

Thorfrida had been a crew member on The Ox for eight years now, and this was the first time she had ever felt uncomfortable on board. It wasn't that Ulfrik's daughter was unpleasant - quite the opposite - but having a Völva aboard ship created a permanent atmosphere of tension. Everyone felt under pressure to be on their best behaviour, and there was none of the laughter and banter so prevalent on previous journeys. In some ways it was like having a queen join the crew; she could smile and be as helpful as she pleased, but she would never be the same as everyone else. She would always be above them; better than them. A Völva commanded too much respect to ever be treated as an equal, and that same respect dictated that the crew could never tell her so. Instead, there existed a constant sense of unease and constraint as all of them tried to keep their distance from the seer. On a crowded ship this was difficult, and their efforts became obvious.

As a mother, it pained Thorfrida to see their captain's awkward attempts at communication with Kadlin. It seemed to her that Ulfrik never knew which role he ought to play. Given his daughter's lofty status the familiarity of a father seemed discourteous somehow, but treating her with the same reverence and respect he showed the rest of the Völur only resulted in creating distance between the two. Thorfrida's heart ached for him every time she witnessed one of their encounters.

Thorfrida had given birth to eight children, three of whom survived to adulthood. Her sons lived in Bramsvik, working the farm their father bequeathed them on his death. Left to themselves, she believed they would be content working together the rest of their lives, but the wife of the eldest was a proud and ambitious woman, constantly complaining that she shouldn't have to share her hearth. She poisoned her husband's ear against his younger brother, and Thorfrida had been eager to return home and keep an eye on things. This new, unexpected journey – unfairly thrust upon them by Jarl Erik – was taking her away from her family when she felt they needed her most. She prayed daily to the All-Mother, Frigga, to maintain the peace between her two sons.

Her daughter had married a cooper from Alfheim, and Thorfrida had not seen the girl for over a year. Gisla and her husband met and fell in love during a pilgrimage to Uppsala, and Thorfrida's eldest son had made the marriage arrangements in place of her late husband. She missed her daughter desperately and was grateful that Ulfrik's trade route took her to Alfheim in Autumn and Spring. Unfortunately, Gisla's new home was several miles inland, and The Ox had not moored at Alfheim long enough this past year for Thorfrida to visit. She wondered if her daughter was a mother yet, and if her husband still treated her well.

The only person on board who didn't seem to mind the Völva's presence was Olvir, the youngest and most recent addition to the crew. While the others did all they could to avoid any contact with Kadlin, Olvir actively sought her out. At sixteen winters, he was only a few months older than her, but Thorfrida believed there was more to his attempts at friendship than simply their age. She caught him staring at the seer when he thought no-one was watching, and more than once he volunteered to instruct her in some task. He blushed when she spoke to him, and Thorfrida would gamble a year's pay that the young man was smitten. From the way Kadlin had begun to look at Asbjorn, though, Thorfrida doubted his chances.

Olvir was the only member of the crew not born in Bramsvik. Ulfrik had met him last autumn in Scania, where he was working as an interpreter for a slave trader. He was a Saxon and had been taken in a raid on his village when he was a small boy. He'd spent his life either on slave ships or in the markets and had quickly proven adept not only at languages but also the diplomacy essential for fruitful trade. Curiously, he was neither enslaved nor beholden to the man who employed him, and so had been free to offer his services to Ulfrik. The Ox was one hand short at the time due to Sibbe's pregnancy, and Ulfrik had quickly been persuaded that this intelligent, eloquent, hard-working young man would be an asset. Olvir always seemed cheerful and never complained about any chore he was given, but he never spoke of his family or his past. Thorfrida got the impression there'd been little joy in his young life, and she always made sure to give him a smile and a hug, and to treat him as her own.

This evening - their second since fleeing King Redbeard's island - she was cooking their meal whilst once again watching Ulfrik and his daughter. Usually, they would find an inlet or cove to moor for the night. The crew would make camp on land and hunt and forage for their food. On a good day, the hunters would return with a deer or a boar, but when game was scarce they could usually rely on an abundance of rabbits and birds. Thorfrida didn't like to cook aboard ship – wood and flame were a dangerous combination - but Ulfrik wanted to put as much distance between The Ox and Tromø as possible, and so she was having to make their meal once more on the open deck. 'Two nights,' he had promised her, 'and then we'll find land.'

This evening Bjarni and Olvir had managed to catch two large bass, and the delicious aroma of freshly cooked fish made her stomach growl. Thorfrida made the bass into a broth, serving it with the last of the bread and being sure to set aside a small share as an offering to the ship's wight. She was about to call the others to come fill their bowls when Magnus gently took her arm and put a finger to his lips.

'Come with me quietly and make no fuss,' he whispered. 'There is a creature concealed behind you. I saw the fire reflected in its eyes when it stole some food a moment ago.'

Thorfrida noticed the portion she had set aside for the ship's gnome had vanished. A sense of dread overtook her, and she gripped Magnus's hand.

'Don't worry, woman, I have you,' he murmured reassuringly in his deep, baritone voice. 'Come with me. I'll let nothing harm you.' His words were strong, but she felt his hands tremble as he helped her to her feet.

Thorfrida's legs were weak with fear, but she managed to stand and walk as calmly as she could over to where the rest of the crew were seated. She tried her best not to look back even though every instinct in her body screamed at her to do so. The sky was almost dark, and a low cloud smothered any cheer that may have been gleaned from the stars. Magnus left her side and she saw him whisper to Ulfrik. Within moments everyone was aware of the potential threat and sat together, alert and afraid, peering into the sinister shadows at the stern. The brightness of the cooking fire made the darkness beyond seem blacker and more menacing.

It was the Völva who first approached it, displaying a bravery that none of the others felt. She stopped a few paces shy of the place where Magnus had seen the intruder, took a pinch of powder from one of the many pouches that hung at her small waist, and muttered some words that were lost to the night air. She threw the powder before her and Thorfrida saw it turn the flames green for an instant. Kadlin cocked her head and stretched a hand toward the fire as if feeling the air for something. After a moment she turned back to them and said, 'I sense no malevolence here.'

'With respect, I know what I saw,' Magnus rumbled, though Thorfrida thought he sounded less certain now.

'I don't doubt you, Magnus,' the seer continued, 'but whatever hides itself here is more afraid of you than you of it.'

'Then it must be shitting itself,' Thorfrida heard the big man mutter beneath his breath.

The Völva strode confidently past the fire and was swallowed by the shadows beyond. For two or three heartbeats, no-one moved or even breathed. The only sound was the creaking of the rigging and the gentle slap of waves against the hull. A chill wind blew suddenly, buffeting the flame beneath the cooking pot.

'Kadlin,' Ulfrik called, concerned. He took a hesitant step toward the stern of the knarr.

His daughter reappeared with a figure at her side and Thorfrida recoiled from what she took to be a *draugr*. The boy was so skinny and wretched looking that it took her an instant to realise he was real and not a spirit. He was wide-eyed with fear as he clung to the Völva's hand. Kadlin brought the boy over to them and Thorfrida could see that he was, indeed, flesh and blood.

'Don't let them throw me to Jormungand, Lady,' he begged.

'Alfgeir?' It was Asbjorn who first recognised the young lad. 'How in the name of Odin…?'

'The gods told me to watch over you, Asbjorn,' Alfgeir replied fervently, tripping over the words in his haste to explain. 'I'm here to protect you.' He thought for a moment before adding 'I'm definitely not here to murder anyone.'

No-one spoke. It was frightening to realise that a person

– albeit a child – had been living amongst them, unnoticed, for the better part of three days and nights. The knarr was small and overcrowded, and yet this boy had managed to conceal himself well enough to avoid detection for so long. He had presumably been eating their food, drinking their ale, and listening to their conversations. They had slept each night, unaware that a stranger was aboard. Thorfrida shivered at the thought.

'I don't like it,' Egil declared, suspicious of the boy's explanation. 'First Jarl Erik threatens our lives unless we leave for Haithabyr, with no explanation. Then we are forced to flee Tromø in the dark of night, again with no explanation.' He nodded at the Völva, adding 'Forgive me, Lady, but it is the truth. And now we find an intruder on the ship who speaks of murder! I say we give him to Rán's Daughters and be done with it before our luck runs out entirely.' There were murmurs of assent.

'I said *not* murder,' Alfgeir protested.

'No-one is killing anyone tonight,' Ulfrik replied sternly, dismissing the suggestion.

Alfgeir looked so small and terrified that Thorfrida was ashamed for having been afraid of him. Her mind conjured the image of her own son, Guthri, who had drowned at the age of six. It had been twenty years since that day, but she still felt the pain of his loss as keenly. This boy was no killer sent to gut them in their sleep. He was just a child in search of adventure, and she would not allow anyone to feed him to the waves.

'I say we should vote on it,' Bjarni Arm-Strong proposed, darkly.

'Leave him be,' Thorfrida said. 'I'm not afraid of a child. He can stay.'

'You don't speak for us all,' Egil countered, heatedly. 'A vote is fair. This voyage is cursed. All our lives are at risk. We should all have a say.'

'The boy has had plenty of chances to kill us in our sleep,' Ulfrik said. 'If he intended harm he'd have done it by now. He says the gods sent him. Perhaps they did. How will they react if we let him drown?'

'What the Daughters choose to do with him is their business,' Egil pushed. 'If the gods want him saved, let them save him.'

'He has had chances to harm us, but he has had chances to reveal himself, also,' Thorvald One-Eye pointed out. 'I would hear a persuasive argument for why he kept himself hid, or let the sea take him.'

'Well, boy?' Ulfrik queried.

The child looked nervously from one hostile face to another. 'I was afraid you would think I was the killer,' he replied in a thin, trembling voice. 'The one the old seer warned Ulfrik about.' Thorfrida noticed that Ulfrik turned pale at these words.

'Who did Yrsa warn you of, Ulfrik? What is the boy talking about?' One-Eye demanded.

'It's too great a risk,' Herdis said, shaking her head. 'Gods forgive me, but let the waves have him. I have children of my own I need to return home to.'

An argument broke out, with many insisting the matter be put to a vote. There had been too much suspicion of late; too many unexplained, seemingly strange decisions by their captain. They were heartbroken at having to leave their homes within hours of their return. They were terrified of the threats made by Jarl Erik and frightened for the families they'd left behind. They were angry that Ulfrik's daughter was travelling with them, impeding their liberty and making them feel trapped. The child, Alfgeir, became a focus for all of this, and many seemed to feel that by eliminating him they may lay a few of their troubles to rest.

'He can't stay!'

'Give him to the Daughters!'

'He is no threat! He's just a child!'

Things became physical very quickly. Egil lunged at Alfgeir, trying to snatch him from the Völva's side. Kadlin pushed him away and put herself between the lad and what was fast becoming an unruly mob. She cast a symbol in the air with her left hand and roared 'Quiet!'

Silence smothered them.

Thorfrida tried to open her mouth but her lips felt sealed by some invisible hand. The feeling of helplessness terrified her and made the hairs on the back of her neck stand on end. All eyes were on the young woman who had tried so hard to be one of them yet was now demonstrating exactly why she could never be.

'I told you I sensed no malevolence.' Kadlin spoke slowly and softly. 'I told you he fears you more than you fear him. There is nothing more to discuss. Thorfrida, please give Alfgeir my meal tonight. He can start earning his way tomorrow.'

There was plenty of stew, and Thorfrida would starve before she allowed the seer to go hungry, but she nodded anyway and hastened to serve the meal. She and the others soon regained the power of speech, yet none had the will to use it. They ate in silence and even Olvir shrank away from Kadlin now. Only Alfgeir sat beside her, his eyes wide and bright as an owl.

They will never accept you now, girl, Thorfrida thought, sadly.

KADLIN

Kadlin found it difficult to sleep aboard ship. The constant motion of the knarr was not so bad when there was something on the horizon to distract her eye, but laying down in the semi-darkness, listening to the slop, slop, slop of the waves and feeling every roll and tilt of the vessel made her nauseous. She'd been relieved when, on the third day, having detected no signs of pursuit, her father finally gave the command to stop at an inlet where they could make camp and restock their supplies.

The crew were careful to remove the prow beast from the front of the ship before coming ashore so as not to present a challenge or cause offence to the wights of the land. The knarr was not as sleek and shallow as a longship and it took skill to see The Ox safely moored close to shore without damaging the hull. Once on land, the crew quickly busied themselves with the task of setting up camp and replenishing their food and water. Magnus untethered the goat from the ships mast and carried it to shore across his shoulders so it could graze.

It had been obvious to Kadlin for some time that none of her companions felt relaxed around her. Her use of magic against them last night had intensified their fear and was not a thing they would soon forgive. Although they maintained a polite and respectful attitude toward her, they avoided speaking to her if they could, and she found herself walking the beach and conversing with Saltfish instead.

'I want to help,' she told him as they watched Thorfrida, Herdis and Alfgeir collect driftwood for the fire, 'but I know they'll see it as an intrusion.'

The ship's gnome shrugged. 'Such tasks are for lower beings than you,' he replied nonchalantly, stooping to pick up an interesting shell. 'Leave them to it, little seer.'

'I collect firewood at home,' Kadlin retaliated, hurt that he would think her too proud for such menial things.

'And a king takes a shit each morning,' Saltfish replied, cleaning the shell on his tunic, 'but never in front of his people. What you do in private has nothing to do with this. You are above these folk, Kadlin Svalasdaughter, whether you wish it or not. Have the wisdom to accept it and play the part they expect from you.'

Although she reluctantly accepted the fundamental truth behind the ship wight's words, her skin pricked at the arrogant way he phrased it. Yrsa had taught her the Völva's place in the hierarchy of men, but she'd also stressed the need to balance it with humility. *Think neither too much, nor too little of yourself. One leads to self-delusion, the other to self-doubt. Only truth, and the acceptance of the truth, creates a strong mind.*

Kadlin stopped to watch Asbjorn as he strapped a quiver of arrows to his hip. He, Egil and Magnus were going hunting and Kadlin found her eyes lingering on the jarl's son. She was unused to spending so much time in the company of men, and lately she found herself thinking more and more about Asbjorn, and wondering what he thought of her. He was probably afraid of her now, like all the rest. She sighed. She'd known at the time that her actions would alienate her still further from her crewmates, but she couldn't regret saving the child's life.

'No,' said Saltfish sternly, following her gaze and wagging a finger. 'No, no, no. That one is far too ugly for you.'

Kadlin felt her cheeks burn. 'You're a poor judge of beauty if you think Asbjorn is ugly,' she said, defensively, embarrassed that he had so easily read her thoughts.

Saltfish sniffed. 'Oh,' said the little gnome, shaking his

head in disappointment. 'You're still only looking at the outside.'

★

Kadlin needed guidance and – without her grandmother's counsel – was feeling lost. She had never been away from home this long before and certainly never this far. The distance unsettled her in a way she couldn't explain. It felt as though, the further she travelled from Bramsvik, the less of a connection she had to Yrsa, Aud and Jofrið. It was almost as if the bonds of family and friendship which bound them were being stretched, like a vine, becoming thinner and thinner the greater the physical distance she put between them. She worried that one day she'd go too far, and the vines would snap. All her life, Kadlin had always known what was expected of her and understood her place in the world, and she'd had the Völur to talk to at the end of each day. Now, she felt alone, unwanted and adrift, and she was afraid. She felt trapped aboard The Ox with a group of strangers.

Kadlin left Saltfish on the beach and ventured inland in search of herbs, roots, and other useful treasures. She needed some time alone with her thoughts and wasn't ready to return to her crewmates yet. It was wonderful to be able to stretch her legs after the confines of the knarr. As she walked, she also looked for a place to safely sit and contact the gods. She had been walking for perhaps five minutes when she found an ash tree that offered decent shade, and which seemed welcoming. Yggdrassil, the World Tree upon which Odin hung himself, was known to be an ash. It was one of the most important trees in magical lore and a perfect choice to watch over her. As she approached the tree, she heard stealthy footfalls behind her.

'You will leave me be, if you value your skin.' Kadlin spoke the words loudly and confidently. She turned, expecting to see a local peasant flee for his life, and was surprised instead to find Olvir standing a short distance away holding a seax. For a moment she thought he meant to use it, but Olvir saw her look and blushed, quickly sheathing the blade.

'I mean no harm, Lady,' he said, raising his empty palms.

'Good,' she replied, curtly. 'I'd hate to have to curse you. Why are you spying on me?'

'I'm not!' He seemed genuinely mortified by the accusation. 'I was worried when I saw you leave the shore. It isn't safe for a woman alone so I...'

'No-one would dare harm a Völva,' Kadlin assured him, interrupting.

'Forgive me, Lady. I'm sure you're right. But how would they know?'

It hadn't occurred to her that, without her staff and wearing Ulfrik's cloak, she looked like any other woman.

They were so much a part of her, her cloak and staff, she'd never considered what people would think of her without them. It had felt like leaving behind an arm when Aud had taken them from her. The realisation that she'd unwittingly put herself in danger came as a shock.

'Thank you,' Kadlin said, hesitantly. 'That was kind. I hadn't thought.'

Olvir smiled. 'I didn't mean to disturb you. Only to follow and keep you safe.'

'In that case,' she said, returning his smile, 'may I ask your protection on my journey?'

Olvir looked flustered. 'I'll follow wherever you go, Lady, but I've brought no food or water. If I'd known you were leaving, I'd at least have packed a…'

Kadlin laughed. 'I shall journey right here, beneath this tree. I'll be gone some time.'

'Oh!' Olvir blushed again, realising his mistake.

Approaching the gods was not a thing to be done on a whim. Like people, they could be cantankerous if caught at a bad time. Some did not like to be bothered at all, whereas others were usually helpful so long as the proper amount of respect and humility was shown. Others, still, required rites to be enacted, and some lived in worlds far too dangerous for most mortals to explore. All, without exception, required an offering or sacrifice.

Kadlin hoped to ask the guidance of Freya, goddess of war, sex, death, and magic, chooser of the slain, and sister of the god Freyr. Freya was reputed to be the most beautiful of goddesses. It was she who had first taught the art of seiðr to mortal women, and as such she was revered by all who worked with the occult. Had she been home at Bramsvik, Kadlin would have buried some amber for Freya, or burned her cat-skin gloves in a ritual fire, but here she had nothing of value to offer except blood. You had to choose your gifts wisely when visiting the gods. A beautiful fish or exquisite seashell would be acceptable to Njörð, god of the sea, for example, but offer the same items to Skaði, his ex-wife, and she would take it as an insult. Blood was easy. Every god was pleased with blood.

Kadlin gathered a handful of twigs from the ground. Using the clay dish, flint and dried grasses that she carried in a large pouch on her belt, she lit a small fire and gave Olvir the task of feeding it the sticks. While it burned, she pulled several clumps of fresh grass and lay them out in a patch of sunlight to dry. It was always wise to restock your supplies when the opportunity arose. Soon, the little fire died down to embers, and Kadlin sprinkled them with a generous pinch of dried mugwort leaves. The resulting smoke was thick and pungent, forcing Olvir to retreat a few paces away. Kadlin removed her shoes, sat on the ground with her back against the tree and inhaled the incense. She took her ritual blade from her belt and made a small cut on her ankle, murmuring a plea to Freya as she did so. The pain was brief, but biting, and she closed her eyes against it, letting the blood run down her foot and into the earth. Her limbs felt heavy, and she allowed herself to drift into the other world, once again closing her hand around the garnet ring and using it to anchor herself to Midgard, the human realm.

She was in a forest.

It was cool in the shade and Kadlin felt comfortable and content as she followed a dirt path. She wasn't certain where the track led, but she was confident she was travelling in the right direction. This is where she was supposed to be.

She walked for what felt like hours. Occasionally the path became blocked by brambles or broken branches and Kadlin had to cut them back or find a way around them. The monotony of her journey started to weigh on her. She found herself taking more interest in the trees on either side rather than the path itself. She began to notice other tracks, and other travellers, and she wanted to call out to them. For some reason she held back from doing so and this made her feel lonely.

The obstacles became more frequent. She snagged her shift while cutting her way through a patch of thorns, and lost a shoe climbing over a tree that was blocking her way. She grew tired of the footpath and decided to try to find another route through the forest. She stepped off the trail and…

She was falling! Kadlin tumbled down an impossibly steep slope, as if the ground had given way beneath her. The trees and rough earth became soft, green grass, yet still she continued to fall. There was snow on the ground when she finally came to a stop. She stood and found herself in a vast, frozen meadow. There was nothing to see for miles in any direction, and Kadlin panicked at the realisation that she had no idea how to return to the forest. As she studied her surroundings, she saw the meadow was littered with the bodies of warriors, their beards frosted with ice.

At the centre of the meadow was a single oak. Kadlin headed toward it, feet crunching in the snow. As she did so a vast eagle with two heads flew from its branches. A man was sat beneath the tree, but as Kaldin approached she could see that he, too, was dead. His death pained her, but she didn't know why. There was something familiar about him…

A woman walked through the field toward her. Her golden hair hung loose and unbraided and her fine clothing clung to her body, emphasising every curve. She glowed with an inner radiance. Brisingamen - the exquisitely crafted gold and amber necklace about her throat - identified her as Freya. The goddess wore a long cloak made of falcon feathers. She plucked one as she approached and held it out to Kadlin.

'Will you fly?'

Freya transformed into a falcon and took to the air. Kadlin felt herself change – becoming smaller, growing wings - and followed the goddess up, up through the clouds toward the sun. The sensation of flight was exhilarating! She had never experienced such a feeling of complete and utter freedom. Looking down, Kadlin could see the frozen carnage far below. She saw the edge of the meadow, and the forest, but she could see other places, too. There was a city to the north, and lakes to the east. Many different lands stretching as far as the horizon. She knew she should return to the forest path, but she was blown away by the magnitude of the world and yearned to explore it.

A shadow fell upon her. Kadlin looked up to see the double-headed eagle. It was several times her size and growing larger with every second. Looking down again, she watched its shadow creep across the land, obscuring everything below. The eagle screeched and tried to snatch her from the sky. She felt its talons graze her back and cried out in pain!

There was an ocean beneath her now. Kadlin folded her wings and plummeted into the water.

It took a few moments to regain her senses. Some of the message had been clear, but so much was a mystery to her still. She wished she could talk to her grandmother. Yrsa could always see things so clearly.

The path through the forest represented her life as a

Völva. Of that she was sure. She had stepped off the path when she boarded The Ox and was feeling lost and out of control. Freya had shown her that her choices were still her own, and she could choose to return to her old life or create a new one. The Norns were weaving her an opportunity. She had not been abandoned by her gods, torn from her home and tossed to the tides. They were granting her the freedom she'd always craved and were watching to see what she did with it.

The meaning of the great eagle, the frozen meadow and the dead man were beyond her. They were part of her future – that much she understood – and were intended as a warning of some kind. She stored their images in her mind, thanked Freya for her insight, and got to her feet. The wound on her ankle had stopped bleeding and she was able to put her shoes back on without causing any further damage.

She'd no idea how much time had passed, but the fire had died out completely and Olvir was nowhere to be found. So much for her protector! She bent to collect the grass she'd laid out to dry earlier and found a falcon feather lying beside it. She thanked Freya for the gift.

Olvir caught up with her as she was heading back to the beach.

'Thank the gods,' he gasped, clearly having run. 'When I returned and found you gone I…'

'Returned from where?' Kadlin asked, bluntly. His face flushed, and she finally understood why the crew had started to call him Olvir Red Face. As someone who had previously worked with slavers, and must have witnessed every kind of human indignity, she found it surprising that he was still so quick to blush.

'I held it as long as I could,' he replied, embarrassed. 'Truly, Lady, my gut was in agony! I didn't want to cause offence by dropping my breeks in front of you, so I went elsewhere. In hindsight perhaps I went a little too far, but I wasn't sure…' He trailed off, his face turning a deeper shade of scarlet. 'I was as quick as the gods allowed.'

'I'm a healer,' Kadlin responded, trying not to laugh. 'You wouldn't be the first man I've witnessed taking a shit.'

'I'll never desert you again. Ever. I swear on my life!'

She saw it then. The look in Olvir's eyes. She saw how he felt about her. And all she could think was *why couldn't it have been Asbjorn?*

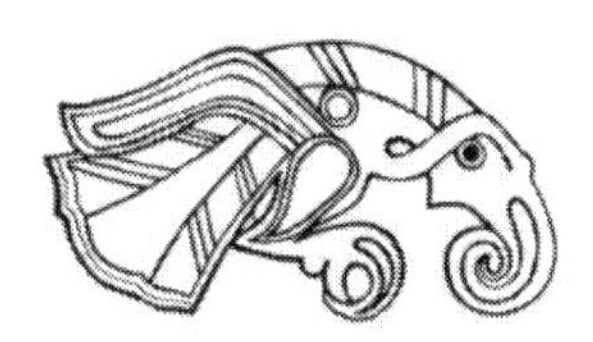

ULFRIK

Ulfrik was still concerned that King Harald may have sent ships after them. They had sailed beyond the borders of Agder, and into the neighbouring kingdom of Geirstad, but that was little comfort. His daughter had yet to confide in him what exactly had happened on Tromø, and although he accepted her right to withhold that information, her doing so didn't make his life any easier. He didn't know, for example, if she'd done something so grievous the king would pursue her the rest of her life, or if it was a minor issue that Redbeard had probably forgotten by now. Knowing them as he did, Ulfrik tended toward the latter. Kadlin was a conscientious young woman, and highly skilled at her craft, whereas the king saw enemies everywhere and could be hot-headed if he didn't get his own way.

In addition to worrying about ambush and execution by Redbeard's soldiers, Ulfrik was also sweating over the silver stored – completely unprotected – in the ships hold. Logically, he knew it was highly unlikely that anyone would open the chest of axe heads and study them, but it vexed him anyway. Only he and Magnus knew the truth, and the fear of discovery was crushing him. Magnus seemed completely unaffected by the subterfuge, but Magnus wasn't the captain and therefore would shoulder none of the blame should the plan fail. Neither was he responsible for the lives of all onboard.

For what felt like the hundredth time since they'd fled the island, Ulfrik went to check on the crates. The three large barrels that had once held the hack silver, but which now contained only rocks, were roped together at the stern. No-one questioned them, and there was no reason why they should. It wasn't unusual for the captain to have personal cargo on board, and he had a good and loyal crew who respected each other's privacy.

Ulfrik climbed down into the hull of the knarr, where the rations and cargo were stored. He made his way past bundles of furs, wool and cloth wrapped in sealskin to keep out the damp, past stacks of walrus ivory, and chests of beads, and opened one of the three crates containing the axe heads. They were still there. He hadn't realised he was holding his breath until he allowed himself to breathe again. He took one of the pieces out of the crate and turned it over in his hands. Ketil Smith had certainly done a fine job considering how rushed he had been. Down here, in the shadows, it was impossible to tell the difference.

'I'm sorry the blacksmith let you down.' Thorvald One-Eye said, swinging himself down into the hold. Ulfrik hadn't realised anyone else was still aboard. Startled, he dropped the axe head, sending it skittering across the floor to where Thorvald now stood.

'Let me down?' He couldn't hide the slight tremor in his voice. He swallowed as Jarl Erik's man picked up the fallen weapon, brushed dirt from it, and handed it back to him. The smuggled silver left a streak of dirt and oil on Thorvald's skin, but he didn't seem to notice.

'The handles,' he remarked. 'You were going to have them attached.'

'Oh that!' Ulfrik felt his confidence return. Once again, he was the merchant, the spinner of tales, and he knew how to play this game. 'We found him well enough, and Yrsa was right… his work was of high quality. Unfortunately for me, so were his prices.'

The other man groaned in sympathy. He ran a hand lightly over the axe heads.

'Can you still sell them, like this?'

'Yes, yes, no problem. And the handles. I already have a buyer in mind. Of course, they'd fetch a much better price if I was able to sell them complete, but I'll not be taken for a fool by a greedy blacksmith.'

'This would be Ketil?' Thorvald asked. Ulfrik's stomach lurched. He closed the lid on the casket and headed back toward the steps.

'Yes, I believe that was his name.'

'Strange,' Thorvald said. 'I've dealt with him before and never found him ungenerous.'

'Then next time we have business there I'll take you with me,' Ulfrik replied coolly, ascending the steps, leading Thorvald back to the main deck and away from the store. 'No doubt Jarl Erik commands a better price than a humble merchant. To be fair, he would have charged a reasonable amount had we been able to wait three days, but he thought he could double it for a quick job. It wasn't worth my while.'

'I shall have words with him next time I visit.'

'It's no matter,' Ulfrik shrugged. 'Every man must earn a living. As I say, I have a buyer in mind. It wounded me more that I wasted a cask of mead trying to change his mind!' One-Eye laughed heartily at this. 'Shouldn't you be watching your peacock?' Ulfrik continued with a slight smile. 'He may encounter a vicious bird, or a particularly voracious nest of ants.'

'I suppose I should,' Thorvald sighed as the two men climbed over the side of the ship. He looked across at the others on the shore. 'I don't see him,' he added, with a touch of concern in his voice.

'He went hunting with Magnus and Egil. That way,' Ulfrik replied, pointing. 'Hopefully the gods went with them and we shall eat meat tonight.'

★

Asbjorn and Egil returned in high spirits, carrying the carcass of a young stag. It hung upside down, feet bound to a pole that they carried between them on their shoulders. Magnus, who had caught a brace of rabbits, was unhappy the younger men had found larger prey.

'Any fool can shoot a stag,' he grumbled. 'It takes greater skill to outwit a rabbit.'

'Your great skill will feed us for a day,' Asbjorn mocked, as he and Egil dumped the stag at Thorfrida's feet. 'We fools have provided for the rest of the week.' There was laughter from the crew, and Magnus retreated in a huff to one of the two, large tents erected earlier by Bjarni, Fromond and Hakon. Ulfrik followed him.

'I don't know why you do that,' he said, half-teasing. 'No-one thinks less of the rabbits. Why make an issue of it?' Magnus waved a dismissive hand, but Ulfrik knew his old friend's pride was wounded and that he was feeling his years. 'It did have a nice set of antlers,' Ulfrik mused. 'I may mount them on the prow and change The Ox's name to The Stag. What do you think?'

'I think you are pissing me off, Ulfrik. That's what I think.'

'Oh, stop sulking, Magnus! It doesn't become you. What in Thor's name will you be like if Thorvald brings back a stag, too?' He grinned.

'One-Eye?' Magnus sounded surprised.

'Yes,' Ulfrik replied. 'He came after you. Did he not find you?'

Magnus shrugged. 'Not me, but I'm not the one he's supposed to be protecting.'

'You didn't stay together?'

'No,' the big man admitted. 'I got tired of hearing Asbjorn brag about his cock. I tell you, Ulfrik, the boy thinks he invented sex. I could tell him a story or two that would…'

'He didn't find either of you?'

Magnus frowned at having been interrupted. 'Why ask me? I've already told you I haven't seen him. I don't know who he found.'

Ulfrik was concerned. He'd sent out scouts to check the area before letting his crew leave the shore, but it was unwise to wander off alone even when there were no settlements nearby. Several hours had passed since he and Thorvald had left the ship. Plenty of time to track Asbjorn down. He strode back outside and found the jarl's son.

'Have you seen One-Eye?'

Asbjorn shook his head. 'Not since we broke fast. Why?'

Ulfrik looked around. 'Has anyone seen Thorvald One-Eye,' he shouted. No-one had. Kadlin, who had been missing for most of the day, and caused tongues to wag by returning with Olvir (he must have a word with that boy…) came over and put a hand on his arm.

'Can I help, Father?'

'It may be nothing,' Ulfrik replied. There was every chance the man had simply gotten lost. But even as he thought those words, Ulfrik knew they were untrue. Thorvald was an expert tracker, and - even if he couldn't locate Asbjorn – would certainly have been able to find his own way back to camp. The most plausible explanation was that someone had intercepted him before he found the others.

'I need two teams to help search for him,' Ulfrik said. The crew were on their feet already, gathering around with concerned faces. 'Bjarni, Hakon, Olvir, go with Egil. Fromond, Herdis, Magnus, come with me. The rest of you stay alert and guard the camp.'

'It's impossible,' Egil complained. 'How would we even know where to begin?'

'I would start there,' Kadlin said, pointing. High in the sky, about a half a mile west of their position, three buzzards were circling.

ALFGEIR

Alfgeir had wanted to go hunting with Asbjorn and Egil that morning but they wouldn't allow it. He'd protested that it was his sacred duty to keep Asbjorn safe, but the men only laughed and sent him to collect firewood with the women. Despite his initial disappointment, Alfgeir enjoyed spending time with Herdis and Thorfrida. He knew the crew were still divided over whether he was a threat, so he pushed himself especially hard and collected an impressive amount of driftwood from the shore and logs from the forest. Thorfrida told him he'd done a fine job, and that made him feel proud. He couldn't remember ever having been praised for anything before, certainly not since his grandparents died. His muscles screamed and his back ached, but it had been worth it.

He wanted to do something nice for Thorfrida. He may not be a hunter like Egil or skilled at poetry like Fromond, but his grandfather had taught him to whittle wood as soon as he was old enough to hold a knife, and he was sure Thorfrida would be happy if he made something for her. He scoured the tree line for a small piece of wood that was just the right size and shape and tucked it safely inside the waistband of his breeks.

When Bjarni Arm Strong returned to camp carrying Thorvald's body, Alfgeir's newfound happiness dissolved and all his fears from the other night instantly returned. Someone had died, just as the old Seer predicted they would, and he was the only outsider in the group. Panic gripped him and he found it hard to breathe. The crew would blame him, and then they would give him to Rán's Daughters to be drowned! He balled his small fists, ready for a fight. Hot tears stung his cheeks and he wiped them angrily away with the back of his hand. If he had to die, he would do it like a man, not crying like a child.

'It wasn't me,' he shouted, but no-one paid him any heed. Instead, they gathered around the body in stunned and fearful silence.

'He was attacked not far from where we found him,' Hakon said solemnly to Ulfrik. 'Two men, on foot. No more. From the footprints and the blood, I'd say he was stabbed in the belly first, then tried to run. No-one gets far with a gut wound. As soon as he fell the cowards ended him with a knife in the back. You can see here that it went up and under the ribs, puncturing his lung. It's a painful way to go, Ulfrik. He didn't deserve this.'

'We should pack up and leave this place,' Herdis said, nervously.

'Fuck that. I'm not spending another night on The Ox,' Egil grumbled.

'Better to sleep aboard ship than wake in the morning to find you've been murdered,' Herdis snapped back. Alfgeir agreed. He thought of the whispered conversation he'd overheard between the captain and Yrsa. *Death will plague you every step of this journey until you are rid of that silver.* That's what she had said. What silver? Alfgeir had seen everything in the hold and there was no silver to be found. He wondered about the three barrels that Ulfrik said were private cargo, but three barrels of silver would be enough to buy every hof and hall in Bramsvik! Ulfrik, a mere merchant, could never command such riches. Not even Jarl Erik could lay hands on a fortune that large.

'Two men are no threat,' Magnus declared. 'Not to a group as big as this. They were thieves who stumbled across an easy target, that's all. Had he not been alone no doubt they would have left him be.'

'Two men may have friends,' Fromond mused.

'And see,' Hakon reached inside Thorvald's tunic and lifted the Thor's hammer from around the dead man's neck. 'He wears a silver Mjöllner - an expensive piece - yet they left it on his body. Neither did they take his arm rings. These were no thieves.'

Alfgeir jumped as an arm slid around his shoulders. Thorfrida pulled him close and kissed his head. 'Don't fret,' she crooned. 'All will be well.' He leaned into her and she began to smooth his hair. It reminded him of his mother, and he found it comforting.

'I didn't do it,' he said again, quieter this time.

'I know,' Thorfrida replied, reassuringly. 'No-one thinks you did.'

★

They felled several young trees to build the funeral pyre for One-Eye. His arm rings were removed and placed in his sea chest along with the rest of his belongings, to be returned to his family. Only his weapons and his Thor's hammer accompanied him into the fire. As captain, Ulfrik made a speech about Thorvald's life, but it was the Völva who performed the funerary rite and asked the gods to receive him.

Alfgeir had witnessed many funerals before, but never for someone who had been murdered. He'd not spoken to Thorvald while aboard The Ox but knew him by reputation and recognised him as Jarl Erik's man. As such, Alfgeir held him in high regard and was sorry for his passing.

That night, as the flames of One-Eye's pyre burned down to ash, the crew ate a stew made from the rabbits Magnus had caught. The stag was skinned and cut into pieces which were then stored in casks of brine to preserve them for the journey. These were taken back to the ship along with anything else that wasn't needed for the night so there would be the minimum left to pack in the morning. There was talk of trying to find Thorvald's killers and avenge his death, but this was voted down as being too risky.

'How would we know them, anyway?' Fromond enquired. 'Or do you suggest we execute every man we find within a mile radius?'

Ulfrik posted two guards to keep watch that night, rotating the shift so that everyone got a chance to lie down. He also gave permission for those who wished to sleep aboard The Ox to do so. Alfgeir would have preferred to stay on land, but he wanted to make a start on his gift for Thorfrida. He didn't have a knife, but he recalled the little seax he had discovered in one of the sea chests. It was too long to be a whittling blade, but it would suffice in the absence of any other option.

Aside from himself, there were only four other people spending the night on the ship. He waited until he was sure that each of them was asleep, then quietly snuck over to the chest containing the seax. He had expected to find the knife secreted at the bottom as before and was surprised to see it clumsily wrapped in a piece of lambskin on top of the other items, as if the owner had been in a hurry to put it away. More surprising was the fact that it was encrusted with recently dried blood. A weak attempt had been made to wipe it clean, but there was no mistaking the residue.

There could be any number of reasons for the blade to have blood on it, he told himself. It may have been used to gut the stag, or to skin the rabbits. But he knew that such a knife would have been properly cleaned and dried afterward. This one had been hidden in haste. Alfgeir thought of One-Eye, and of the stab wounds that had ended his life. He put the seax back and closed the sea chest as gently as possible so as not to wake the others. He knew to whom the box belonged, but they could not have had anything to do with One-Eye's death. There must be some other explanation.

He curled up on the floor and closed his eyes, but sleep didn't come easily to him that night.

KADLIN

The death of Thorvald One-Eye had a sobering effect on the crew. Many felt an attempt should have been made to find his killers, and that sailing away without doing so dishonoured him in some way. Others - encouraged in no small part by Egil - believed their journey was cursed, and that a sacrifice was necessary to restore their luck. The boy, Alfgeir, had kept to himself and been silently sullen all day. He seemed troubled, and Kadlin guessed he still worried the crew may sacrifice him.

They crossed into the kingdom of Vestfold later that day, and the mood noticeably lifted when Ulfrik gave the order to make port at Lutshavn. Lutshavn was larger than Bramsvik with a harbour incorporating several long docks, each capable of mooring three ships either side. It was a relatively new yet thriving place to trade. The crew of The Ox were regular visitors and had many friends and contacts in the town. They were met at the dock by a portly, ruddy faced man who greeted them as family.

'Ulfrik! Did you get lost? Your home is the other way,' he ribbed, grinning broadly and exchanging hugs with Ulfrik. 'Back so soon, my friend? Is this a good thing or should I worry?' His smile faltered a little. Her father laughed and deflected the question.

'You haven't met my eldest daughter, Kadlin. Kadlin, this is our good friend, Knut Stout-Belly.'

The man turned his attention to her. His eyes shone with genuine warmth and he took her slender hand in both of his, patting it gently.

'Welcome, Kadlin Ulfriksdaughter,' he beamed. 'Your father is a great man. A very great man. If you need anything while you are here, let Knut know. Are you training with him? He will teach you to be a very fine merchant.'

Kadlin wasn't used to being greeted in such a relaxed and informal way. Usually people were unwilling to look her in the eye and speak above a whisper, let alone take her by the hand and ask about her personal life. She much preferred this casual manner, although it felt strange to be addressed as the daughter of her father rather than her mother.

'Kadlin is a Völva,' Ulfrik replied, before she had a chance to form her own response. Stout-Belly looked aghast. He released her hand as if he'd been burned and took a step back, hastily lowering his gaze.

'Forgive me, Lady,' he said. 'I didn't know. Ulfrik has never mentioned.' He licked his lips, finding them suddenly dry. 'I would never have been so familiar.'

'I appreciate the warm welcome,' Kadlin said, reassuringly. She reached for Knut's hand and clasped it briefly to show there was no ill feeling. She felt him relax a little. 'I'm in need of a new cloak,' she continued. 'Perhaps you could advise me who to see.' She was still wearing her father's cloak as he had refused to take it back, but she could tell he was cold without it and she'd resolved to purchase another as soon as possible. She had nothing of value, other than Yrsa's ring, but a Völva was always in demand and there would be no shortage of people willing to trade for a fortune, a hex or a remedy. Then there was the matter of her staff. A decent staff should be stored and dried in a barn for at least a full year before it could be used. Cut a branch and put it to work too soon and you risked it bending, splitting or breaking. A good, strong staff needed to be seasoned if it was to last. Usually she would do this herself, but she required one now, not in a year's time. She must find a stick seller as well as a cloak maker.

'I know a good seamstress who has many cloaks, Lady. I will bring her to you.' Knut replied earnestly. 'Please, allow me to escort you to Jarl Thorstein. He will want to meet you. I will catch up with you later, Ulfrik.'

Kadlin was disappointed, but not surprised, that their friend had reverted to formal speech. Neither was she surprised that he insisted on escorting her to see the jarl. It was usual for the leader of a community to offer hospitality to a travelling Völva. There was never any worry of having to sleep beneath the sky. People felt privileged to play host to one of the Völur and would compete for the honour, each trying to impress their guest with the generosity of their welcome. She said goodbye to Ulfrik and left him and the crew to their trade. She had no doubt they would be more comfortable without her.

⋆

Despite the relative size of Lutshavn to Bramsvik, Jarl Thorstein's hall was no grander than that of Jarl Erik. It had no wind-holes, as the hall on Tromø had done, and the only source of light was a circular hole cut centrally in the roof, over the firepit. To Kadlin, who had become accustomed to life onboard ship, it felt stuffy and poorly aired. She tried not to wrinkle her nose as she was introduced to the jarl.

'Jarl Thorstein, may I present the Völva, Kadlin, daughter of Svala, daughter of Yrsa,' Stout-Belly said, having asked her proper name on the way. 'She is here for one night, travelling with her father, the merchant, Ulfrik of Bramsvik.'

'My Hall is yours, Lady.' The jarl took her hand and kissed it, but his lips were slightly too damp and lingered a fraction too long for her comfort. She withdrew her hand and resisted the urge to wipe it on her shift. Thorstein gestured for thralls to bring food and drink. 'The gods have heard our prayers, sending you here,' he continued. 'One of my men left his home two days ago and has not been seen since. It's not like him. If you can see where he is, or what has happened, many here will owe you a debt. Please, name your price.'

'I'm in need of a new cloak and staff,' Kadlin replied.

'They are yours,' he agreed.

'I thought to fetch Helga, Lord,' Stout-Belly said, making it sound more like a question than a statement of intent.

'Yes, do that,' the jarl agreed. 'And tell Anders to bring what staffs he has.'

Knut Stout-Belly nodded and excused himself before leaving. Kadlin's host showed her to a table where several thralls had hastily set out a jug of mead, a basket of bread, some fruits and a platter of fish. Kadlin sat and helped herself.

'Thank you for your hospitality, Jarl Thorstein,' she

began, as she poured a cup of mead. 'I look forward to seeing more of Lutshavn before we leave.' The jarl took a seat opposite her and tore off some bread. 'I will need something personal belonging to the man who is missing,' Kadlin continued. 'A ring. A shirt. Something he would have touched often.'

'I will send word to his wife,' the jarl replied solemnly. 'She will know what to bring.'

★

Helga, the seamstress, was the first to arrive at the hall. She was older than Kadlin - perhaps forty winters - and her hands were beginning to show the first signs of arthritis. Kadlin doubted that Helga would have more than five more years of being able to hold a needle, and thus support herself. She hoped the old woman had a good family on whom she could rely.

Stout-Belly had informed Helga that her client was a Völva, and the seamstress knew enough to only bring cloaks of blue for Kadlin to choose from. There were four in total; one the colour of cornflowers, another the rich blue of the herb, hyssop, and two the indigo blue of an autumn night sky. All were made of soft, boiled wool, and were the right length to fall just above her ankles. She chose the cornflower cloak.

As she donned the cloak of a Völva once more, it seemed to Kadlin that it lay heavy upon her shoulders, as if the fabric had been weighted with the burden of duty. Ulfrik's cloak had allowed her some anonymity, something she craved, and it felt a huge sacrifice to give that up and become so visible once again.

Ada, the wife of the missing man, arrived looking pinched and pale. She was clearly concerned about her husband, and Kadlin sensed a terrible fear emanating from her. She had brought a pair of naalbinded socks that belonged to him, and Kadlin noticed many repairs to the toe and heel. The socks had been worn well and often. They would do.

'Give me your hand,' she instructed the woman, 'and keep an image of your husband in your thoughts.'

Ada offered her hand as if to a snake, and visibly flinched when Kadlin clasped it firmly. Kadlin held the pair of socks in her left hand, closed her eyes and focused her mind. She rarely got images when divining information this way. Instead, it came to her as physical sensations, and as emotions.

Had she known that Olaf Boatbuilder was dead, she probably would have tried to find him another way. As it was, the knowledge caught her unaware.

Kadlin shivered. She was cold. Very cold. Her teeth began to chatter uncontrollably, and her jaw felt rigid as her facial muscles froze. She was afraid. More than fear – it was panic. Shock. Shock that this could be happening!

She forced her mind to remember who it was and to distance itself from what she was experiencing, but it was difficult to push Olaf's terror aside.

She was wet. Soaked from head to toe. It poured down her face and ran into her mouth. She choked, coughing up water as it filled her lungs. She couldn't breathe! Her vision blurred as she felt a hand on her head, pushing her under once more...

Kadlin vomited water onto the floor. She fell to her knees, gasping for breath and clutching at her throat. She was safe, she reminded herself. She was safe. She stood, shakily, and felt Jarl Thorstein's arm around her. Supporting her.

'I'm sorry,' she said to Ada. 'Your husband's spirit has passed.'

Ada let out a feral cry that was more animal than human. The jarl seated Kaldin back at the table and looked at her with concern.

'What did you see?'

'He is drowned,' Kadlin replied, still trying to catch her breath.

Ada was sobbing hysterically now, drawing women from the square outside. Others came, too, hearing the noise and concerned for the safety of their jarl.

'He was a boat builder,' Jarl Thorstein said. 'I will have men search the harbour for his body.'

'No,' Kadlin held up a hand. 'I tasted no salt. This wasn't sea water. It was fresh, like a pool or spring. Neither was it an accident,' she added. 'Your man was murdered.'

ULFRIK

Ulfrik was troubled by the death of One-Eye. Although no credible explanation had been found for the murder, he couldn't help but feel that he himself bore some of the responsibility. It had been his suggestion that Thorvald go after Asbjorn, and he knew better than to let any crew member venture out alone. He had simply wanted rid of the man; to get him away from The Ox and stop him asking questions that Ulfrik didn't want to answer. He hadn't thought for one minute that his solution would become so permanent. Yrsa had warned him that people would die until the silver was delivered. Getting to Haithabyr as soon as possible must be his priority from now on. If the crew had to sleep at sea a few more times to accomplish that, so be it.

He wondered if Egil and Bjarni were right when they insisted the journey was cursed. His usual recourse would be to discuss the matter with Yrsa. Strange that he had not considered talking to Kadlin about it. That would seem the obvious thing to do. He smiled as he imagined Svala shaking her head and sighing at him for not thinking of it sooner. He would talk to his daughter and ask if she could sense a curse on their voyage. If so, he had every faith she'd be able to break it, and then their worries would be over.

He gave Hakon and Fromond first watch on the ship, promising to return by midday to take second shift with Magnus. The big man accompanied him to the marketplace, and he found himself wanting to purchase a gift for Kadlin.

'What do you buy a Seer,' he asked his friend.

'Whatever she wants if you value your hide,' Magnus replied, scrutinising a small, copper brooch with a green stone. 'Do you think Brunhilde would like this?' He held it up for Ulfrik to see.

'She's your wife. What do you think?'

'I think she would like it.'

'Then get it for her.'

Magnus studied the brooch a little longer. 'The green would match her eyes,' he mused, turning it over in his palm. 'What about a brooch for your daughter?'

'Perhaps,' Ulfrik said, noncommittally. Trinkets weren't exactly what he had in mind. He wanted to find something meaningful. He moved on to the next stall while Magnus handed over some pieces of hack silver for the seller to weigh. He looked at the wares of several traders before he found something that caught his eye - a small figure of a shieldmaiden cast in silver. She was quite tiny, only two thirds the length of his thumb, but there was something about the simplistic features of her face, and the lines of her clothes, that appealed to him. Despite wearing a long, elaborate dress, she carried an upright sword in one hand and an embossed shield in the other. Her long, straight hair was knotted at the back of her head in a functional, yet fashionable, style. The sculptor had created a hole between her neck and hair through which a leather cord had been threaded so she could be worn as a charm.

'A Valkyrie to watch over you in battle, Lord?' The trader saw the interest in Ulfrik's eye. Ulfrik shook his head.

'I'm no warrior, friend. Nor am I a Lord,' he replied, and made as if to move on. He'd already decided to buy the piece, but knew he'd get a better price if he feigned disinterest.

'For your son, then? For protection?'

Ulfrik wrinkled his nose in mock indecision. 'If she was bronze, perhaps, but my pockets don't run to silver. A beautiful piece, though! My compliments.'

'You can't put a price on protection,' the man insisted. 'Let me tell you the story of this little Valkyrie. She is real, you know! She came to our goði in a dream and told him to sculpt her, and to have her cast. Her purpose, she said, was to protect a mighty warrior! She instructed the goði to melt down his own silver arm ring to create her, and that is why only this one was ever made.'

Ulfrik was certain it was a tale. He was used to weaving such words himself. The merchant probably had a chest full of these charms beneath his stall. Despite this, he still felt compelled to buy the pendant for his daughter. He must have hesitated too long for the trader continued 'I feel that she wants to go with you. For you, I am willing to drop my price.'

Ulfrik would look back on this moment over the coming days and wonder how he, an experienced merchant, had been talked into parting with such a large sum. Never at any time, however, would he regret the purchase. It felt right. Perhaps there was something in the story the man had relayed, and a Valkyrie truly was watching over the bearer.

He thought nothing of the fact that Kadlin didn't return that afternoon. Given the choice of being entertained by a jarl, or keeping watch aboard The Ox, he would probably have chosen the former, too. Magnus had brought a 'tafl board along on the journey, and the two men spent most of their shift engaged in strategic battle. Ulfrik was three moves from defeating his opponent when Olvir Red Face came racing down the dock yelling Ulfrik's name.

'Ulfrik! Ulfrik!' Olvir ran up the gangplank then doubled over with his hands on his knees, gasping for breath. 'In the square… A murder… They said something about a Völva.'

Ulfrik's heart stopped. The world began to spin. He tried to get to his feet, but his legs would not support him. He put a hand on the 'tafl board to brace himself, scattering pieces everywhere.

'She's dead?' His tongue could barely form the words.

'I don't know,' Olvir admitted. 'I saw a crowd of people running behind a cart. They were saying that someone had been murdered, and I heard another person mention a Völva. I wasn't close enough to hear them properly before they were gone. There was… there was a body on the cart, but there were too many people. I couldn't see. I wanted to follow but I thought I should let you know.'

'Thank you. Good man. Thank you.' Ulfrik started unsteadily toward the gangplank. 'Show me where.'

'They were heading for the mead hall,' Olvir said, following him.

'Go. I'll watch the ship,' Magnus volunteered.

'Fuck the ship,' Ulfrik snapped. 'I need you.' He felt in his pouch for the Valkyrie pendant. 'If you are real,' he murmured, 'let her live.'

*

Ulfrik had travelled most of the known world, but the walk from the dock to the mead hall was the longest journey of his life. There was a large crowd gathered by the time he, Olvir and Magnus arrived. They pushed their way to the front but were denied entry by Jarl Thorstein's guards.

'I need to see her,' Ulfrik said. 'Kadlin. The Völva.'

'Yeah, you and everyone else,' one of the guards retorted. He gestured to the crowd. 'You may have noticed, unless you're blind, or deaf, or…'

'Or fucking stupid,' added another guard.

'Or fucking stupid,' the first agreed.

'She's his daughter, you putrid troll turds!' Magnus yelled, diplomatic as ever. Ulfrik raised his hands as the angry, insulted guards drew their weapons.

'Friends, please,' he said, placatingly. 'I just need to see the body.'

'Father?' Ulfrik's heart raced at the sound of her voice.

He looked beyond the guards to where Kadlin now stood, resplendent in a new cloak. 'Let them through,' she commanded, and the guards stepped aside. Ulfrik threw his arms around her and kissed her forehead. She seemed utterly shocked by this greeting, as was everyone who witnessed it. Men had been killed for less. He realised his mistake and instantly released her.

'Forgive him, Lady. He thought you were dead,' Magnus explained.

'Dead? Why?' Kadlin asked, surprised.

'Because some witless bastard told him you were,' Magnus replied, cuffing Olvir around the head.

KADLIN

She could have broken the news a little more gently. That she knew. At the time, though, the remembrance of drowning was fresh in her mind and she'd thought of little other than delivering the facts. She could still feel the hand on her head, pushing her under, long fingers tightly gripping her skull. There was something there, in that memory. Something she was missing…

Had she known that Olaf Boatbuilder was the younger brother of the jarl, she would have taken more care with her words. People lashed out when they were grieving. When a man with power lashed out the consequences were deadly.

Jarl Thorstein was certain he knew who had killed his

sibling, and why, and sent armed men to find the culprit. He also sent people to check every freshwater pool and spring within a mile radius. It wasn't long before the body was found. News spread quickly, and by the time Olaf's body reached the mead hall a large crowd had gathered outside. Some were simply there to satisfy their curiosity. Others tried to gain favour by pointing fingers at their neighbours, and many had come to seek the aid of the Völva. If she could find a missing man, perhaps she could locate the jewellery they had misplaced, or predict the outcome of a voyage, or tell if a marriage would be fruitful.

Kadlin would willingly have helped them but reaching out for answers from the other side used energy, and she only had a finite amount of that. Contacting the dead – reliving their last moments – that was especially draining work, not to mention the emotional toll it took on her. She had felt Olaf's terror as if it was her own. She'd felt his panic as water filled his lungs, and the pain of his body being deprived of oxygen. She would never forget that, nor any of the other deaths she had experienced over the years.

'Are you okay, daughter?'

Ulfrik's voice pulled her from her thoughts. He'd sent Magnus and Olvir back to the ship but had opted to stay with her awhile.

'Just a little tired,' she replied, smiling in what she hoped was a reassuring way. Ulfrik returned the smile but she could see there was something troubling him. 'Talk to me, Father,' she said. 'What worries you?'

'I need your help,' he confessed. In a hushed voice he told her of the death of Gunnar, and of the horde of silver disguised in the hold. He told her of their secret mission, and how Jarl Erik had threatened the lives of Ulfrik's family and crew if he did not set sail for Haithabyr. And finally, he told her of Yrsa's warning and how he now feared they were under a curse. As her father spoke, Kadlin thought of the tear she had shed into the blessing bowl and how the journey had been tainted by it, but she also thought of Yrsa's words, and how her grandmother had known The Ox was sailing a dark and dangerous path long before they left Bramsvik. It seemed there may be greater forces at work here than a simple curse or a tainted blessing.

'We must leave before nightfall,' Ulfrik concluded. 'The crew will be angry, but rather that than I watch them all die by some misfortune. We need to reach Haithabyr and be rid of the silver as soon as the gods allow. I won't risk the death of anyone else by tarrying longer.'

Before Kadlin could respond, five of Jarl Thorstein's men came in dragging another man. He'd been badly beaten and was loudly protesting his innocence. Ada, the dead man's widow, ran at him, screaming, and began hitting him with her fists. Despite her small size it took two of

Thorstein's men to restrain her. The man was thrown to his knees before the jarl, bleeding and trembling in fear.

'I've done nothing, Lord,' he said. 'I had no reason to quarrel with Olaf.' The jarl silenced him with a punch that left him on the floor.

'Every man here knows he was ploughing Thordis,' Jarl Thorstein bellowed. 'You are stupid, Jorund, but you are not blind.'

Kadlin felt a wave of pain and disbelief coming from Jorund as he reacted to this news. The man had not known. Not until this moment. Of that she was certain.

'Thordis,' he said. 'No. No, Lord.' He shook his head. 'She would not. She would never.' Jorund cowered as the jarl raised his fist again. 'I swear it before Tyr,' he cried. 'May he tear out my heart if I don't speak the truth! Olaf was twice my size. How could I have killed him?'

'It was two of you, then,' Jarl Thorstein snarled. 'You will confess what you did to my brother, and then you will tell me who helped you do it.' He signalled to his men and they hauled Jorund to his feet.

'Wait,' Kadlin commanded. 'Jarl Thorstein, I believe he is speaking the truth.'

'No. He killed my brother,' the jarl declared, determined. 'Before he dies, he will admit it.' His men hesitated, loyal to their jarl but unwilling to defy a seer.

'You will leave him be,' Kadlin demanded, firmly. She heard a sharp intake of breath from her father, and the hall became silent. It was dangerous to challenge a leader, but she felt with certainty that Jorund had nothing to do with the boatbuilder's death and she could not, in all conscience, allow an innocent man to be tortured. Most leaders, even kings and queens, would defer to the wisdom of a Völva. The Völur could influence the fate of men and lay a curse upon those who offended them. Cursed men did not retain their power for long...

Thorstein stared at her and Kadlin could see that reason was battling the raw emotions inside him.

'It has to be Jorund,' he insisted, his voice cracking. 'Olaf had no enemies. Not one. No-one but this man had any reason to wish him dead.'

'You want justice for your brother. I understand,' Kadlin replied, 'but there is no justice in punishing an innocent man.'

'Then find me the guilty one,' Jarl Thorstein said. 'You are the one who said Olaf was murdered. Find me his killer and Jorund goes free. If not, I go with what my gut is telling me – that this worthless nithing killed my brother.'

Kadlin looked at her father and saw him pleading with her to refuse the jarl's request. She knew he wanted to leave Lutshaven by nightfall and how important it was for him to do so. But Jorund was also silently pleading, and Kadlin knew she couldn't abandon him to be tortured and executed.

'Agreed,' she said, and heard her father groan. 'First, I have a task to do for my father, but after that I will do what I can to find your brother's killer.'

*

The stick seller, Anders, arrived shortly after Jorund was taken away. He brought a vast selection of staffs with him – over forty – and Kadlin spent a while running her hands over the wood and seeing which of them felt right. There were straight sticks, some with kinks or twists, some with root balls at one end or other natural, decorative features. She chose a hazel staff, almost her own height, which had grown with honeysuckle spiralling around it. She thanked Anders for his excellent work in cutting and seasoning the staff, then took her leave of Jarl Thorstein and walked back to the docks with Ulfrik.

'I don't ask you to wait for me,' she said as soon as they left the mead hall. 'I know your business is urgent, so leave tonight and come back for me on your way home. It seems there's no shortage of people wanting my services here.'

'I'm not leaving you…' Ulfrik began.

'It's my fault,' Kadlin interrupted. 'If I hadn't spoken out the jarl would have taken Olaf's death to be an accident.'

'You may be wise, daughter, but you are not yet worldly,' Ulfrik replied. 'A jarl like Thorstein will always look for someone to blame. Jorund's life was over as soon as Olaf breathed his last. Accept that you cannot help this man.' Kadlin opened her mouth to respond but Ulfrik held up a hand and continued. 'If you can't accept this, however, then understand that I will never leave you behind. You are my daughter. What kind of man would that make me?'

'I will be fine,' she assured him.

'I don't doubt it,' he agreed, 'but you'll also be alone and friendless in a strange town, and there is a killer among these people who now knows you've been set against him. The crew will be glad of a night here. We will wait.'

Most of the crew were still ashore when she and Ulfrik returned to The Ox. Kadlin was pleased as she needed space if she was to check the ship for signs of a curse. At her request, her father removed those still aboard and waited with them on the dock, leaving her alone on the knarr. Well, almost...

'You look different,' Saltfish said, studying her.

'I have a new cloak,' Kadlin replied with a smile. 'And a staff.'

'Still only looking at the outside,' Saltfish tutted. He

tapped her chest with a finger. 'I mean in here. What have you done now?' The look on the little wight's face made Kadlin feel she'd let him down in some way. She told him of Jarl Thorstein's request, how she'd experienced the death of his brother and how Jorund's life was now forfeit unless she could find the real killer. Saltfish shook his head. 'You really don't know when to keep things to yourself, do you.'

'I did my duty and I spoke the truth,' Kadlin replied defensively.

'Oh yes, I remember how well that worked out for you with King Harald. How is your grandmother these days,' the ship's wight said, stroking his beard. 'Just because a thing is true, that does not give you leave to go vomiting it at people! Some truths must be digested slowly and in small bites, or they come back upon you covered in bile.'

Kadlin was stung by the mention of Yrsa. She had tried not to think about those she'd left behind, as wondering at their fate only caused her pain. Had the Völur suffered because of her actions? Were they even still alive?

'I don't understand,' she said wretchedly. 'You think I should have lied to Jarl Thorstein about what I saw?'

'Why is telling the truth so important to you,' Saltfish asked. 'If knowing a thing will only bring pain and heartache, why say it at all?'

'But Olaf was murdered,' Kadlin cried. 'Should I let his murderer go free rather than hurt his brother's feelings? Where's the justice in that?'

'Oh, you want justice. Is that what you think you've achieved?'

Kadlin's cheeks burned. She felt responsible for Jorund's predicament but didn't understand what she could have done differently.

'Look again at what you saw, little seer,' Saltfish said, patting her hand. 'Look with fresh eyes.' He went back to his favourite spot at the prow, turned his back on her, and began to sing softly to himself.

Kadlin was confused and afraid. She didn't want to experience the boat builder's death again, but something had been nagging her about it and now Saltfish was suggesting she'd read it wrong. If she let it go, and spared herself this, Jorund would almost certainly die. She wished Yrsa were here, or Aud or Jofrið. She didn't want to do this alone. Kadlin rested her staff against the hull of the ship and sat cross-legged on the deck. She pulled her hood down to shield her face from anyone who may be watching. *Never show fear.* She remembered that much. She slowed her heartbeat and let her mind reach out. It was easier the second time, and she didn't need the presence of his wife or socks to reconnect with Olaf's spirit. Pay attention to detail, she instructed herself. What did I miss?

She was going under again! Kadlin spluttered, trying to keep her head above the surface of the pool. It was no use. She felt the firm grip of the hand upon her head, pushing her down. She tried to separate her feelings from Olaf's – to control the panic so that she could focus.

Her assailant was incredibly strong! Olaf had been a muscular man, but they were holding him beneath the surface with just one hand. Kadlin's lungs were on fire, trying to suck in air but finding only water instead. Her body began to buck, yet still the fingers held Olaf fast.

Through the fear, and the pain, Kadlin's mind realised what she had missed before. The fingers were long and elegant, like those of a woman, yet they reached down either side of the boat builder's face, gripping him tightly below the cheekbones. His whole head was held firmly in the palm of his killer's hand. No human had hands that large!

Kadlin forced herself to stay with Olaf, to feel the final spasms of his dying body. The hand released him, and he floated, face down, on the surface of the water. The last thing he saw before death clouded his vision was hundreds of skulls screaming back at him from the bottom of the pool, each one green with age and algae.

Kadlin coughed up a lungful of water and took several shuddering gasps. She lay down, rolling onto her side and hugging her chest as she shivered. The physical symptoms would fade quickly once her mind realised she was safe.

Deep breaths, she told herself. You will be fine. She thought about what she had seen at the bottom of the pool. Olaf's killer had not been human, and the pool was its lair. No doubt, centuries ago, people had made sacrifices to it there. Now, in this modern age, it had to do the killing itself.

After a few moments Kadlin felt able to get to her feet. She was still a little shaky but hadn't forgotten what she'd come here for. She was certain she would have noticed if a curse had been placed upon their voyage or the ship, but she'd promised Ulfrik that she would check, and she always kept her word.

Kadlin searched every place where a talisman could be hidden, or a bindrune or sigil carved or painted. There was nothing. Whatever black fate Yrsa had foreseen, it would not be brought about by magic, but by the acts of men.

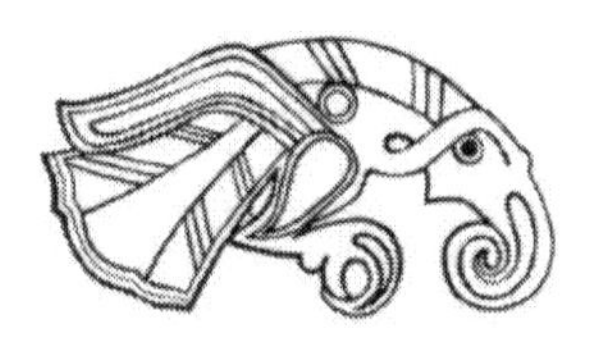

ASBJORN

The market at Lutshaven was tiny compared to the great trading centres at Birka and Haithabyr, so he really shouldn't have expected too much. Even so, Asbjorn was disappointed as he surveyed the stalls. There were perhaps two dozen traders, most of whom sold only items of food or drink. A handful of butchers, three bakers, a rather promising cheesemaker and two brewers of ales and meads. A couple of stalls sold dyed cloth, but there was nothing of sufficient quality to catch his eye. Even the jewellery makers had nothing special.

'What do you think,' he asked, turning to Alfgeir. 'Can you see anything she would like?'

The boy shrugged without even looking. He had been

sullen and moody all day, and not at all his usual self. Asbjorn had brought him to the market to help choose a gift for Ragnfrið, but so far Alfgeir had shown little enthusiasm for the task and said barely a word. It was no matter. Asbjorn was certain he'd find nothing suitable here anyway.

'What is wrong with you today?' The boy would be family one day, so he tried to make an effort, but sulky children were something Asbjorn never had much tolerance for and his patience was wearing thin. He smacked Alfgeir round the ear. 'Talk. Or go back to the ship. I thought you were a man, Alfgeir. Should I have left you with the women?'

That seemed to strike a chord. Alfgeir met his eyes for the first time that day. 'I saw the knife,' he mumbled. 'I know what you did.'

Asbjorn was certain his heart stopped beating for a moment. He felt as though a frost giant had reached inside his chest, for he was suddenly chilled all over. He glanced around anxiously to see who else was listening to their conversation, but no-one seemed to be paying them any heed. He grabbed Alfgeir's tunic and dragged the boy away from the market, not stopping until he found a secluded place away from prying eyes and ears.

'What are you talking about,' he demanded.

'Don't worry. I haven't told anyone,' Alfgeir said,

miserably. 'I know you must have had a good reason for killing Thorvald…'

Asbjorn clamped a hand over the boy's mouth. He looked around nervously again, but no-one was near. 'You don't know what you're talking about,' he hissed, removing his hand. 'I didn't do anything to One-Eye. He was attacked by thieves and everyone knows it.'

The child said nothing, but the look on his face spoke for him. He knew.

'Listen, Alfgeir,' Asbjorn crouched down and spoke softly. 'You and I are going to be family soon. You want that, don't you?' The boy nodded. 'Well, then there are things you need to understand. But this is a secret. Just between us men. Okay?' Alfgeir nodded again, and Asbjorn could sense a rekindling of the trust between them. He sighed. 'My father is old,' he said, 'and he is not a good jarl. Not like I would be. You want me to be jarl, don't you, so your sister can be a jarl's wife?'

'She would like that,' Alfgeir agreed.

'She would, and we want that for her, don't we? We want her to be happy.'

The boy nodded.

'Sometimes, in order to become jarl, you have to kill the old jarl.' The boy started at this, and Asbjorn feared he may be losing him. 'My father won't let me marry

Ragnfrið,' he lied, 'so I have to choose between him and her.' He could see Alfgeir mulling this over. 'I can't defeat him by myself,' he continued, 'because Jarl Erik has too many men, but I met some warriors from Frankia and they're going to help me. I just have to do something for them first.'

'They wanted you to kill Thorvald?'

'No. I had to kill Thorvald because he heard me talking to Egil about all of this. He would have tried to stop me, and then Ragnfrið would be unhappy. So, do you see why I had to kill him? Do you understand? Because I love her so much.'

His decision to kill One Eye actually had nothing to do with love and everything to do with self-preservation. His father's man had come upon them as he and Egil were discussing what to do once they reached Haithabyr. A smarter man would have run back to camp and warned the others, but Thorvald One Eye had always been an over-confident bastard and had challenged them both on the spot. They'd had no option but to kill the fool.

'So, what do they want you to do,' Alfgeir asked, hesitantly.

'They want me to stop Ulfrik from giving something to the King of the Danes. That's all.'

'How? How will you stop him?'

'Well, I may have to kill Ulfrik, too.' He watched the child's reaction. 'The gods want me to be jarl. They sent you to help me, didn't they?' Alfgeir nodded uncertainly. 'Then you have to trust that this is what I need to do. If the crew try to stop me, I may have to kill them, too. But this is what the gods want me to do. And it is for Ragnfrið.'

Alfgeir was silent for a while. 'I don't believe you,' he said, finally. 'Why would the gods want you to kill our friends? I won't let you do it. I'll tell Ulfrik.'

Asbjorn slowly reached inside his cloak and closed his hand around the hilt of the small seax. 'I have something for you, Alfgeir,' he replied, gently. 'Trust me. This will make everything clear.'

★

The crew of The Ox were gathered on the dock when Asbjorn arrived back at the knarr. 'Asbjorn! Thank the gods,' Ulfrik called out, as soon as he spotted him. 'I need you to go with Kadlin.'

'Where,' Asbjorn enquired, irritated. 'And why me?' He needed to speak with Egil and didn't have time to run errands.

'The jarl's brother was killed. Drowned in a pool just outside of Lutshaven. Kadlin believes it was a nekk, so I want you to go with her for protection.'

The Völva, standing beside her father, blushed a little. Asbjorn had noticed her growing interest in him over the past week. It was hard not to. He'd seen that doe-eyed look on countless maidens before and had spent many a lonely hour wondering what it would be like to have a seer. However, given her connection to the gods, and her uncanny ability to sniff out the truth, he'd felt it prudent not to pursue the idea.

'If it's a nekk then what protection can I offer? My arrows will be useless,' Asbjorn replied. Nekken were shapeshifters who dwelled in ponds and pools. Mostly they kept to themselves, but occasionally one developed a taste for humans. Assuming a pleasing form, they enticed their prey into the pool and drowned them there. Asbjorn would rather stand naked against an army of berserkers than face such a creature! There was no defence against magic but magic itself.

'I will deal with the nekk,' the Völva said. 'I need you to protect me from Jarl Thorstein's men if necessary. The creature will try to defend itself and I need someone there I can trust.'

'Have you considered going without Thorstein's men,' Asbjorn suggested.

'Odin's beard! Just do as you're told,' Ulfrik snapped, losing his patience.

'We need them to show us where the pool is,' his

daughter replied, coolly, 'and I need them to witness what happens. The jarl is set on killing a man, and my word may not be enough for him in his grief.'

Asbjorn could see there was no way out of this. To argue further would raise suspicion. He gave her his most charming smile. 'Then I am yours, Lady.'

'Bring your bow,' the Völva replied. 'And find me a blacksmith.'

KADLIN

The pool where Olaf Boatbuilder's body had been found was a ten minute ride outside the main town. Jarl Thorstein had been surprisingly open to the idea that his brother's killer was a fae and insisted on being there to see it slain. Kadlin suspected he harboured a notion that he himself could kill the creature, and she hoped he would have the sense to stand aside when the time came. He also provided horses, food and ale, and two armed guards.

The land was gloriously verdant and perfumed with the scent of spring flowers. They passed several smallholdings where lambs or calves played, piglets dozed by their mother's side, and newly hatched chicks darted here and there like tufts of wool caught on the breeze. The air was alive with the song of birds and the hum of insects. It seemed wrong to think of death on a day like this when there was such an abundance of life.

The pool was located within a birch grove. It was much larger than Kadlin had imagined and was bordered by smooth, white boulders of quartzite, which glistened in the dappled sunlight. On one of these rocks sat a young girl, about seven years old, sobbing so hard that her tiny frame shook with each shuddering breath. Beside her, on the sparkling rock, was a ball of soap and a basket of wet clothes. She hugged her knees and hid her face at their approach, too afraid to speak. It was unlikely that such a young child was out here alone washing clothes, yet Kadlin could see no sign of an adult.

'Where is your mother, child,' Jarl Thorstein queried. The question brought a fresh bout of sobbing from the girl. She pointed weakly toward the centre of the pool, where a woman was floating, face down, unnoticed by them until this moment. One of the guards immediately began taking off his boots but Kadlin stopped him.

'No-one enters the water,' she commanded sharply.

'It isn't decent to leave her there, Lady,' he said. 'Please, for the child's sake.'

'No-one enters the water. Not for any reason,' Kadlin repeated firmly. 'What is your name?'

'Gils, son of Anders,' he replied.

'And do you have family, Gils Andersson?'

'A wife and three boys.'

'Do you think your wife and children would understand if you risk your life for the sake of decency? The poor woman is beyond our aid. The best we can do for her now is avenge her death and protect her daughter. Do you not agree?'

Gils bowed his head and nodded solemnly.

Kadlin dismounted, tethered her horse to a tree, and climbed up on the rock to sit beside the girl. The child's clothes were soaking wet, and she was shivering. The warmth of the spring sun was not strong enough to penetrate the canopy of birch leaves, and there was a slight chill in the air. Kadlin put her arm around the girl so that her cloak covered them both.

'You are very brave,' Kadlin said. 'Your mother would be proud.' The girl began picking nervously at the hem of her shift. 'I am Kadlin Svalasdaughter,' Kadlin continued. 'Do you have a name?'

'Eva, daughter of Karl.' The child's voice was barely more than a whisper. With gentle questions, Kadlin found out that she lived nearby on one of the farms they had passed. Her father and younger siblings were at home, and she had come here with her mother to wash the clothes.

'There was a man,' Eva said, pointing to the other side of the pool. 'He talked to Mama and she went into the water with him. I kept calling, but she wouldn't come back, and I can't swim.'

'What did he look like,' Jarl Thorstein asked.

'A nekk can take any form it chooses,' Kadlin explained. 'To Olaf, it probably looked like a beautiful woman, enticing him to swim with her. It has no power over us as long as we stay out of the water, so no-one goes in no matter what you think you see.'

The next hour passed slowly. Kadlin was conscious of the waning light and knew they would have to leave if the creature didn't show itself by sunset. Only a fool would set themselves against a fae in the dark. She thought of Ulfrik, and how he had delayed his departure because of her. She hoped they would be able to leave on the morrow, and, with good winds, make up the time. Asbjorn brought her some bread and a flask of ale, and she took them gratefully.

'Do you think it will come,' he asked.

'It has little incentive,' Kadlin responded. 'It's outnumbered and we know what it is, so we're unlikely to fall for its tricks. Most likely it will stay hidden.'

'Surely that depends on how good a predator it is,' Asbjorn mused.

'How so?'

'Perhaps it thinks it can take us all,' he replied. 'Maybe it likes a challenge.'

A sudden scream, followed by a splash, had them all on their feet.

'It took her,' yelled Gils, who had been sitting near Eva. There was no sign of the little girl other than ripples on the surface of the pond.

'Do you see it,' Thorstein barked.

'No, Lord.' The guard quickly stripped off his boots and coat.

'Stay where you are,' Kadlin shouted, but this time he ignored her. Eva came up, spluttering for air, a few feet from her mother's body. She screamed at the sight of the corpse. Gils dove into the pool and swam toward her just as she was dragged under again. In a few strong strokes he reached the place where she'd disappeared and frantically dove down to try and find her. He came up for air empty-handed, with a look of despair in his eyes.

'Get out,' Kadlin yelled, rushing to the edge of the pool. Turning to the jarl, she said urgently 'A nekk has no power over those on land. It couldn't have taken Eva. She must have thrown herself in. It fooled us!'

'Gils,' Jarl Thorstein roared, drawing his sword, 'it's her!

Get out, now!'

Something that had once been Eva, but was now morphing into a monster, broke the surface behind Gils. The child's head elongated, shedding its hair, and smoothing out to become almost featureless. Black eyes sparkled above a grinning mouth full of needle-like teeth. It's nose and ears were little more than slits. The nekk's body was strong and powerful - no longer that of a child - and it reached out with one formidable hand and seized Gils, wrapping its long fingers around his skull as it had done with Olaf. The second guard took one look at their monstrous foe and ran, screaming, from the grove.

'Release him,' Kadlin commanded. She hadn't had time to carve any symbols of power into her new staff, but she resolved to do so as soon as she was back aboard The Ox. With her old staff, this creature would be easier to handle.

'He came into the water of his own free will,' the nekk replied as it pushed Gils under. 'He is mine, witch.'

Kadlin took her knife and plunged it into the pool, gripping the hilt tightly so as not to lose it. It was a risky move as her arm went in the water up to her elbow, making her vulnerable. The knife blade was small, but made of steel, and the creature screamed in pain. The effect was only temporary, but it was enough to make the nekk release its victim for a moment. Gils came up, coughing for air, and started to swim for shore.

'Kill it,' Thorstein shouted. 'Kill it!'

The nekk turned its attention to Kadlin. The pain the blade inflicted had already passed, and Kadlin knew it wouldn't work a second time. She locked eyes with the creature and could tell it was trying to assess if it could reach her before she withdrew her arm.

'You're not fast enough,' she taunted, with a smile. Gils was almost at the edge of the pool; if she could distract the nekk for just a few more seconds he would be safe. The nekk's grin became a snarl. It dove beneath the surface and covered the distance between them with incredible speed. Kadlin felt a hand on her shoulder as Asbjorn hauled her clear of the water just in time. Her heart pounded at the near miss. She'd never seen anything move so fast!

With a shriek of anger, the nekk dove once again, this time appearing behind Gils and dragging him back from the edge. Jarl Thorstein swung his sword but wasn't close enough to inflict any damage. The thing that had been Eva lifted Gils clear of the water and dangled him by his head while he screamed.

'Your weapons can't harm me, impotent jarl,' it jeered.

Kadlin hurriedly opened the pouch of iron dust she'd bought from the blacksmith earlier. He'd taken the minute shavings left over from other jobs and ground them to dust at her instruction. Before they left, she'd mixed half the dust with a few drops of water, then dipped each of Asbjorn's arrows into it and allowed them to dry. Kadlin tipped the remaining dust into her palm and blew it toward the nekk with all the breath she could muster! The monster dropped Gils and began to gasp and clutch at its throat.

'I will kill you,' it shrieked. 'I will drown you! I will entomb you in water for eternity, Völur bitch!'

'Asbjorn!' Kadlin shouted. Asbjorn, who was waiting for her instruction, drew his bow and nocked one of the iron-dipped arrows. He took aim, but before he could loose the arrow Jarl Thorstein leaped into the pool in a mad rage, hacking and slashing at the water with his sword.

'Get out of the way,' Asbjorn shouted, but the jarl was beyond hearing.

Kadlin jumped into the pool after him and swiped her staff at the back of his knees, taking his legs away and plunging him under the water just as the nekk lunged at him. She threw herself sideways, creating a clear line of sight for Asbjorn. He fired, but his hands were shaking so badly that the arrow completely missed its mark. He nocked a second, fired, and this one hit the nekk directly between the eyes.

'Help me. Quickly,' Kadlin called to Gils, 'before it recovers.' Her cloak and shift were heavy with water, making her movements slow and clumsy.

'It's not dead?' Gils looked horrified as he hastened to do as she asked.

'Not until we decapitate it,' Kadlin replied as she and Gils dragged the creature to the water's edge. 'That was just enough to stun it. My Lord, time to avenge your brother!'

The nekk opened its eyes. Gils cried out in fear and released his hold.

'For Olaf,' snarled Jarl Thorstein. He swung his sword and cleaved the creature's head from its body.

THORFRIDA

'I can't find Alfgeir.'

The Völva and Asbjorn had returned to the ship the previous evening just as the setting sun turned red on the horizon. They were successful in their hunt, it seemed, for the jarl sent several jars of dried fish, a sack of oats, and a barrel of ale as a gift, and Ulfrik's daughter had been wearing a new cloak. Now, in the morning light, Thorfrida could see it was a cornflower blue that complimented the girl's eyes. Killing monsters obviously agreed with her as she looked rosy-cheeked and beautiful today. Asbjorn, in contrast, had returned looking pale and shaken. The dark circles around his eyes this morning gave testament to a sleepless night.

Most of the crew had found lodgings in Lutshaven for the night and returned at first light to ready The Ox for their journey. All, that is, except for Alfgeir. It wasn't like him to sleep ashore, and Thorfrida had worried about him last night. Now, as the sun crept higher in the sky, she was certain something was wrong.

'It isn't like him, Ulfrik,' she said to the captain. 'Something's not right. I feel it in my bones.'

'We can't wait for him,' Ulfrik replied. 'Whatever mischief he's gotten himself into is on his own head. I've delayed long enough.'

There was a haunted look on the captain's face and Thorfrida refrained from pushing him further. Still, she couldn't stop the nagging feeling that something terrible had happened to the lad. She'd become very fond of Alfgeir and worried about him like a mother.

'Cast off,' Ulfrik called. Hakon leapt onto the dock and began to untie the thick rope that bound them there, while Bjarni and Egil hauled up the stone anchor.

'No. Wait! Please.' Thorfrida scanned the port for any sign of the boy. 'Has anyone seen Alfgeir,' she shouted.

'Not since yesterday,' Fromond replied. 'Asbjorn took him to the market.'

'How much did he get for him, I wonder,' Herdis ribbed. The others laughed. How could they joke when a child was missing? Thorfrida's heart thumped as she pushed her way to the other end of the knarr, where Asbjorn stood.

'Where is Alfgeir?'

'How would I know,' he responded. 'There was nothing at the market for Ragnfrið so the boy and I went our separate ways. The last time I saw him he was speaking to the captain of another ship.'

'Probably booking passage back to Bramsvik,' Egil added. 'He was a miserable shit yesterday morning. I reckon he was homesick.'

'He wouldn't leave without saying goodbye,' Thorfrida challenged, 'and he has no silver, nor skills, to barter passage with.'

'Didn't stop him getting a free ride with us, now, did it,' Egil sneered.

Hakon coiled the rope and tossed it onto the deck. He and Bjarni Arm-Strong shoved their weight against the knarr, pushing the prow away from shore before quickly climbing back aboard The Ox. The crew took to their oars and used them to push away from the dock.

'Wait,' Thorfrida begged, making her way back to Ulfrik at the steer board. 'We can't just leave him! Something terrible has happened. I know it.'

'We'll look for him on our return,' Ulfrik said. 'I'm sorry,

'Frida.'

Tears welled in her eyes and she felt the emptiness of despair in her heart. She wanted to scream at him that something was very wrong, but he was too distracted to heed her words.

The crew rowed until The Ox was far enough out to sea to catch a breeze, then Ulfrik gave the order to set sail. With a sense of grief and loss, Thorfrida watched Lutshaven shrink behind them until it was no longer even a dot on the horizon.

Ulfrik pushed them hard over the next few weeks. They slept aboard ship most nights, going ashore only when dwindling food and water supplies made it necessary. He took greater risks to increase their speed, sailing further out to sea to catch the winds when they dropped nearer land. His daughter made offerings to the ocean gods Njörð, Rán, and Ægir, asking for safe passage across the seas. Deeper waters put them not only at the mercy of the gods, but also Rán's daughters, and every eye aboard The Ox anxiously scoured the waves for a sign that the sisters had noticed them. The mood of the crew was low, and resentments ran deep as the ocean beneath them.

'What's the great hurry,' Fromond asked as they ate their supper one stormy evening, voicing the concerns of the whole crew. 'We're all eager to return home, Ulfrik, but keep up this pace and either the ship will break, or we will.'

Thorfrida grieved for Alfgeir as if he were dead, and most nights she sobbed quietly over the wooden bird the boy had carved for her. By the time they made port at Eiriksvik she had come to a decision.

'I need to see Gisla,' she said to Ulfrik. 'I need to see my daughter.' Eiriksvik was a fishing village in the kingdom of Alfheim, close to the border with the Geats. Past the village was a dense forest, and somewhere beyond that lived Gisla and her husband. Eiriksvik was a beautiful place, and - when her daughter had lived in the village itself - Ulfrik had been happy to spend a few days exploring the area and trading with the locals while she visited her child. There were ancient carvings in the rocks here, pictures made by the ancestors, and Ulfrik never seemed to tire of looking at them. Since Gisla and her husband had built their own home and moved further away, however, he had not been willing to justify the extra days it would take.

'I'm not asking you to wait,' Thorfrida continued solemnly, not meeting his eye. 'I'm telling you I'm leaving. I can't do this anymore, Ulfrik. This life. It's too much. I want to spend time with my children, and my grandchildren. We have one too many on board ship anyway since your daughter joined us, so I'll not be leaving you short-handed.'

Ulfrik took her hands in his and squeezed them gently. 'I know you're upset about Alfgeir,' he said. 'I know you miss him. I promise we will stop at Lutshaven on our way home. We've not abandoned him.'

'That's exactly what we've done,' Thorfrida breathed, letting her tears fall. She withdrew her hands from his and wiped the tears away. 'Something terrible happened to that boy. I feel it in the very marrow of me, but you wouldn't listen. We forsook him, just as we forsook One-Eye when his ashes were not yet cold. There will be no justice for either of them because we, their friends, could not trouble ourselves to bring them justice. We have changed, Ulfrik, since we left Bramsvik, and I do not like who we are becoming.'

By the time they set sail without her the next day, Thorfrida was already halfway through the forest. Her conscience still weighed heavy, but her heart was a little lighter.

ULFRIK

As if he didn't have enough to worry about with the hidden silver, the threats of Jark Erik and King Redbeard, the urgency of their mission, the antipathy of his crew, and the shadow of death looming over them all, Ulfrik also had concerns about the budding friendship between his daughter and Asbjorn. Anyone with eyes and ears could tell that Kadlin was falling for him, though Ulfrik was at a loss to explain why. Asbjorn was handsome, a good hunter, a decent warrior, and yes, one day he would probably be jarl, but he was also a self-obsessed, vain, arrogant man who never put anyone else before himself and wasn't good enough for Kadlin! Ulfrik could have overlooked his personal feelings if he believed Asbjorn would make her happy, but that could never be. A Völva could not marry, and a jarl's son had a duty to do so. The best his daughter could hope for was a lifetime as Asbjorn's mistress. Any children she bore him would be a threat to his legitimate heirs, and as such would have a target on their backs from the day they were born. No, Ulfrik did not want this life for Kadlin, and he pleaded with the Norns daily not to weave this fate for her.

Of course, there was always a small chance he was completely overreacting. So far, he had never so much as seen them holding hands, and yet Kadlin followed Asbjorn around like a freshly hatched duckling. Olvir, too, was clearly feeling the strain of seeing the two of them together. His feelings for Kadlin were obvious, as were his feelings toward Asbjorn. To his credit, he showed no animosity, but he was silent and withdrawn and did his best to stay away from them both - not an easy task on a little knarr encircled by water.

With all the drama surrounding the nekk, the disappearance of Alfgeir, and the loss of Thorfrida from the crew, Ulfrik completely forgot about the Valkyrie until he found her, wrapped in a piece of linen, in a corner of his chest.

'I have something for you,' he said to his daughter.

Kadlin seemed genuinely pleased with the gift and it lifted Ulfrik's spirits to see her smile. She ran her fingertips lightly over the pendant. 'There's power in this,' she said. 'Where did you get it?'

'At Lutshaven. In the market,' Ulfrik responded. 'The seller told me she was created from the arm ring of a goði and that she contains a real Valkyrie.'

'Perhaps it is true,' Kadlin replied.

'He also said she was intended for a great warrior,' Ulfrik added.

'Then I shall keep her safe until we meet,' his daughter laughed, tying the cord around her neck. She tucked the pendant inside her clothing, wearing it as a talisman, against the skin, rather than a decoration.

The marketplace of Haithabyr was reached by navigating a long and narrow inlet off the Baltic coast of Jutland. There were many other merchants on the river travelling to and from the market, and occasionally Ulfrik would hail a passing vessel and exchange information with its captain.

'The price of ivory is low,' one told him. 'Not worth the taxes.'

'Good weapons are in demand,' encouraged another.

'Don't trust Bothvar the Geat! The bastard's scales are weighted!'

They also talked of world events, sharing news from countries they had visited. Ulfrik was particularly interested in reports from Saxony. According to all accounts, the conquered Saxons had attempted no major rebellions against the invading Franks for the past two years. The Saxon people were far from happy under the rule of Charlemagne. They still worshipped the pagan gods of their land in private, but publicly they were forced to pay homage to the Christian god and to pay Frankian taxes. Olvir, too, was interested in news of Saxony. He never spoke of his early life other than to say he'd been taken during a raid on his community when he was seven years old. That was nine years ago, and he had not set foot on his native soil since. Ulfrik had never pressed him on the subject, but it intrigued him to know the young man still cared so deeply about his homeland.

The port at Haithabyr had dozens of long jetties at which several ships could dock at once. By the time The Ox was safely moored, and the port officials had inspected and taxed their cargo, the sun was already low in the sky. There would be no point in trying to set up stall tonight, so Ulfrik sent Olvir and Fromond to scout a good location and secure a pitch for the morning.

Now that they were finally here, Ulfrik was keen to be rid of the silver as soon as possible. He was certain the men who had attacked them and killed Gunnar in Birka were waiting for them here. Somewhere, in this tide of human faces, assassins lurked. Ulfrik drew Asbjorn, Magnus and Kadlin to one side and spoke to them in a low voice.

'We'll not be safe until the tribute is delivered,' he warned. 'I want it gone tonight. Asbjorn and I will go to the tavern and meet our contact. Magnus, I leave you and Kadlin here to guard the silver.' The father in him wanted to leave his daughter out of this, but even the bravest of warriors would think twice before attacking a Völva. The silver was safest with her guarding it.

'Why do I have to stay,' Magnus growled. 'Let Asbjorn be the guard dog. I need ale to wash away the taste of salt in my mouth.'

'You ask too much of an old man, Ulfrik,' Asbjorn quipped. 'The Lady and I can watch the barrels. Take Magnus with you. At his age you really shouldn't leave him unattended.'

'Age may have slowed my body, but it hasn't slowed my wits, you little shit,' Magnus snapped before Ulfrik could correct Asbjorn about the barrels. 'Stay here if you wish. Don't expect my thanks. Come, Ulfrik, we're wasting valuable drinking time.'

Ulfrik patted the piece of carved whale bone he'd tucked inside his tunic. He wondered if their contact would still be waiting, or if they'd given up on him by now. If so, what then? He coughed nervously, finding his throat suddenly dry. If they didn't show, he decided, at least there would be ale.

The harbour was at the eastern end of Haithabyr, with

defensive earthworks erected to the north, south and west of the town. The people lived in small houses tightly packed together in rows that stretched from east to west. The whole town was organised in a grid, with all the blacksmiths in one area, the bakers in another, and so on. The air carried the scent of exotic spices, of meads and honeys and tanned leather hides.

The tavern to which Ulfrik led them was toward the southern end of the market. It was less crowded than he had expected, but he still saw every face as a potential enemy and every movement as a possible threat. He was a merchant, not a warrior, and although he knew how to use the short blade at his hip, he doubted his ability to adequately defend himself against trained men. Magnus found them somewhere to sit with a good view of the entrance while Ulfrik purchased a jug of ale.

'Friend,' Ulfrik said, catching the landlord's arm. 'I'm looking for someone who may be interested in this.' He unwrapped the whalebone. The man looked at it a moment, then glanced around furtively to see who else may be watching.

'I know someone,' he said. 'They've been waiting quite some time. I can't guarantee they're still interested, but I will send a boy.'

'My thanks,' Ulfrik replied. He took the jug of ale and two cups and went to join Magnus.

KADLIN

Kadlin was disappointed at having to wait with the crew rather than accompany her father and Magnus. She'd heard so much about Haithabyr and was excited to experience it for herself. She understood, though, that duty came first, and reasoned that she could visit the market tomorrow.

Asbjorn was strangely uncommunicative. He stood by the gangplank, watching over the harbour and scrutinising each new face as if looking for someone. She had hoped – when he'd volunteered to stay aboard ship – it was because he wanted to spend some time with her without the watchful eye of her father. Kadlin wasn't sure what their relationship was; it wasn't exactly a friendship, and neither was it sexual, but a definite closeness had developed since they'd slain the nekk. She liked having the attention of a man, especially one as fine as Asbjorn, but she knew he had a woman waiting for him back in Bramsvik, and for that reason she'd drawn very clear boundaries. She could hear Yrsa's voice in her head. *Be honourable in all things. Don't expect to be treated with respect if you can't behave respectably!*

Kadlin allowed her thoughts to turn, once again, to her grandmother. She ardently hoped Yrsa was alive and well, and that the events at Tromø had not had a lasting negative impact. Her father only intended to stay a few days in Haithabyr – just long enough to make the journey worthwhile – and then they would begin the voyage home. It seemed years since she'd seen her family, and her heart yearned for them. Even austere Aud would be a welcome sight.

Will you fly? She pondered the words the goddess, Freya, had spoken to her. It was neither a command, nor a statement. Rather, it implied she had a choice. There had been no opportunities, thus far, to spread her metaphorical wings. Perhaps, on the return journey, Freya's meaning would be revealed.

'Wherever your thoughts are, I guarantee it's the wrong place.'

Kadlin turned to see Saltfish sitting on Ulfrik's sea chest. His face was pinched, and there was a look of sadness about him. Kadlin inclined her head politely. 'And where should they be, Master Wight,' she enquired.

Saltfish glanced at Asbjorn, then back to her. He drummed his gnarled fingers on the lid of the chest as if deciding something. Then, decision made, he climbed up on it, so they were almost face to face. 'This is a lesson your grandmother could not teach you,' he sighed. 'It's something every seer has to learn for herself, through experience. Love makes you blind.'

'I'm not in love,' Kadlin replied, feeling her cheeks flush.

'No,' he agreed. 'You are not. But you've allowed yourself to become infatuated. With your keen senses you should have been the first to notice the rot aboard this ship. I smelled the stench of it long ago.' He looked at Asbjorn again. 'Time to stop blocking yourself, little seer. Open your eye.'

Without warning, the wight reached up and pressed his palm against her forehead. She felt a surge of energy that took her breath away, as if a bucket of ice-cold water had been thrown over her. Kadlin felt it coursing through her body, cleansing her spirit and freeing her mind. She gasped at the sudden sense of clarity, like waking abruptly from a dream.

'It's important you see this as a lesson, and only a lesson, or you'll bind yourself further,' Saltfish counselled. 'Don't blame yourself for what happens next. Don't let it consume you.' He removed his hand.

Kadlin felt it almost immediately. The air around the ship crackled with malice, and it was coming from Asbjorn. As she looked at him – truly looked at him – his face seemed to twist and contort, becoming ugly and repulsive. How had she blinded herself to this? How had she not seen the corruption inside him?

Kadlin reached for her staff, into which she had carved runes, and sigils of power and protection. As she gripped it, the runes hagalaz and thurisaz began to glow. Hail and thorn. Pain was coming. Pain and suffering.

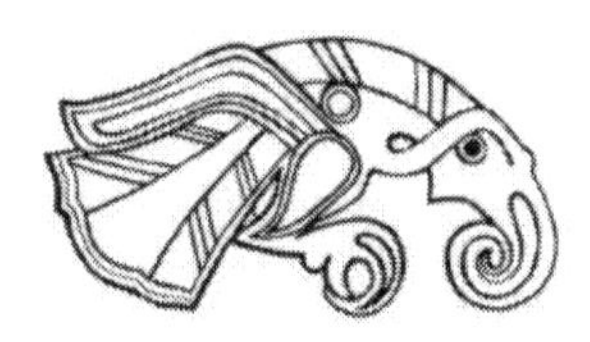

ULFRIK

There was still no sign of their contact. The faintest glimmer of light remained outside, and Ulfrik did not relish the prospect of walking back to The Ox in darkness. Magnus was slumped forward on the table, snoring loudly beside a tankard of ale. He had not consumed enough to be drunk, so Ulfrik surmised his friend was simply exhausted and had allowed him to sleep.

He shook the big man's shoulder. 'Magnus.'

Magnus lifted his head a hand's span off the table and opened bleary eyes. It took him a moment to get his bearings and recall where he was. He sat up, wincing at a sudden pain in his neck, and wiping drool from his chin with a sleeve.

'What? Are they here?' Magnus looked around the crowded tavern.

'No. But it's getting dark and I think we should leave,' Ulfrik said, getting to his feet. He told the landlord they'd be back on the morrow should their contact arrive, then he and Magnus stepped outside into the gathering gloom.

In all the scenarios Ulfrik had run through in his head, none of them accounted for the possibility that no-one would show up. What was he supposed to do with the silver now? Sitric had given him the piece of carved whalebone and the name of this tavern. That was all. If their contact didn't show, he had absolutely no idea what he should do. Had they grown tired of waiting all these weeks, with no sign of him? He should have delivered the silver in the spring and it was summer now. Or had they assumed, as Jark Erik feared, that Ulfrik had stolen it? Worse still, had the Franks gotten to them first?

As if his thoughts had called them forth, two Frankish warriors emerged from the shadows to block their path. Ulfrik stopped, putting out a hand to halt Magnus, who was practically sleep-walking beside him.

'Perhaps we should go back inside,' Ulfrik murmured. They turned around slowly, being careful not to make any sudden or threatening movements, only to find two more men behind them.

'Fuck,' Magnus muttered, becoming more alert by the second.

'I don't like being made to wait,' their leader said loudly in a thick accent. 'And we've waited a long time for you.'

'You have us confused with someone else, friend,' Ulfrik replied, cordially. 'We are merchants. Here to trade. We only arrived this afternoon.'

'I know when you arrived, Ulfrik Varinsson of The Ox,' the man said, smiling coldly. Ulfrik felt a chill at the mention of his name. 'I've had men watching the docks for you for many moons now. I know who you are, and I know what cargo you carry.'

'Then you will know I no longer have it,' Ulfrik bluffed, changing tactic. 'It was delivered as soon as we got here. My friend and I have just been celebrating.'

'Yes,' agreed Magnus, unconvincingly. 'With ale,' he added.

'We have the silver,' the man replied. 'It's being removed from your ship as we speak. All we want from you is the name of your contact.'

The warriors behind them let out strangled cries. Ulfrik turned to see them clutching their throats as blood gushed through their fingers. A short, slender woman with long, raven hair ran at him, brandishing an axe in each hand. Before he had time to react, she landed one foot on

Magnus's thigh and another on Ulfrik's shoulder, launching herself into the air. She brought the axes down, hacking them into the heads of the two remaining Franks. It was all over in a matter of seconds. Ulfrik stared in shock at the four bloody bodies twitching on the ground.

Their saviour tossed something to him - a second piece of whalebone. Ulfrik straightened his tunic, composed himself, and put the two carved pieces together. They fit perfectly, completing the design.

'I'm Sólveig,' the woman said. 'And you are late.'

'Fuck,' said Magnus again.

For once, Ulfrik could think of nothing better to say.

★

Sólveig was captain of the Sea Serpent, a Danish longship. She and her crew were in the service of King Sigfrid and were far from happy to have been kept waiting so many moons. Two of her crew - a dark-haired man, and a flame-haired woman who looked to be a Celt - were waiting with an ox and cart not far from where Sólveig had slain the Franks.

'Meet us at The Ox,' she called, not stopping to explain further as she, Ulfrik and Magnus ran past. Any other day, Ulfrik would have told her that he was too old to run, but he was afraid for Kadlin and his crew, and he, too, wanted to reach the ship faster than a cart could have carried them. Even Magnus did not complain as he jogged back to the jetty.

Kadlin was waiting on the dock when they arrived. She held a lantern in one hand and her staff in the other.

'Men took the barrels,' she warned in a low voice. 'They didn't know about the axe heads. It's Asbjorn, Father. Asbjorn betrayed us.'

Ulfrik's stomach churned. On the one hand he was relieved to hear the crew and the silver were safe, but on the other he realised a jarl's son was a powerful enemy, and Asbjorn was unlikely to let any of them leave Haithabyr alive if his treachery was exposed.

'This is Sólveig,' Ulfrik said hastily, introducing their companion to Kadlin. 'She saved our lives.' To Sólveig he added 'Have that cart ready to leave.'

The crew got to their feet as soon as Ulfrik and Magnus boarded the ship. Lanterns had been hung fore and aft, illuminating angry and concerned faces.

'What's going on,' Herdis demanded. 'Asbjorn said no-one could leave until you returned. We're hungry, Ulfrik.'

'A misunderstanding, I'm sure,' Ulfrik replied with a brief smile. 'I have no problem with you leaving the ship. Why don't you all go now?' If he could get them off The Ox, at least they stood a chance. He stood to one side, allowing the crew to file past. 'Asbjorn,' he added, 'we need to talk.'

'Is that your contact,' Asbjorn demanded, staring at Sólveig waiting on the jetty.

'He didn't show,' Ulfrik lied. 'Kadlin said they came here instead and took the barrels.' He allowed a little of the anxiety he was feeling to show in his voice. 'It was the Danes, wasn't it? You made sure it was the right people?'

'Of course,' Asbjorn confirmed. 'Who is she?'

'Thank the gods.' Ulfrik forced himself to look relieved. 'Well done.' He clapped Asbjorn on the back, resisting the urge to draw his knife and gut the boy. He had to get Kadlin and the silver away from here as soon as possible. Out of the corner of his eye he spied the ox and cart at the end of the jetty. 'Olvir,' he called. Olvir Red-Face was on the gangplank, but he stopped at mention of his name. 'Help Magnus, will you, before you leave? I've traded the axe heads. They need to be loaded onto that cart before she changes her mind.'

Magnus glared at him, unwilling to leave his captain, but he did as he was bid and went with Olvir to fetch the silver.

Asbjorn saw the ox and cart, and his face tensed.

'Who are these people? Who is that woman,' he snapped.

'I think you're forgetting which one of us is captain,' Ulfrik replied, tartly. 'I don't need to explain myself to you. She's the woman who is going to exchange three chests of axe heads for eight rolls of silk. Eight! One of them even has gold thread if she's to be believed! The woman is mad. I've persuaded her to do the exchange tonight before she realises what a bad deal this is and changes her mind. Magnus and Kadlin will go with her and bring back the silk.'

'Magnus will not,' Magnus said, emerging from the hold. He and Olvir were carrying a chest between them. He scowled at Ulfrik.

'It seems I'm not the only one who's forgotten you're the captain,' Asbjorn sneered. Ulfrik's heart sank. Magnus was a good friend but a stubborn bastard. The Franks would discover their deception soon and then they'd return. Ulfrik feared for the lives of anyone left aboard when they did.

'Wait,' Asbjorn said. He lifted the lid on the chest and looked inside. Seeing only axe heads, he lowered it again, allowing them to continue.

'Odin's arse,' Magnus muttered.

As Magnus and Olvir were carrying the third and final chest to the cart, a commotion began at the end of the docks. Ulfrik couldn't make out much in the darkness, but he could see flaming torches and hear raised voices.

He hastened down to the jetty to join his daughter.

'Hurry,' he urged Magnus. 'Let's get this lady on her way.' He forced a smile. 'I need you to go with Sólveig,' he said to Kadlin.

She shook her head. 'You're going to need me.'

'What I need right now is someone I can trust to deliver this safely,' he assured her. 'Please, I am asking as your father. Let me deal with these men. Once the silver is gone, we shall all be safe, and this will be over.' Kadlin could see he was not telling the truth, but she nodded reluctantly and climbed up on the cart.

'As you wish. I'll be back as soon as I can,' she promised.

The crowd of angry people had reached the end of the jetty, and by the light of their torches Ulfrik could see that around twelve armed warriors were herding the crew of The Ox back to the ship.

'Go with Kadlin,' he said to Olvir, hastily. 'I need someone to check the quality of the silk and she has no experience in such matters.'

Sólveig leapt up onto the cart and barked a command at her two crew members. The man seized the ring in the ox's nose and started to pull, while the red-haired woman slapped the reigns. Slowly, grudgingly, the ox began to move.

Ulfrik seized Olvir's arm and pulled him close. In the language of the Saxons - a language he knew Asbjorn would not understand - he said 'Don't let her return to the ship! Do you understand me? Do not come back! Give me your oath you will see her safely away from here.' Olvir looked shocked. His eyes flicked to Asbjorn, and then he nodded.

'I swear it,' Olvir replied in the same tongue. 'I'll protect her with my life. May the gods be with you, Ulfrik.' He ran after the cart and jumped on the back beside the silver.

The Franks were blocking the end of the jetty. *Mighty Thor, see them safely through. Protect my child.* Ulfrik prayed. As he watched, he saw Kadlin stand and raise her staff. He thought how magnificent she looked. Just like her mother. She said something to the men, who practically tripped over themselves in their haste to get out of the way. Kadlin sat back down as the cart began to move. It was soon swallowed by darkness.

Ulfrik allowed himself to breathe again. Whatever came next, at least his daughter was safe. *Thank you*, he murmured, to whatever gods were listening.

ASBJORN

Asbjorn had made offerings to the god, Loki, every time The Ox made port. As a master manipulator and dealer in deceit, Loki was the perfect god to guide a young man seeking to overthrow his captain and depose his father. Asbjorn had dedicated the death of Thorvald to the trickster god, and at Lutshaven had buried one of his own arm rings with Alfgeir, as an offering, asking Loki to keep the boy's body concealed. So far, his god had been good to him.

The Völva was the only person who posed a threat to his scheme. He'd seen first-hand what she could do, and he feared her for it. He'd gone out of his way to flatter and enchant her, using his charm and charisma to keep her distracted. She may be a witch, but she was also a woman, and young women eventually did whatever Asbjorn wanted them to. He and Kadlin had grown close, but not close enough, and he knew he did not yet wield enough influence over her heart to command her loyalty. She remained a problem, but – just as he'd been pondering how to solve it – Ulfrik had returned and sent his daughter to exchange axe heads for rolls of silk. Asbjorn had rejoiced in the power of his god, convinced that Loki had solved the problem for him. Now, though, as he watched the commotion on the jetty with growing unease, he couldn't help but wonder if the trickster was still on his side.

The Franks were supposed to have killed Ulfrik and his contact, leaving Asbjorn in command of the ship. So why was Ulfrik still alive, and why were Frankish warriors herding the crew back toward The Ox? He recognised them as the men who'd collected the barrels earlier. This was not the plan! He'd given them the silver and in exchange they were supposed to attack Bramsvik and kill his father. Why had they returned?

'What happened,' he hissed, grabbing Egil's arm as his friend was ushered back aboard the ship.

'They pointed lances at us. We did what they said,' Egil replied tersely.

The Franks stayed on the jetty, ensuring no-one left The Ox. Their leader, a short, stocky man who was missing two fingers on his left hand, approached the gangplank, but Ulfrik stepped forward to block his path.

'By what right do you treat my crew this way,' Ulfrik demanded. 'What law have we broken? I'm captain here. I am responsible for anything that has happened. Let them leave and we can talk.' Fingers ignored him, waving him aside and directing his comments to Asbjorn instead.

'Did you think we would not notice, Asbjorn Eriksson,' he called. 'Did you think you could cheat us without repercussions? I'm curious. What did you think was going to happen next?'

It was slowly dawning on the crew that their predicament was somehow Asbjorn's fault. His stomach pitched.

'What is this about? What have you done,' Fromond spat, accusingly.

'I gave you what you wanted,' Asbjorn replied to the Frank. 'We had a deal.'

'Our deal was for silver,' the man answered angrily, 'not for stone. The barrels you gave us contained only rocks and air.'

Rocks? How could this be? Asbjorn had seen the contents of the barrels himself and supervised the loading of them onto the ship. No-one could have switched them without his knowledge. It must be some enchantment. Had the Völva done this? Had Kadlin seen through him after all?

'It seems your quarrel is with Asbjorn,' Ulfrik said to Fingers. 'Perhaps we should leave and give you some privacy.' There was a smugness in his voice, a sense of victory that made Asbjorn suspicious.

'What did you do,' Asbjorn growled. 'Where is the silver?'

'You were guarding it,' Ulfrik replied with an innocent smile. 'You insisted on doing so, if I recall. What did *you* do with it?'

'Someone needs to explain,' Hakon said. 'What silver? Who are these men?'

'Whatever this is, it has nothing to do with any of us,' Herdis stated.

'Where is it, old man,' Asbjorn repeated, ignoring them. He continued in a loud voice, not taking his eyes from Ulfrik. 'The captain has stolen something from me. If he returns it, I'm sure these gentlemen will leave us in peace.' Perhaps he could still get the crew on his side if he could shift the blame onto Ulfrik. 'Give it back,' he demanded. 'Give it back and you may yet walk away from this.'

'I don't know what you're talking about,' Ulfrik replied calmly, looking him straight in the eye. 'We left the silver here, with you, at your insistence. Now, I don't know who these men are, or what kind of a deal you've made with them, but I will not let my crew be put at risk because of you. Clearly, you've conned these people, and you appear to be out of your depth. Leave my ship and sort it out with them elsewhere.' Despite his strong words, Asbjorn noticed sweat on Ulfrik's brow. The captain was afraid.

'Where is it,' Asbjorn yelled. 'I will kill you, Ulfrik. I swear it by the gods!'

'Enough of this,' Hakon bellowed, striding angrily toward Asbjorn. A Frankish warrior's lance hit him before he could get within five paces. The long, thin spearhead pierced Hakon's chest, spitting his heart and throwing him backward. There were screams and yells from the remaining crew, who cowered at the steer board end of The Ox. Some pulled blades and stood defensively between the Franks and their crewmates, but Asbjorn knew that even the best of them stood no chance against trained warriors. Killing the crew had never been part of the plan, but plans change. Asbjorn seized his bow, nocked an arrow, and aimed it at Ulfrik's heart.

'I will kill you,' he threatened. 'Or him.' He turned the arrow on Magnus.

Magnus laughed. Asbjorn had hoped for fear, or pleading, but he had not expected laughter. His stunned expression made Magnus laugh even harder - a big belly laugh that brought tears of mirth to his eyes.

'Do you think you scare me, you little turd,' he snorted.

Asbjorn could contain his anger no longer. He loosed the arrow.

Magnus's laughter became a gurgle as the arrow hit him in the throat. At such short distance it ripped right through him and out the other side, the fletching tearing a hole three fingers wide in his oesophagus. Ulfrik cried out and tried to catch his friend as he fell, dropping to his knees and cradling Magnus as the big man choked on his own blood. Asbjorn nocked a second arrow and aimed it directly at Ulfrik's face.

No-one was laughing now.

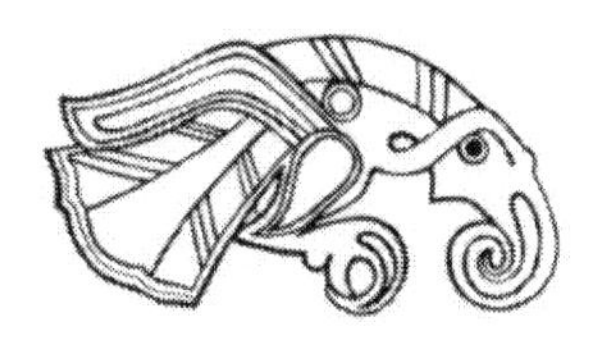

OLVIR

Sólveig's ship, Sea Serpent, was moored only a few jetties further along the dock. There were no lamps lit on board, and none on the cart, so darkness hid them even though they were close enough to hear the raised voices aboard The Ox. The moon was new, no more than a sliver in the sky, and provided little light. Sólvieg's crew were waiting for them, and five men slipped from the shadows of the ship as soon as the cart came to a halt.

Olvir jumped lightly down and held out a hand to help Kadlin. His eyes were still adjusting to the dark and he could barely make out the expression on her usually impassive face. She was fearful – not for herself, but for those they had left behind.

'Quickly,' she urged, as Sólveig's crew carried the chests from the cart. 'I must get back to my father.'

Sólveig put up a hand and motioned for her men to wait. She reached out and lifted the lid on the first chest, then drew a sharp intake of breath. Her hands moved to the weapons at her hip.

'These are axe heads. Where's the silver,' she demanded, looking at Olvir. Her night vision must have been better than his, as he could barely see the outline of the box, let alone its contents.

'Trust me, that is your silver, and nothing is missing,' Kadlin responded. 'It was the only way to conceal it.'

Sólveig hesitated a moment longer, then quietly closed the lid on the chest. She nodded for the men to continue loading them.

'Take us with you,' Olvir blurted. He had been trying to think of an appropriate way to broach the subject, but time was against him and so were his nerves.

'That wasn't our agreement,' Sólveig replied, following her crew onto the ship. Kadlin, no doubt thinking him a coward, regarded him with disgust.

'Please, Ulfrik asked it…' Olvir began as she walked away from him. His mouth ran dry as he realised that keeping his oath may mean physically restraining a member of the Völur. Would the gods forgive such irreverent action?

Would she? At that moment, screams and shouts from The Ox drew their attention. By the light of the lamps on board, they saw Hakon collapse on the deck, speared through the heart by a Frankish lance. Kadlin hoisted her skirts and started to run. Instinctively, Olvir ran after her and grabbed her wrist.

'Please, Lady,' he begged, his heart racing from fear.

She tried to pull away and he tightened his grip, dragging her back toward the Sea Serpent. At any moment he expected to be struck down by the gods, or have his insides turned outside.

'Release me!' The enraged seer began beating him with her free hand.

He saw Sólveig watching from her ship, unable to believe what was she seeing, yet reluctant to involve herself. Several of her crew raced down the gangplank as soon as he laid hands on Kadlin, but Sólveig sharply called them back and given the command to cast off.

'Wait,' Olvir called. 'I gave him my oath I would see her safe.'

'Coward!' Kadlin spat at him.

'He said not to return. Keep you safe. He made me swear.'

More shouting from The Ox drew their attention.

Asbjorn had drawn his bow and was pointing it directly at Ulfrik. He changed target and murdered Magnus before their eyes. Ulfrik cried out and dropped to his knees to cradle his dying friend. Kadlin redoubled her efforts to pull away.

'Let me go! He needs me!'

There were tears of desperation on her cheeks, but Magnus' death made Olvir more determined. Ulfrik had been right to send his daughter away. Asbjorn would not leave any witnesses.

Olvir looked back at Sólveig and saw she understood that, too. She beckoned to him and barked an order as the ship began to pull away. None of the men were willing to assist in the abduction of a Völva, and it was Vendi – the red-haired woman who had driven the cart – who reached out to help him.

Olvir had plenty of practice at restraining struggling women during his years with the slavers. He tried to think of Kadlin as just another woman, rather than a powerful sorceress, as he picked her up and threw her over his shoulder.

'I will curse you! I will curse you! Let me go!'

He raced back along the jetty with her beating her fists against his back. Sea Serpent was already moving, and he had to leap the last few feet onto the deck. Vendi was waiting to grab him, and steady them both, as he landed.

Sólveig ordered that no-one speak until the docks were behind them. Olvir wrestled Kadlin to the ground and clamped a hand over her mouth. The ship moved almost silently through the water, the only sound being the slow dip of the oars as they rose and fell.

As they passed The Ox, they could hear conversation aboard. Asbjorn's bow was once again aimed at Ulfrik.

'You're too late,' Olvir heard his captain say, smiling calmly. Asbjorn followed his gaze toward the river and saw the Danish longship gliding by. He dropped his bow, seized the oil lantern from the prow and raised it higher. Enraged, he let out a roar of fury and hurled the lamp at Ulfrik's feet. It smashed on impact, engulfing Ulfrik and Magnus in a fireball and sending rivers of liquid flame along the deck! Ulfrik writhed and screamed as he was consumed by the fire.

It spread through the ship faster than Olvir would have thought possible, igniting the folded sailcloth and coiled rigging, and trapping the terrified crew aft. The heat was instant, and overpowering.

"No survivors,' Asbjorn yelled as he and Egil ran down the gangplank toward the Franks. The air was filled with tortured screams as the closest thing Olvir had to family burned alive. He felt Kadlin go slack in his arms.

KADLIN

Sea Serpent was a longship called a snekkja, meaning 'snake', because of its long and slender shape. It was built for speed and warfare, being fifty-six feet in length but only eight feet across the beam. To Kadlin, it felt very cramped after the comparative width of a knarr. The Ox had been literally twice as broad. Privacy was out of the question with forty crew, one captain and two passengers all occupying such a narrow space. No-one could cough, sneeze, piss or shit without everyone else knowing about it.

Although Kadlin knew that Olvir Red Face had simply done as his captain commanded and bore no blame for the burning of her father and their crew, she found herself unable to even look at him. Logically, she knew it was not his fault, but her grief and anguish distorted her thoughts and she was afraid of unleashing her fury. Instead, she kept silent for fear of what wounding words her grieving tongue might speak.

Olvir himself was content to keep out of her way and seemed relieved that she had not yet killed or maimed him, nor carried out her threat of a curse. Much as they tried to avoid each other, it was impossible aboard such a slight ship. Instead, Kadlin kept her eyes down and her mouth shut, and mentally rehearsed every torture she would inflict upon Asbjorn Eriksson when she found him. The gods would bring them together again one day. She was sure of that. They would not let such a betrayal go unpunished.

Sea Serpent had no wight and Kadlin missed her daily talks with Saltfish. She guessed the little gnome would have burned with his ship, and she grieved for him, too. Any other wights at the docks that night would have taken note of what happened, though. They may not get involved in the affairs of men, but they would have mourned the death of one of their own and noted who caused it. The chances of Asbjorn finding safe passage back to Bramsvik by sea, now, were slim. If he were forced to travel by land it would be close to the Winter Solstice before he reached home. With luck, she could be there before him and arrange an appropriate welcome.

It seemed an age since Arni, son of Andvett, had called at their hov in the middle of the night with a summons from King Redbeard. Kadlin wondered what would have happened if Yrsa had declined the invitation. Would Ulfrik still be alive if the Völur had never travelled with him to Tromø? But no, the threads that had bound her father's fate were already being woven long before the birth of Redbeard's daughter.

Every time Kadlin closed her eyes she saw her father burning. She heard the crackle of the flames, felt their heat, and watched as fire engulfed The Ox. The groans of the dying ship and the screams of the crew replayed in her head over and over, and she resorted to using herbs to help her sleep.

The past was carved in stone and could not be altered. The 'What has been' was the realm of the Norn, Urðr, and was unchangeable. Kadlin had witnessed many people waste their lives by dwelling there. They became trapped, doomed to relive events of the past and never move forward - alive, but not living - forever looking back with regret.

There were three realms of time; 'What has been', 'What is becoming' and 'What is due'. 'What is becoming' was the most powerful, being the only time that could directly influence the other two. Her actions in the 'What is becoming' simultaneously created the 'What has been' on which she would be judged, and thereby determined opportunities to be found - or consequences to be faced - in the 'What is due'. If she hoped to create a chance to avenge her father in the latter, she must create it with her deeds in the former.

'Are you well, Lady? You haven't eaten since we left Haithabyr.' Vendi woke Kadlin from her thoughts. The crew of Sea Serpent had come ashore for the night, and a meal of fish broth had been prepared. Vendi held a bowl of food in each hand. She offered one to Kadlin, who took it appreciatively. They hadn't spoken much, but Kadlin already liked this woman. She had a soft, lilting voice, and beautiful green eyes that conveyed genuine warmth and empathy. Her hair was long and tousled, falling in flame-coloured curls. Vendi honoured the gods of her homeland rather than the Aesir, but her tender and caring manner reminded Kadlin of Odin's wife, Frigga, the All-Mother. Despite her apparent gentleness, Kadlin saw true strength in Vendi. They had only met three nights ago, yet she already felt a kinship with her. For someone who had never known friendship outside of the Völur, it was a rare and precious thing.

'I am well enough,' Kadlin replied noncommittally, not wishing to be drawn into another discussion about the tragedy. 'Thank you,' she added, indicating the food. The crew of Sea Serpent always spent the night ashore, and Kadlin had been surprised the first evening when they'd sailed the ship straight onto the sand. A snekkja was shallow enough to ride the waves right up on the beach, so the crew had no need to wade ashore – a blessing in colder months. It also gave an advantage when mounting an attack, as there was less time for their quarry to raise the alarm or prepare a defense.

'May I sit,' Vendi asked. 'I don't wish to intrude.'

'Please,' Kadlin said, genuinely grateful for the company. They ate in silence for a while, and Kadlin noticed Vendi's husband, Ragnar, watching them from the campfire. He was around twenty years old, a few years younger than his wife, but the two seemed well matched and clearly doted on each other. Ragnar was from the province of Westphalia in Saxony. He was tall and muscular, with deep brown eyes and long, black hair that he wore loosely pulled back at the nape of his neck. Like Vendi, he seemed gentle and compassionate, yet didn't shy from confrontation. Kadlin had seen him step between two drunken warriors the previous night and had been impressed with how calmly and skilfully he had resolved the situation. Like the rest of the men aboard Sea Serpent, Ragnar always kept a respectful distance from Kadlin and tried not to catch her eye. Men were usually less comfortable than women around practitioners of witchcraft and disliked any interaction with the supernatural.

'Your man is pretending not to watch us,' Kadlin remarked, amused.

'He is… concerned,' Vendi said, carefully. 'He thinks I

should leave you alone and not bother you.'

'And what do you think?'

Vendi smiled. 'I think you have a tongue and will say if you are bothered.'

★

The following morning, having set sail again with the dawn, they reached their destination just a short distance further along the coast. They moored Sea Serpent at the town of Ingisbruk, where their return drew a small crowd and was cause for celebration. An ox cart was brought, and the three chests of silver axe heads loaded upon it.

'Sólveig!' An older gentleman greeted their captain affectionately. Kadlin guessed, from the warmth of his welcome and the way the two embraced, that this was Sólveig's father. His face was reddish brown, and flatter than most, with high, rounded cheekbones and almond eyes like his daughter's. His long, poker-straight hair and wispy beard were pure white, but his bushy eyebrows were still as black as a winter's night. He said something to Sólveig in a language Kadlin did not understand, and his daughter hugged him.

'He's a Uyghur,' Vendi explained, noting Kadlin's interest. 'His people live far to the east of here. Don't let the white hair fool you. Ehmet is one of the toughest warriors I've ever met.'

'What brought him this far west,' Kadlin asked.

'Love,' Vendi replied, smiling. 'The Danes encountered his tribe while exploring trade routes. He fell in love with Sólveig's mother, but she wouldn't stay, so he followed her here. I think you would like him – he's a shaman. But first you should meet the King. He'll be able to find you passage home.'

'Is that what happened with you and Ragnar,' Kadlin queried. 'You fell in love and followed him here?'

'No,' Vendi said, a little too abruptly. Her smile vanished. 'Come, Lady. Let's find you a place to ride.'

King Sigfrid lived within a vast ring fortress. The circular ramparts around the encampment were the height of three men, with the outside ditch being equal in depth. Four entrances, facing north, south, east and west, had been tunnelled through the walls so the top of the henge formed one, unbroken circle upon which armed guards patrolled. Each entrance was secured with a large, oak and iron gate manned by sentries.

Sólvieg led them through the north gate, and once through the tunnel Kadlin saw that the encampment was filled with many longhouses and smaller hovs. The longhouses were strangely shaped compared to the rectangular ones of her homeland. These were thatched, and the walls bowed out in the middle like the sides of a ship. Instead of one main entrance, there was a doorway in the centre of each wall. The hovs were also thatched but lacked the decorative features displayed on the longhouses.

Central to the encampment was a huge mead hall with entwined serpents carved into its doors and along its beams. Once again, there was an entrance in the centre of each wall, with the main doors in the longer, bowed walls of the dwelling. Sólveig had given permission for the crew to reunite with their families, bringing only Kadlin, Olvir, and two others to the mead hall.

Kodran, Sólvieg's second in command, was clearly in love with his captain. Kadlin didn't think they were wed, but they were certainly a couple. Kodran and his twin sister, Inga, were Danes, and had grown up in Ingisbruk. Sólveig left the twins outside to guard the cart and led the Kadlin and Olvir inside to meet the king.

King Sigfrid was younger than Kadlin expected. He looked to be around thirty, of medium build, with mouse coloured hair which he wore in a single long braid. His beard was short and neat, and he wore several finger rings as well as his many arm rings. The large, heavy, golden torc the king wore around his neck was a testament to the immense wealth he commanded.

'I thought you were dead,' he said to Sólveig, making it sound like an accusation. Before she could reply, the king turned to Kadlin with a smile. 'It's an honour to welcome a member of the Völur to my home. I am King Sigfrid, and it would be my privilege to have you as a guest while you are here.'

Kadlin thanked him and introduced herself. She was reasonably fluent in the language of the Danes as her father had taught her when she was a child. The memory of Ulfrik pricked at her heart.

'Your arrival is timely, Lady, as I could do with your skills,' the king continued. Kadlin gave a wry smile. No matter where she went, people always said the same thing – that she had shown up just when they needed her. They often read some supernatural significance into this, either crediting her with the ability to sense their hardship or believing the gods had sent her. The truth was more mundane; people were forever in need, and constantly desired guidance.

'I would be happy to help, King Sigfrid,' she replied, but thoughts of her father threatened to overwhelm her, and she could feel tears forming in her eyes. 'Perhaps we could talk later. Is there somewhere I could rest?'

The king noticed her unshed tears, but, to his credit, pretended not to.

'Of course. You must be exhausted,' he said. He snapped his fingers and a couple of thralls came running. Sólveig was speaking but Kadlin couldn't hear the words. The only sound in her ears was the pounding of her own heart as she tried not to let the tears fall. Yrsa would be so ashamed, she told herself, if she failed to retain her composure, especially in front of royalty. Kadlin murmured her thanks and followed the thralls.

The mead hall consisted of a large, central hall, with private chambers at either end. She was led to one of these, provided with a platter of food and some ale, and left in peace. As soon as she was alone, Kadlin threw off her cloak, collapsed onto the bed of furs, and gave in to her grief.

OLVIR

It would have been impossible for Olvir to feel any more wretched. He had done what Ulfrik asked, and protected Kadlin, but had that been the right thing to do? Could she have used her magic to protect the crew? Would they still be alive if he had disobeyed his captain's command? Would Asbjorn have dared to torch the ship if the Völva had been there? Olvir thought not. His brain hurt so much from thinking on it that he wanted to rip it from his skull!

The only thing that made him even more miserable was the fact that Kadlin blamed him, too. She'd barely been able to look at him since the fire, and when she did it was with such loathing that it shrivelled his heart.

He had fallen in love with her months ago, before they ever met. He'd seen her speaking with Ulfrik and been struck by how beautiful she was, and the way the sunlight turned her hair to molten bronze. He loved the smile he'd glimpsed, just for a moment, before her face regained its practiced composure. Having worked for slavers most of his life, Olvir understood all about the masks that people wore and was pretty good at seeing beneath them. He'd been surprised at the softness and vulnerability he had seen beneath Kadlin's mask and was awed at the strength it took to wear it. She was the most intriguing and magnificent woman he had ever seen, and he spent the next few months at sea praying for the chance just to speak with her. When they had returned to Bramsvik, and the very next day set sail again with Kadlin aboard, Olvir felt certain the gods had answered his prayers! Now, though, he wondered if he shouldn't have been a bit clearer about his desires. There had been plenty of opportunities for conversation on their journey, but Kadlin only had eyes for Asbjorn. Unfortunately for Olvir, their talks and proximity only served to strengthen his feelings. Being rejected and despised by her now wounded him deeply.

He had consoled himself these past three days by talking with Gretter and Ragnar. Both were Saxons, like himself, from the province of Westphalia. It felt good to converse freely, and at length, in his native tongue, and it raised his spirits to hear news of his homeland and the ongoing rebellions there.

For the past ten years there had been conflict between the invading armies of Charlemagne, leader of the Franks, and the people of Saxony. Charlemagne kept winning victories and forcing the conquered Saxons to convert to his Christian faith, but as soon as his attention was diverted elsewhere, the people fought back and reclaimed their stolen lands and religion.

Saxony was divided into four main provinces; Nordalbania in the north, Westphalia to the west, Angria in the centre and Eastphalia to the east. Chief among the rebel leaders was a Westphalian Saxon noble known only by his *nom du guerre*, Widukind, meaning 'child of the forest'. Most Saxon nobles had embraced Christianity and submitted to Frankish rule in order to retain their lands and titles, but Widukind encouraged the middle and lower classes to rise up against their oppressors. He had become something of a legend over the past decade, always evading capture and refusing to back down or negotiate.

News from Saxony over recent years had been disheartening, as Charlemagne's troops defeated the rebels at every turn and captured all the Westphalian leaders except for Widukind. With the eventual submission of the Eastphalians two years ago, all seemed lost. According to Ragnar, Widukind had used that time to regroup and raise funds for a new rebellion. Somehow, the chests of axe heads they had brought with them were part of that plan.

Olvir tried to speak with Kadlin on the way to the fortress of the Danes, but she rode on a cart while he walked behind, making conversation awkward. He had quit after his tentative attempts to engage her attention failed.

Olvir had never met royalty before. He'd expected to be told to wait outside or be given the task of guarding the chests. He was surprised, therefore, when Sólveig brought him into the mead hall, along with Kadlin, to meet the king. His primary concern was Kadlin's safety and he was uncomfortable with her being led away, alone, to a private chamber. Logic told him that King Sigfrid would see her well-treated, and that a member of the Völur would be afforded every comfort and courtesy, but his stomach lurched as he watched her walk away and he couldn't help but feel nervous about it. She had lost everything and been helpless while her father was murdered before her eyes. Olvir knew exactly how that felt and he desperately wanted to comfort and console her. Most of all, he wanted to make sure she felt safe. He had been just a child when Charlemagne's troops had killed his parents; too small to help them and too weak to defend himself against the men who'd taken him captive and sold him into slavery. It had taken all his wit and cunning just to stay alive, and he had never felt safe – not for a moment – since the day his parents died. He remembered the feel of his mother's arms around him and how, as a child, he would close his eyes and lean his head upon her shoulder and know with certainty that he was loved and protected. He'd had no-one to rely on but himself since their deaths, and he struggled to recall what safety felt like.

When King Sigfrid dismissed him so that he and Sólveig could talk privately, Olvir wanted to wait outside in case Kadlin needed anything, but he found Ragnar and Gretter waiting for him.

'Come, meet my father,' Ragnar said eagerly.

'You'll like him,' Gretter grinned. 'Everyone loves the Raven.'

'The Raven?' Olvir wasn't sure he should be leaving Kadlin. He hesitated, but Gretter put an arm around his shoulders and steered him away from the mead hall. The midday sun threatened to blind them with its intensity.

'Niklaus the Raven,' Gretter said. 'Many songs have been written about his fight against the Franks.' He pointed to one of the longhouses, which was flying a scarlet banner with two black ravens. 'That's our banner. Raven's Kin - the family of the raven.'

'You're all related?' Olvir was surprised. 'How many sons does he have?'

Gretter chuckled. 'Five, as far as I know, but there's many

here who look to him as a father. You'll understand when you meet him. He's… he's Niklaus.' He shrugged and smiled. They heard raucous laughter as they approached the longhouse, and Olvir's companions looked at each other and grinned. 'He's home,' they said in unison.

It was cool inside the longhouse, away from the heat of the summer sun, and Olvir's eyes took a moment to adjust to the shade. A group of men and women were seated at a table, drinking ale and engrossed in a story being told by their host. Niklaus was in his late thirties, with long, corn-coloured hair, untameable eyebrows and a bushy beard. His handsome face was creased with laughter lines, and his grey-green eyes sparkled with mischief as he spun his tale. He was stripped to the waist, revealing a powerful, tanned body, inked with many different designs and images. A heavy Thor's hammer hung around his neck on a braided, leather cord, and he wore numerous arm rings of silver and bronze.

'I looked him in the eye,' Niklaus proclaimed, 'and I said, 'I wasn't lying, Lord, and I'm rather insulted you would even suggest it.' So, he snaps his fingers, and his thrall comes running and drops a bunch of clothes at my feet. This Lord points at me and he says 'I traded a good pig for these, you bastard! You told me they were the shifts of three young virgins.' So, I look all offended and tell him I can prove it, and then me and Cuney went outside and came back in with…'

'…the three, naked, Christian monks you stole them from.' Ragnar finished. Everyone turned to look at him. Niklaus broke into a broad grin.

'My son,' he boomed, standing and throwing his arms wide. 'My son has returned!' He crossed the room to greet them, giving Ragnar a mighty hug, and kissing him on the cheek. 'Where the fuck have you been,' he asked, jovially. 'You were only meant to be gone a week! Welcome back, my lucky lads,' he said, embracing Gretter. 'I hope he didn't get you into any trouble.' Niklaus reached out and clasped Olvir's hand in a strong grip. 'Welcome, my friend,' he said. His eyes continued to smile and there was genuine warmth in his greeting. 'My name is Niklaus. They call me the Raven. Come and sit.' He led them over to the table. 'Cuney,' he continued, 'this is my good friend… uh…' He looked at Olvir. 'What's your name?'

'Olvir, Lord. Olvir son of Ludin.'

'There's no lords here,' the Raven said. 'We're all family. Cuney, this is my good friend, Olvir Ludinsson.' He introduced Olvir to a well-groomed, slender man with brown hair and intelligent blue eyes. 'Olvir, this is Cuneglas the Celt. He's my righthand man. I'd be lost without him. Quite literally, sometimes.'

Cuneglas was impeccably dressed in a deep red tunic with knotwork embroidery around the neckline and cuffs, grey linen breeks, and grey leg bindings. He wore several arm and finger rings, and his facial hair was neatly trimmed and oiled. He got to his feet and briefly clasped Olvir's hand.

'And this is his lovely wife, Maida,' Niklaus went on, introducing Olvir to a beautiful, elfin woman with sleek, dark hair and eyes the colour of the earth in autumn. Her arms were decorated with inked designs and she wore several finger rings on her delicate hands. Niklaus continued in this way, making sure Olvir got to know everyone around the table. Food was brought, and ale continued to flow.

Niklaus was one of the main Westphalian Saxon warlords under Widukind and had played a significant part so far in the rebellion against the Franks. The Raven's Kin were his warband, a group of Saxons and Celts dedicated to freeing their lands from the tyranny of Christian rule. They exchanged stories, telling Olvir of their battles, and he, in turn, told them of his life and how he came to be at the home of King Sigfrid. In all his time aboard The Ox he had never felt able to confide the things he told them now. It was true what Gretter said, Niklaus made him feel like family. He instinctively trusted this man and felt safe in his company.

'What are your plans now,' Cuneglas enquired. 'Where will you go.'

'I don't know,' Olvir replied, surprised that he hadn't pondered this before. He had been so pre-occupied with worrying about Kadlin that he hadn't really given much thought to his own predicament. He had no master, no job, no family to return to and no home. He was adrift, like a rudderless ship on the ocean, at the mercy of the winds and tides.

'I feel the gods at work here,' Niklaus ruminated, stroking his beard. Many around the table murmured their agreement. 'They have freed you of all obligation and brought you to us. Join our cause, Olvir, son of Ludin, and fight for our home. For your home. Fight for Saxony.'

'I don't know how, Lord,' Olvir admitted.

'We can teach you,' Niklaus offered, banging his fist on the table. 'Think on it. No need to rush the decision. No-one is pushing you, here. The gods have cut your bonds and made you master of your own life again. Whatever you decide to do with it, I'll help if I can. You have the protection of the Raven's Kin and you're welcome to sleep here, with us, for as long as you stay.'

Olvir nodded gratefully and smiled. Ragnar clapped him on the back. 'Drink,' he said. Ragnar refilled his tankard and raised it in a toast. 'To Saxony!' Those assembled banged their hands on the table and cheered. Olvir drank deeply, enjoying the feeling of camaraderie.

'To absent friends,' Niklaus said soberly, raising his horn. The table fell silent, and Olvir realised that everyone here had lost people dear to them in this war. One by one, they raised their drinks and toasted the memory of those who had fallen, speaking their names and honouring their sacrifice. Olvir thought of his parents, and of his siblings. What would they think of how he had lived his life since their passing? Would they be proud? Would it be enough for them that he survived, or would they want him to take up arms and avenge them? Was he right to have kept running, or should he have returned here long ago and laid his ghosts to rest? Olvir raised his tankard, spoke their names, and drank.

He had much to think about.

KADLIN

It was late afternoon when Kadlin awoke. Someone had brought a bowl of water and a cloth to her room while she slept, and she felt better having cleansed herself, and combed and re-braided her hair. Performed slowly and purposefully, the process was almost meditative. She wove her mother's blue bead and the falcon feather into her braid and slipped Yrsa's ring onto her finger.

There were two exits from the room, one of which would take her back into the mead hall and the other led outside. Kadlin chose the latter and was surprised to find Olvir waiting on the grass for her. He was crouched with his back against the wall and scrambled to his feet looking apologetic as she stepped out.

'I've no wish to make you uncomfortable, Lady,' he said, seeing her reaction. 'I gave my oath to see you safe and I mean to keep it if you'll let me.'

Kadlin felt a wave of anger as she looked at him. Throughout her entire voyage with The Ox, Olvir had been the one person on whom she could depend. Whether she had needed instruction, assistance, conversation or company, he had always been there, yet no-one had ever laid hands upon her as he had done or treated her with so little respect. He had humiliated her in front of witnesses and prevented her from helping her father. A part of her still believed she could have saved Ulfrik had she been there. She had wanted to kill Olvir that night. The only reason he still breathed was because she knew he was following orders. Her father's orders.

'Leave me,' she snapped, 'I can't look at you.'

'Lady, please…'

Kadlin pulled the small dagger from her girdle. Her knuckles turned white and her hand trembled as she resisted the urge to use it. 'Leave,' she growled. To her relief, he acquiesced and slunk away like a kicked dog. Kadlin sheathed her dagger, noting that her hands still shook as she did so. She took a few calming breaths, dropped her shoulders and forced herself to relax. Her desire for fresh air had gone, replaced by a need to be safe within four walls.

She found the mead hall empty save for King Sigfrid, Ragnar and a man she did not recognise. The three were in deep discussion but stopped at her arrival.

'I hope you're feeling better, Lady,' the king said, smiling. 'Kadlin Svalasdaughter of Agder, this is my good friend Niklaus the Raven, of Westphalia. You know his son, Ragnar.'

'Always an honour to meet one of the Völur,' the Raven said, inclining his head. 'I was sorry to hear about your father and crew, Lady. My condolences.'

'Thank you,' Kadlin replied, taking a seat beside them.

'Sólveig tells me you need passage back to Agder,' King Sigfrid began. 'How soon do you wish to leave?'

'As soon as possible,' Kadlin answered. She missed her home and family and yearned to return to the quiet life she once sought to escape. This adventure had come at too high a cost.

Her reply annoyed the king and he looked affronted. Kadlin recalled Yrsa's warning that kings were not like other men; they saw enemies everywhere and valued flattery over forthrightness.

'Of course,' Sigfrid said, stiffly. 'You will stay for the Solstice, though. I insist.'

The summer Solstice was five days away and Kadlin had

hoped to be on a ship before then. She was, however, completely at Sigfrid's mercy. Nothing happened here without his permission, and passage to Agder would not come cheap. She had the garnet ring and silver Valkyrie to barter with if it became necessary, but both had significant sentimental value and she hoped it would not come to that. If the king would not provide her with transport in exchange for her services then she would have to earn her way, but that, too, was dependent upon his consent.

'My Lord is too kind,' she said, trying to hide her concern.

'This could be to our mutual benefit,' King Sigfrid added. He smiled. 'You provide me with insight and guidance from the gods and I will provide you with comfort and safety. A fair exchange. I'll see that you have your own hov and thralls to attend you.'

'The King is very generous,' Kadlin replied, tightly. It was not, in fact, a fair exchange. Hospitality was the very least he could offer a woman of her standing. It was an honour to have a member of the Völur under your roof, and payment for her services was always in addition to basic comforts.

'I need the gods' advice on an important matter,' King Sigfrid continued. 'I'd like you to cast the runes for me and see what counsel they give.'

'Would you prefer privacy?' Kadlin asked, glancing at Niklaus and Ragnar.

'This involves the Raven's Kin, too, so speak freely,' the king instructed. 'You are aware, I'm sure, of the situation in Saxony. I need to know if another campaign against the Franks will be successful. Will the gods support us?'

Kadlin removed a white cloth from one of the pouches that hung at her waist. She unfolded it, laid it on the table and did her best to smooth out the creases. Next, she tipped her runes into her right hand and concentrated her mind until she could feel the energy of each one. She held them over the cloth and let them fall. Kadlin ignored the runestaves that fell outside the cloth, and those that landed face down. She studied those that remained, and her heart sank as she interpreted their message. Keeping her face as passive as possible, she attempted to relay the news as positively as she could.

'I see many coming together to fight for this cause,' she began. 'A strong leader rises, and they will follow.'

'Widukind,' the Raven murmured. In her gut, Kadlin knew that he was wrong, but she refrained from correcting him. It was not Widukind the runes spoke of.

'There will be victories,' she said, hesitantly, 'but at great cost. Perhaps too high a cost, my king. Many will die. I see whole fields stained red with blood.'

'Death is inevitable in war,' King Sigfrid mused.

'The gods do not favour an assault now,' Kadlin replied bluntly. 'Perhaps in a few months...'

'In a few months we shall be staring at the face of winter,' Sigfrid countered.

'You asked the counsel of the gods, Lord King, and I have provided it,' Kadlin said. 'Any rebellion begun this side of winter will fail. I see victories for a campaign mounted later, but there is no clear outcome yet. Much may change between now and then.'

'If I may, Lord King,' the Raven interjected, 'if the Lady says the gods counsel waiting, it would be wise to wait. Let's return to Saxony in the spring, when the weather - and the gods - will be on our side.'

Kadlin was certain she had given no such assurances of the gods' favour, but she was grateful to Niklaus for helping their host see sense. What was the point of seeking answers from the gods if you ignored their advice?

'Can you guarantee success if we wait until spring,' Sigfrid asked.

'No, Lord King,' Kadlin responded firmly. 'It is too far ahead to see clearly. Further rune castings nearer the time would be necessary.'

'It is settled then,' King Sigfrid replied, standing. 'Niklaus, you will leave as soon as the winter frosts are over.'

'And my passage home?' Kadlin wanted nothing more than to be back at Yrsa's hov, with all its familiar sights and smells. She wanted her family. Needed them.

'Fishing season begins after the Solstice,' the King replied. 'I'm sure there will be vessels heading that way. We will talk again.'

Kadlin's heart sank. Yrsa would not stand for this. She would demand proper payment and issue veiled threats of curses and plagues should her words go unheeded. Kadlin had been trained to think this way, too, but the events of the past week had sapped her strength and her will. She was mentally exhausted and doubted she could challenge a king at the moment without breaking down in tears. Better, for now, to accept his terms and keep her dignity.

★

Once word spread there was a member of the Völur within the ring fort, Kadlin found a steady stream of folk in need of her skills and services. She was kept busy with new clients, and took daily walks with Vendi, who knew the area well, and was able to show Kadlin the best places to find the herbs she required. She was excited to discover some – quite difficult to find in Bramsvik – growing in abundance here. Cuneglas' wife, Maida often accompanied them, too, and although Kadlin's heart still ached for Ulfrik, for her grandmother, and for Jofrið and

Aud, the companionship of her new friends helped to ease that pain a little.

On the eve of the Solstice, it was Niklaus the Raven who turned up at her door. She had not spoken to him since their meeting with King Sigfrid and was surprised to see him smiling warmly as if they were old friends. From any other man this might be taken as insolence, but Niklaus made her feel comfortable and at ease, and she knew he meant no disrespect.

'Forgive the intrusion, Lady,' he began. 'I know you've been busy.'

'No intrusion at all,' Kadlin replied. 'Come in.' She stood back, holding the door ajar. Niklaus hesitated, and his hand involuntarily went to his Thor's hammer. He was comfortable conversing with her, it seemed, but not enough to cross her threshold. 'Or we could talk here,' she conceded. 'What do you need of me?' Niklaus visibly relaxed and smiled gratefully.

'I have a charm that was made for me by a dear friend, many years ago. She was not a Völva, but she was skilled in magic.' He reached inside his tunic, removed a pendant from around his neck and held it out. 'I hoped you may be able to recharge it. I've felt less of a spark from it of late.'

Kadlin reached out and took the pendant. It was a smooth piece of oak with a bindrune carved on one side and the hammer of Thor on the other. It was crude, but effective.

'This is for the protection of family,' she observed. Niklaus nodded.

'All under my roof are family,' he said, solemnly. 'I do what I can to keep them safe. I've somehow managed to promise boar meat for the festival, and the hunt will likely be a dangerous one.'

'Somehow managed?' Kadlin raised an eyebrow.

'A tedious tale, Lady, involving the consumption of copious amounts of mead and ale.' Niklaus grinned. 'I've asked Ullr's blessing and made an offering.'

'How soon do you leave,' Kadlin asked.

'As soon as I return. Is this a thing you can do?'

'The bindrune is simple,' she replied. 'Simple, but it will do. If I had more time, I'd prefer to make you another and improve on the design.' She closed her left hand around the pendant, feeling a faint hum as she did so. She crouched down and pressed her right hand flat on the ground, envisioning roots growing out of her palm and fingertips and pushing down into the earth. Kadlin focused on sending the roots deeper, connecting with Nerthus, the earth goddess. She felt the earth's energy, drawing it up through the roots and into her body, allowing herself to become a conduit, letting the energy flow in through her right hand and out of her left hand into the charm. It only took a few moments to recharge the pendant and she felt invigorated by the process. Kadlin stood and handed it back to Niklaus.

'I'm grateful,' he said, placing the talisman back around his neck and tucking it within his tunic. 'What do I owe?'

Kadlin smiled and shook her head. 'It was no trouble.'

'Then eat with us tonight,' he insisted. 'I must repay you in some way.'

'I would like that,' she agreed.

NIKLAUS

There was nothing quite like a hunt to forge bonds of friendship between men, and nothing like a boar hunt to test their valour. For that reason, Niklaus invited the young Saxon, Olvir Ludinsson, to join the party. The lad had been with them a few days now and had grasped the basics of wielding a spear. Of equal importance, he was well liked by the Raven's Kin.

'This is folly, Nik. He's not ready,' Cuneglas cautioned. 'He still aims wide most of the time and we've no idea how he'll react under threat.'

'Exactly,' Niklaus replied. 'What better way to find out?'

Cuneglas muttered that he could think of several more

appropriate ways, none of which were likely to result in death or dismemberment. Hunting boar was every bit as dangerous as facing a foe on the field of battle. Lives could be lost to tooth and tusk as easily as to sword and spear. Niklaus understood Cuneglas' concern but reasoned that - if Olvir's courage failed to hold - he would rather find out now, when their foe was outnumbered, than in a shieldwall when one weak link could cost many lives.

There were eight men in the hunting party. They rode in silence through the forest until Ragnar, at the head of the group, held up a hand to signal they should dismount. He had found tell-tale signs of boar activity in this area the previous day and was confident there was a den nearby. If they were lucky, it would be a solitary male, providing meat aplenty for the Solstice feast. If they were unlucky, it would be a female with offspring. A wild sow protecting her young was a fearsome adversary and likely to take some of the hunters down with her.

Female boars lived in small, family groups for most of the year, but in autumn - the mating season - these groups united, forming a sounder of up to fifty animals. Male boars formed 'batchelor groups' until they reached sexual maturity and then lived solitary lives, only joining the sounder in autumn in order to breed. This time of year, Midsummer, was a good time to find a lone male.

They hobbled the horses and left them to graze, following

Ragnar on foot. Boar were destructive in their habits and it was not difficult to spot the large areas of rooted soil where the animals had been feeding.

'Definitely more than one,' Cuneglas said, crouching down to examine the ground. Niklaus grimaced as he looked at the swirling mess of hoofprints.

'It's a bloody female, isn't it,' he grumbled. 'This is not good.'

'One sow and seven or eight young, at a guess,' his companion replied. Cuneglas stood, brushing dirt from his hands. He was the only man the Raven had ever known who could return from a hunt immaculately clean.

'Fuck,' Niklaus muttered. 'He couldn't have found us a nice, elderly male?'

Cuney laughed. 'With bad eyesight and a dodgy leg? Wheezes when he runs…'

'That's the one,' Niklaus grinned. 'He'd do nicely.'

Ragnar hefted his spear and held it at the ready as he pointed toward a group of leafy shrubs some distance away. The long grass in front of them was cut and matted, a sure sign of a nesting boar. Niklaus and Cuneglas took up position facing the den whilst the others crept closer. The men formed two lines, three either side, creating a narrowing channel. If all went well, their quarry would be funnelled toward Niklaus and Cuneglas. Theirs was the most dangerous task – bring the beast down.

'Best of luck, Nik,' Cuneglas murmured, raising his spear.

'Don't need it,' Niklaus replied with a wink. 'The gods love me.' He lifted the bindrune charm to his lips and kissed it, then did the same with his Thor's hammer before tucking both back inside his tunic. He drew his seax.

At his signal, the men began shouting and beating their shields with their spears. Within seconds there came a high-pitched squeal, and an enraged boar charged from the shrubbery directly at Olvir.

Olvir froze.

Ragnar threw himself into the path of the beast, deflecting its tusks with his shield, saving Olvir from being disembowled. The sow's momentum lifted Ragnar off his feet and sent him sprawling. Olvir recovered his wits in time to hurl his spear at the raging animal. He missed his target, but the throw was enough to change her course and save Ragnar, giving him time to scramble to his feet.

'Told you he aims wide,' Cuney yelled, as several furry piglets shot out of the den and raced after their mother, squealing and grunting.

'Think positive, Cune. No-one's dead yet,' Niklaus

shouted, bracing himself as the sow and her brood stampeded toward them. Seeing her path blocked, she veered sharply to the left, knocking Gretter to the ground and trampling over him. Ragnar threw his spear, striking the boar in the shoulder. It was not enough to pierce the coarse bristles and hide but did succeed in bringing the animal back on course. Niklaus crouched low, waiting until the creature was almost upon them. He threw himself sideways, rolling clear of the charge and slashing at the sow's legs as he did so. She stumbled and fell, momentarily exposing her chest and underbelly. Striking swift as a snake, Cuneglas thrust his spear through the thinner hide on the side of her body and into her heart. Death was almost instant.

'Gretter!'

With the immediate danger over, Niklaus called out to their fallen friend. He was relieved to see Gretter raise a hand, signaling that he still lived. The others were busy rounding up and dispatching the piglets. Niklaus bent down to clean his blade on the grass, and as he did so something barrelled into his leg, almost knocking him off balance. He looked down to see a small piglet repeatedly butt its head against his boot, squealing angrily. She tried to bite his ankle, found the leather of his boots too tough for her tiny teeth, and resumed butting and grunting instead.

'Ragnar, look at this,' Niklaus called, laughing heartily.

The piglet was only a few months old and still had stripes along its back.

'A vicious beast,' Ragnar grinned. 'Do you need help?'

'I might need saving. Yeah. Look at her go!' The baby boar managed to get a grip on the end of Niklaus' boot, and began snorting and shaking her head, like a dog with a rat. Cuneglas, having pulled his spear free from the sow, stepped forward to dispatch the raging piglet.

'Don't do that! Don't kill it,' Niklaus said, mortified. 'Look how brave she is! You can't kill something as courageous as that.'

'It's not brave,' Cuneglas countered. 'It's mad. It's a mad, brown thing, Nik. It won't survive by itself if we leave it. Kinder to kill it now.'

'Kinder, and tastier,' Ragnar agreed.

'Mad, brown thing,' Niklaus chuckled. 'Mad Brown. I love it.'

'No,' Cuneglas said firmly, recognising the look on his friend's face. 'You can't keep it, Nik. It's not a hound! Ragnar, talk some sense into your father.'

Ragnar shrugged. 'It is appealing,' he smiled. 'Besides, we have a whole boar and eight other piglets. More than enough for the feast.'

'The ninth boar,' Niklaus pondered, stroking his beard

thoughtfully. 'That settles it, Cuney. Nine is an auspicious number. She's coming with us.'

'Actually, she's the tenth boar,' Cuneglas reasoned. 'She's the ninth piglet.'

'The gods have given her to me,' Niklaus said.

'Yes,' Cuneglas agreed. 'To eat!'

'She's a gift from Freyr himself, and you'll not be turning her into a snack.' Niklaus roped the animal's legs together and swung her across his broad shoulders. 'Mad Brown is Raven's Kin, now, until I understand her purpose.'

'It's a piglet. A mad piglet. You can't seriously think there is anything special about it,' Cuneglas said, exasperated. He looked to Ragnar for support, but Ragnar simply shrugged.

'She's not just any old piglet, though, Cuney,' Niklaus replied, tapping his nose knowingly. 'She's the ninth piglet.'

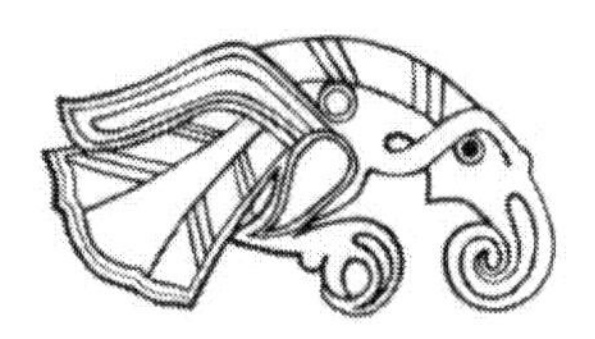

OLVIR

Olvir had hoped his inclusion in the hunting party would be a chance to prove his worth. Instead, he rode back with cheeks burning in shame, certain Niklaus would ask him to leave the Kin after his dismal performance today. He was not surprised, therefore, when the Raven slowed his horse to ride alongside him.

'You did well today,' Niklaus said. Olvir was sure this must be sarcasm.

'I'm sorry,' he apologised.

'I thought you was a linguist,' Nik replied, frowning. 'So how come you're not understanding your own mother tongue? I said you did well.'

'Ragnar nearly died because of me,' Olvir confessed, miserably, unable to meet the other man's eye.

'No, Gretter almost died,' the Raven corrected him, pointing to Inga's husband. The boar's attack had left him with a fractured wrist and two broken ribs, yet he insisted on riding back to the ring fort rather than allowing them to construct a stretcher for him. 'But then Gretter's a stubborn bastard. I reckon if Hel herself turned up to take him to the next life, he'd say "Fuck off. It's just a scratch.".'

'Your son risked his life because of me,' Olvir said.

'Says who? Maybe he's had a hard day and decided "Fuck it, I'm going to jump in front of a boar." You never know what's going on in another man's head.'

Olvir couldn't help but laugh at that. The Raven smiled. 'You could have run, but you threw your spear and saved his life.'

'After he saved mine.'

'Odin's balls! Who cares who did what first? You saved my son. And that's the version I'll be telling the little Seer when she eats with us tonight.' Olvir felt his face redden even more at mention of Kadlin. Niklaus chuckled gleefully. 'I knew it! I knew you liked her.'

'She should hear the truth,' Olvir countered.

Niklaus looked serious for a moment. 'Did you shit your breeks?'

'What? No!'

'Then you did better than most for your first time. Now stop feeling sorry for yourself, and smile. She's not going to want to kiss you while you've got a face like a slapped arse.'

*

Olvir would have liked to learn how to use the seax, or scramasax, the traditional weapon of his people. The single bladed knife varied in length from a dagger to a short sword, and was a multifunctional tool now widely used throughout the northern lands for skinning deer, chopping vegetables, digging turnips, and anything else that a person may need a knife for. The Saxons, though, had perfected its use in warfare. So synonymous were they with the blade, they had taken their name from it. During his time with the slavers, Olvir had not been permitted to own tools or weapons of any kind. As a free man, working for Ulfrik, he had been unable to afford one.

A spear was the cheapest and most widely available weapon, and the easiest to master. One could be fashioned, if necessary, purely from wood, and even a basic, metal-tipped spear required relatively little in the way of smithcraft when compared to an axe or sword.

Niklaus had gifted Olvir an iron-tipped spear with an ash shaft when he joined the Raven's Kin, and Ragnar had been happy to instruct him in its use.

Olvir was in better mood by the time they returned to the ring fort. The hunt had been invigorating and he felt ready to tackle whatever the day threw at him. He was therefore disappointed when Niklaus advised him to get some sleep.

'Big night, tonight,' Nik said, as they dismounted outside the longhouse. 'Ragnar, fetch Ehmet and see what he can do for Gretter. Then I suggest we all get some rest.'

'I'm fine,' Gretter argued, wincing in pain as they helped him from his horse.

'You'll be finer if you shut up and let someone help. Ragnar, fetch Ehmet,' the Raven instructed. He untied Mad Brown, who had been roped across his horse, and fashioned a crude leash from her bindings. A small boy was playing nearby and he summoned the lad over. 'You look like a capable young man. Can I trust you with an important job?' The boy nodded eagerly. Niklaus stroked his beard, thoughtfully. 'Hmm. I'm not sure,' he deliberated. 'You'll need to be strong, and very sensible, and brave.'

'I am,' the boy said. 'I'm very strong.'

'Ok. I believe you are,' Niklaus crouched down so that

he was at the same eye level as the child. 'I need an official Piglet Wrangler. Someone to take care of Mad Brown while I go have a sleep. Do you think you can do that? She's a very special animal. A gift from the gods themselves.' The boy's eyes widened as he was handed the piglet's leash. He grinned as if he'd been given a great treasure. 'Now, go see about getting her something to eat and drink, and if you do a good job, I'll let you be my Piglet Wrangler again tomorrow.' The boy hurried off with Mad Brown in tow, each looking as wide-eyed as the other.

'That was clever,' Olvir said, admiringly.

Niklaus frowned, uncomprehending. 'Oh, you think I just conned that boy into taking care of my pig.' He shook his head. 'No. That was Frodi. Did you notice his foot?'

'I didn't,' Olvir admitted.

'Well next time you see him, have a sneaky look. He was born with a twisted foot. Means he can't run very fast and the other kids don't always let him play. That doesn't do much for his self-confidence. But now he's my official Piglet Wrangler. That's an important job, so he must be an important man. He knows I trust him, so he's feeling pretty happy and confident at the moment. And, for the rest of the day, he's running around with a wild boar on a rope. Every child here is going to want to be his friend. Today, he's a fucking god.'

'I'm sorry,' Olvir said. 'I misjudged your intention.'

Niklaus clapped him on the back and grinned. 'You're always bloody apologising. Do you know that? I think we need to do some work on your self-confidence. How do you fancy being my official Mead Taster this evening? It's an important job.'

Olvir laughed.

'Come on,' Niklaus said, heading inside the longhouse. 'Let's get some sleep while we have the chance. I'm fucking knackered.'

VENDI

The festivities would last twelve days and nights, with the Solstice Eve being the start of the celebrations. Every man, woman and child would aim to wait up all night and greet the rising sun on the Solstice morn. Not all would succeed. Some, due to their advanced (or tender) years, would succumb to sleep before the sun arose. Others, having quaffed too much mead, and with bellies full after feasting, would be found the next day, slumbering beneath tables or in other unlikely places. Many, though, bolstered by adrenaline or sheer youthful excitement, would make it through the 'shortest night' and be ready to greet Sól's chariot as she rose in the sky.

Vendi spent the morning of the Solstice Eve baking bread

and checking the food supplies to ensure there was enough for tonight's feast. Other members of the Raven's Kin provided apples, cheeses, freshly churned butter, nuts and berries. Inga had taken several of the older children fishing and returned in the afternoon with a plentiful catch which she set about gutting, cleaning and seasoning. Long trestle tables were brought out of the longhouse and set on the grass, beneath the summer sun, with benches for their guests. Large vats of mead and ale, having been made several weeks in advance, were rolled out and set in the shade.

When Ragnar returned with the hunting party, there had been nine boar carcasses to prepare. The sow was skinned and then spit roast, which would take the rest of the day and most of the evening to cook through. Vendi hung the piglets in the store, saving them to be served as broths, or as sliced meat on platters, over the duration of the festival. Then there were vegetables to be dug, cleaned, chopped, and boiled or roasted. Even with Vendi, Inga and Maida working together with five thralls, it was late afternoon before everything was organised, and Vendi had a chance to cleanse her face and dress her hair. She picked scented blossoms and wove them into her braids and chose her brightest beads to wear. Only then did she wake the men folk.

'Look at them,' Vendi said. She and Maida stood, hands on hips, staring down at their sleeping men snoring on the floor. 'One hunt and they think the work is over. It's a good thing us women have some stamina, or nothing would get done around here.'

'I often think it must have been the goddesses who made the world,' Maida mused with a wry smile. 'The gods probably said they were going to, but never got around to it.'

Vendi laughed.

A furious mass of brown bristles streaked through the longhouse, stampeding over the sleeping Ragnar and squealing at the top of its little lungs. It was followed by several small children who were equally as excited.

'What is that?' Vendi demanded as the furry creature raced in circles around the room. 'And what is it doing in here? Out. Out!'

'Sorry, Vendi,' the eldest of the children panted, flush-cheeked and grinning. 'Mad Brown chewed through the rope! Frodi, wait!' As quickly as they had entered, the children and baby boar were gone. Ragnar sat up, rubbing his chest where he had been trampled by tiny trotters. He regarded his wife through sleepy eyes.

'Did you say something, Vend? Do you need me?'

'Time to get washed, my love,' Vendi replied. 'Blessed Solstice.'

★

Typically, Niklaus neglected to mention that he had invited the Völva to join them, so it was a pleasant surprise when Kadlin arrived. She brought a gift of seven posies of fragrant herbs to place on the tables and asked the blessing of the gods for the celebrations. Her tawny hair was more elaborately braided than usual and adorned with the same, sweet smelling herbs as the posies, which perfumed the air as she walked. Despite the obvious effort, she looked drawn and tired.

'It's good to see you, Lady,' Vendi beamed. She had become very fond of the young seer over the past few days. 'Blessed Solstice to you.' She spoke in the language of the Danes, as she knew Kadlin couldn't speak the native tongue of the Saxons in which she usually conversed.

'Blessed Solstice,' the Völva replied, returning the smile. There was an awkward moment as Vendi instinctively moved to hug her friend, then – realising the impropriety of such an action – stopped herself before doing so. 'Can I do anything,' Kadlin asked, politely.

'Yes,' Vendi replied, taking her by the hand and leading her outside to join the others. 'You can sit, and you can eat, and you can drink.'

The Raven's Kin, their families and friends, were gathered on the grass outside the longhouse listening to a skald recite the tale of Máni and Sól, the brother and sister who were the moon and sun. Each raced through the sky on horse drawn chariots, endlessly pursued by the ravenous wolves, Skoll and Hati, who would eventually catch and consume them at Ragnarok, the end of the world.

After the tale, there was singing and dancing. Niklaus volunteered a bawdy song that Vendi considered highly inappropriate, followed by a ballad so sweet, so sad, that it reduced those assembled to tears.

Cuneglas, resplendent in a fine, embroidered tunic, recited an epic poem of his own creation, resulting in much banging of fists on tables and calls for more. He obliged with another three poems, the equal of any bard or skald, and Vendi smiled to see Maida positively glowing with pride at her husband's performance.

The evening was still bright and warm by the time they settled down to feasting. Vendi had a reputation, within the Raven's Kin, for brewing marvellous meads and magnificent ales. Never one to follow the flow, she had experimented with different ingredients and methods over the years and become something of an expert. For the Summer Solstice she created a sweet, floral mead flavoured with marigold and honeysuckle, with a clear, golden colour in honour of Sól's shining rays. For those who preferred a berry mead, she had prepared a heady concoction from a blend of elderberries and strawberries, which had a wonderfully thick consistency that was pleasing to the tongue. It was darker than the floral mead, with a rich, ruby shade. There were three ales, of varying strengths. Vendi also liked to create herbal meads, which – in addition to their superb flavour – had added health benefits when consumed consistently. Honey, the main ingredient of any mead, was known to have many healing qualities and be good for staving off common ailments. It could even be smeared on wounds to prevent infection. When combined with certain herbs, it was possible to brew concoctions that not only tasted delicious but could also be used to treat illnesses and boost vitality. Vendi had learned much about healing herbs, over the past five days, from her new friend. She looked forward to learning more.

The feast went on for most of the evening, as did the entertainment. Mad Brown caused chaos by snuffling beneath the tables for scraps and butting her head at those who didn't drop enough food. One of the dogs tried to muscle in on the action, and she saw it off with a bleeding ear and its tail between its legs much to Niklaus' amusement. Having tasted a little spilled ale, the piglet decided to chase the thrall whose job it was to refill the cups, terrifying the poor woman and making her drop and break the jug.

It was dark by the time the feasting was over. The night was still warm, and the herbal posies provided by Kadlin perfumed the air and cleaned away the smell of food. People began drifting from the tables to sit in cosy groups, or gathered around the large, Solstice fire that had been lit.

'You must meet Ehmet,' Vendi said, when she had the chance to speak with Kadlin again. Sólveig's father was the local healer and had been tending Gretter's injuries today. It was unusual for a man to be accepted as a healer or practitioner of magic. This was considered women's territory and an 'unmanly' pursuit. Men who dabbled in the occult were generally looked down upon and ostracised. Perhaps it was due to the fact that Ehmet came from a different cultural background, or because he physically looked so different to them, but he had been accepted as a healer and shaman by those within the ring fort, and none who needed his services ever had any complaint.

'How is Gretter,' Vendi asked when she finally found the elderly Uyghur. Gretter's wife, Inga, had been absent from the festivities, so Vendi assumed the news was not good.

'Stubborn, stupid and in need of a bath,' Ehmet replied. 'His arm will be fine, but his ribs will never set properly. He should not have insisted on riding home. It did more damage than the boar.'

Vendi thought of Inga and wondered if she would manage to join them for the sunrise. It seemed unlikely.

'Ehmet, I wanted you to meet the Völva, Kadlin Svalasdaughter,' Vendi said, introducing them. 'She'll be leaving us once Solstice has passed and I wanted you two to have a chance to speak.'

Ehmet reached out and gently touched Kadlin's brow with the back of his hand. It was an intimate but respectful gesture, and his face reflected great empathy. 'I am sorry for your suffering, Lady,' he said. 'What will you do now?'

'I'm returning home, to Agder,' Kadlin replied. 'My life is there. My family.'

'And the one who caused this pain for you? He will be there, too?'

'He will,' Kadlin confirmed. Ehmet nodded sagely.

'May I offer some advice, Lady, based on personal experience? And I mean no offence by this. Learn a weapon. Magic cannot stop the thrust of a spear, nor the path of an arrow. If you want your vengeance, make sure you live long enough to deliver it.'

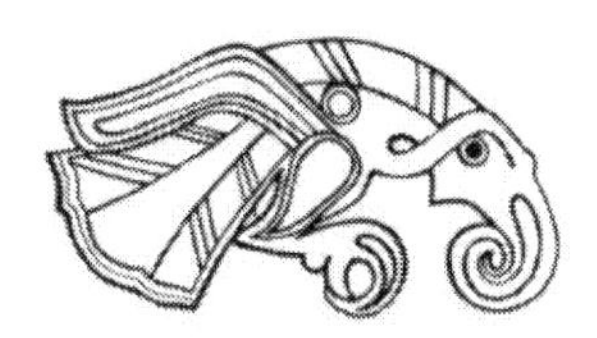

KADLIN

The hov provided by King Sigfrid was modest, yet comfortable, and furnished to meet Kadlin's basic needs. Lisetta, the olive-skinned thrall who prepared her meals and kept the place clean, was only ten years older than Kadlin, but her face was already lined, and her long, dark hair was heavily streaked with grey. She wore it as a single plait, coiled into a knot at the nape of her neck. When Kadlin arrived home in the early hours of the morning, exhausted and chilled having stayed up all night to greet the dawn, she found Lisetta waiting beside the hearth and looking just as tired as her mistress.

'Would you like me to fetch your drink, Lady?'

'I don't think I'll need it today, Lisetta,' Kadlin replied

with a yawn. She had been taking a tea of chamomile flowers and crushed valerian root each night to help her sleep, and to avoid the nightmares that inevitably followed. This morning, though, she wasn't certain she would even make it to the bed before she slept. 'You get some rest. I can see myself to bed,' she instructed. She managed to remove her shoes and jewellery but slept in her clothes as she was simply too tired to undress. It was a deep and dream-filled sleep.

She dreamed she was a Valkyrie, fighting at the side of Odin, the All-father. He handed her an axe and bid her return home to Bramsvik and chop down the first tree that she saw. She climbed the hill to Yrsa's hof and found her grandmother, Aud and Jofrið lying dead beneath the linden tree. Only it wasn't a tree anymore. It was Asbjorn.

He laughed at her. As he did so, the Asbjorn-tree shook, and more dead bodies rained from his branches. Her brother, Ingvar, was amongst them, as were her younger siblings, Leif and Greta. Everyone she had ever cared about fell from the tree as a corpse, and Asbjorn continued to laugh.

Kadlin swung the axe…

⋆

It was afternoon when Kadlin awoke. For the first time since leaving Haithabyr she felt rested and refreshed.

Lisetta was already up and made her a breakfast of elderflower pottage with a cup of nettle tea.

'Will you be needing a meal this evening, Lady,' she asked.

'No, thank you,' Kadlin replied as she savoured the brew. 'King Sigfrid has asked me to celebrate with him tonight. Take the rest of the day as your own, Lisetta. Enjoy the Solstice.' Kadlin pondered her conversation with Ehmet as she ate her breakfast. Her dream confirmed the gods would support her if she tried to avenge her father, but she was troubled by the sight of the dead Völur. Until recently, she had never felt afraid of mortal men. Her status as a Völva gave her protection and she had always taken that for granted. There had never seemed a need to arm herself or learn any defence other than magic. Why swing a sword when you can conjure a curse?

Now, she felt differently.

Niklaus had tried to heal the rift between herself and Olvir last night. He had found her beside the fire and guessed at her thoughts as she watched the flames.

'He feels their loss as you do, Lady,' the Raven had said, gently. 'It's eating him alive that he has caused you extra pain. Can't you forgive?'

Kadlin understood this. She did not say as much, but she had already forgiven Olvir for making her board Sea

Serpent that night. He was only following orders and had probably saved both their lives. What she could not forgive – what she could never explain to anyone else – was that Olvir was the first person to ever make her feel vulnerable and afraid. She had been helpless when he seized her and dragged her back to the ship. She had felt the weakness of her body and realised just how much she relied on the fear of others to keep herself safe. Without that fear she was helpless. It had been a terrifying and humiliating experience, and she could not yet forgive him for that. He had bruised her confidence so badly that she'd failed to stand up to the king. *Give them reason to doubt your strength and they will cease to stand behind you.* Yrsa's wise words had plagued her thoughts these past few days.

Perhaps she would not have given so much weight to Ehmet's advice had she never had that experience. She had thought herself untouchable until now. By the time she had eaten, cleansed her face and re-braided her hair, Kadlin had resolved to speak to Sólveig about where and how to gain weapons training.

The Solstice festivities continued with wrestling matches, Skaldic songs and tales, and games of skill. Kadlin was watching a kubb match when Vendi and Maida asked if she would like to join them collecting flowers and foliage to make head wreaths. She would have liked to see the end of the game, but having friends was still a very new experience, and she was happy to have been invited.

They walked the meadows beyond the ring fort, gathering white marguerites, blue cornflowers and irises, fragrant orchids and elegant summer grasses. There was plenty of greenery for the men at the edge of the woodland. Young oak branches, now bearing acorns, were still pliable enough to be used. There was an abundance of trailing ivy, hazel leaves, and forget-me-nots. The three women filled their baskets and returned to the longhouse of the Raven's Kin.

It seemed like years since Kadlin had sat, in the company of women, and woven a festive head wreath. Memories of her mother made her smile and brought a lump to her throat. She remembered the excitement, as a small child, of wearing her first wreath and attending her first celebration. The sounds and scents came back to her as if it were yesterday. She wiped a tear from her cheek and realised that Maida was staring at her.

'Forgive me,' Kadlin said, smiling reassuringly. 'I was thinking of the first time I wore one of these, and of my mother.'

'You miss her, Lady,' Maida asked, softly.

'Kadlin, please,' Kadlin said. 'Let's not be so formal. Call me Kadlin, at least when it's just us. Let me be a friend here, not a Völva.'

'Is your mother waiting for you at Bramsvik,' Vendi asked.

'No.' It felt strange to talk about this. 'She died trying to birth my brother when I was five. We were alone at the time and I was too young to save her.' She could see empathy in the faces of her friends and felt it radiating from them. Their compassion was comforting. It occurred to Kadlin that she had never discussed that night with anyone outside of the Völur. She had been so young when Svala died that the memories she had of her mother, such as they were, were faded and incomplete. On occasion, a scent or sound stirred a vague remembrance of her, but the image of Svala's face always evaded her, elusive as smoke on the breeze.

'I'm so sorry,' Vendi said.

'That was the first time I ever saw one of the gods,' Kadlin continued. 'Hel claimed them both. She took my mother's hand from mine and carried her, screaming, to the Otherworld. My grandmother found me that night, crouched beside my mother's body, the tiny corpse of my brother between her thighs. It's the last and clearest memory of her that I have.'

'You actually saw the goddess?' Maida looked pale. Kadlin nodded.

'Yes. Just the one time. I've not seen her since and nor do I wish to. She told my mother not to worry – that she wasn't there for me.'

'She spoke?' Vendi's eye were wide in amazement. Kadlin

found it liberating to talk of her life and experiences with people for whom this was not 'normal'.

'In my head. Yes,' she replied.

'Weren't you afraid,' Maida asked.

'Terrifed!' It felt good to admit that. 'I was terrified,' Kadlin repeated. She smiled. 'I'm not supposed to say things like that.'

'But you are not a Völva here,' Vendi said, gently, putting a reassuring hand on Kadlin's arm. 'You are just a woman amongst friends.'

★

The Solstice celebration at the mead hall was more elaborate and formal than the one hosted by Niklaus the previous night. In addition to ales and mead, the king provided jugs of wine, something Kadlin had never tasted before. It was dry and sour to her palette, compared to the honeyed sweetness of mead, and she wondered why wine was so expensive and highly prized. She was lauded as a guest of honour, asked to perform the blessing rite, and she loathed every minute of it. She longed to rejoin her friends and just be Kadlin once again.

King Sigfrid slaughtered his favourite horse as an offering to the gods, asking for a good harvest and fair summer, and the meat was prepared and consumed during the feast along with platters of beef, pork, several fish dishes, fruit, cheeses and vegetables. Horses were highly prized, and the offering of a horse, especially a beloved one, was second only to a human sacrifice.

After the feast there was music, dancing, and competitions. Kadlin found Sólveig watching Kodran in a knife throwing contest. He seemed to be winning.

'Axes, without doubt,' Sólveig replied when asked what weapon she would recommend. She didn't seem at all surprised to be asked the question, and even offered herself as a tutor. 'You won't have the power to wield a sword. It takes years to develop that kind of muscle. A seax would suit you, but against a larger and stronger foe you'd most likely lose. You're too small for a spear. I mean, you could use one well enough, but it wouldn't play to your strengths.'

'I have strengths,' Kadlin asked, sardonically. 'You almost have me convinced not to bother trying.'

'Forgive me, Lady,' Sólveig said, smiling. 'Of course you have strengths. You are small and light, so you should be swift and agile. If not yet, then you will be with training. You need a weapon that exploits this and can be used at close range. Get through their defences, attack, retreat. Kill before they have time to react. A normal axe would be too cumbersome and heavy for you, but these…' She drew the small, throwing axes that were sheathed at her hips, and handed them to Kadlin. 'I think something like these would be perfect for you.'

Kadlin felt a thrill as she held the axes in her hands. They felt right. Each was approximately the length of her elbow to her fingertips. They were light, yet solid. A deadly extension of herself rather than a separate, weighty weapon.

'Close quarter arms that can also be used from a distance,' Sólveig continued. She took one of the axes from Kadlin's hands, turned and hurled it in one swift movement. It embedded itself in a post several feet away. Kadlin's heart raced.

'Will you teach me,' she asked. 'Name your price.'

'This is not a skill you can learn overnight,' Sólveig warned, retrieving the thrown axe. She slipped it back into its leather sheath and held out her hand for its twin. Kadlin reluctantly returned it. Sólveig studied her a moment. 'Give me six weeks,' she suggested. 'Sea Serpent is raiding after the Solstice. We head west and will return by next harvest. Come with me. Join my crew. I will train you every day and I give my oath you will return as a warrior.'

Six weeks! She had hoped to be back in Bramsvik by then. Kadlin's brow furrowed as she weighed her options. She thought again of how easily she had been overpowered by Olvir, and how weak and terrified she had felt. She would never give anyone the chance to make her feel that way again. Although her heart ached for home, and for the people she had left there, she knew with certainty that she would regret allowing this opportunity to pass.

'And your price?'

'My price,' Sólveig replied, 'is that you work as a member of the crew. I'm one hand short now Gretter is injured, and I don't have room for passengers. You want to learn, then I will teach you. But you earn your place aboard my ship.'

Kadlin thought of how the crew of The Ox had reacted to her presence, and their resentment of her. They had not been willing to treat her as an equal, and it hadn't been fair to expect it of them.

'Your crew will not accept a Völva as one of them,' she said.

'Then you have some decisions to make, Lady,' Sólveig replied.

★

Kadlin's heart was pounding the next day when she called upon King Sigfrid. She took a moment to compose herself before entering the mead hall, summoning thoughts of her ancestors to give herself courage.

'Are you enjoying the Solstice, Lady,' the king said, smiling, when he saw her.

'I am, thank you,' she replied. 'Though Sól is fierce this

year.'

She had questioned Lisetta last night and discovered that she was usually a house thrall to King Sigfrid's wife. Lisetta said there had been no rain for several weeks, and the king was under pressure from local jarls who were concerned about the crops. The sacrifice of his best horse had been an attempt to placate them. Kadlin hoped to use this knowledge to her advantage.

'I've come to offer a trade,' she began, accepting the cup of weak ale that he handed her. 'I find myself in need of some items, but without the means to purchase them, and you are in need of rain but without the means to produce it. It seems to me that we are each potentially able to solve the other's problem.' She took a sip of her drink, allowing him time to digest her words. Sigfrid raised a hand and motioned for the room to be cleared. He waited until they were alone before responding.

'You can guarantee rain?'

'There are no guarantees with the gods, Lord King. They do as they wish. But I can make offerings on your behalf and I can try to draw the rain here. I can also speak with the land wights about the crops.'

The king ruminated a moment. 'And the items you require?'

'I shall be leaving aboard Sea Serpent in ten days,' Kadlin

replied, trying to keep her voice calm. 'Sólveig tells me we shall return by the next harvest. As you are no doubt aware, the possessions I had – other than what you see – were destroyed in the fire at Haithabyr. I'm in need of new clothing and some weapons. A set of throwing axes, to be precise.'

'What does a Völva need with weapons,' King Sigfrid asked.

'Do we have an agreement,' Kadlin replied, holding his gaze.

'You make it rain within a week and you shall have your clothing and your weapons. Lisetta will know who to see.'

'I can give you no guarantees,' Kadlin said.

'Rain within a week,' the king repeated. 'That is the agreement.' Kadlin's heart thundered, but she thought of Yrsa and stood her ground.

'I can give you my oath that I will do everything in my power to bring you rain and protect your harvest,' she began, 'but if the gods wish a drought for you they will not be persuaded by my intervention. You noticed my tears when I first arrived here, but don't mistake grief for weakness. I am a strong ally to have, King Sigfrid, and if rain can be brought here, I will do it.'

The king studied her, thoughtfully. After what felt like an

age, he asked her to wait and disappeared into one of the private chambers. He returned moments later with a weighty pouch of hack silver which he gave to her.

'I've offended you, Lady,' he said, solemnly. 'I have the highest regard for the Völur, and I meant no disrespect. This will be more than enough to pay for what you need. Please accept the rest as an apology.'

Kadlin waited until early evening, when the sun was weaker, before setting out into the fields to perform her magic. She brought with her a pitcher of water, her knife, a switch of willow and a piece of fruit. She placed the fruit in the centre of a field and left it as an offering to the land wights. She could see them peering at her through the barley stalks, and hear their whispers, but they didn't make themselves known and so she respectfully left them in peace. They had heard her plea for a good harvest. If they chose not to speak with her directly then that was their choice.

A slight breeze began to blow, cool and refreshing, as Kadlin set the pitcher down. She had given a lot of thought to which god she should sacrifice to, and what the sacrifice should be. She could ask Freyr, brother of Freya, Lord of the Elves and God of the Harvest. She could have asked Thor, Protector and Defender, and God of Thunder. Instead she sent a plea to Odin. He had many names and many faces. He was the Wanderer, the Poet, the All-Father, the God of War and the Hanged

God. He was also the Bringer of Rain.

Kadlin took her knife and carefully carved the symbol for 'water' into the ground. She poured just enough water over the symbol to soak the ground without erasing the mark, then set the pitcher down.

'Odin,' she called. 'Bringer of Rain I call upon you to let the rains flow. Drench the earth with the gift of rain so the land will flourish.' She dipped the willow switch into the pitcher three times, each time flicking water into the air so that it fell upon her face and shoulders as a light shower. She then repeated this twice more. Three times three – the number of Odin. 'I offer myself as sacrifice. For the next six weeks I will dedicate my life to you, The Wanderer and God of War. I will perform no magic. I shall use no divination tools. I will travel and devote myself to the study of weapons and warfare.'

Kadlin thrust her right hand toward the sky, reaching out with her senses to the small clouds so high above. She closed her eyes, feeling the drops of water on her skin from the willow switch, and searching for moisture within the clouds. When she found it, she focused on intensifying that feeling. She conjured images in her mind of great, grey storm clouds, swollen with rain. When the vision was so intense that she could actually feel vapour on her fingertips, she stooped to press her left palm on the ground over the water symbol. One hand stretched to the sky, the other touching the earth. 'All-father,' she cried, 'you see my heart. You know how much I want to return to my home and family. I sacrifice this for the next six weeks to be yours instead. Mold me, Odin. Make me your weapon and I will have my revenge in your name.'

Pain shot through her as if she had been struck by lightning. Her left palm was rooted to the earth and her right was being pulled upward, stretching her muscles until she thought they would snap. All the strength was sapped from her body in an instant. She collapsed on the ground and let darkness claim her.

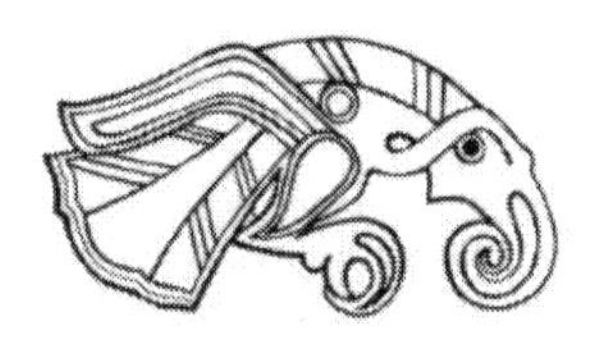

SÓLVEIG

It had been two weeks since her conversation with the Völva, and Sólveig had started to ready her ship and crew for the voyage. They would be raiding to the west, along the shores of Frankia and beyond, but their departure had been delayed due to a sudden and unexpected rainstorm that lasted several days. Gretter was still recovering from the injuries he sustained during the Solstice boar hunt. He could neither fight nor row and so was of no use to her at the moment. Inga had wanted to stay behind and take care of her husband, but Gretter would not hear of it. At first, he had refused to accept that he was too unwell to raid with them but conceded when Niklaus threatened to have him physically restrained if he tried to board.

'Risk your own life if you want to,' the Raven had warned. 'It's none of my business if you want to go tempting the gods like you do. But I won't keep my peace when your stubbornness puts the lives of others at risk. Sit down, or I shall put you down and have you bound until they've sailed.'

Sólveig was pleased, but surprised, to find the Völva ready and waiting beside the ship. She almost didn't recognise her. Instead of her fine dress, Kadlin wore linen breeks, soft leather boots and a blood red tunic. Over the tunic was a fitted, sleeveless vest of woven leather, and a belt hung at her small hips, holstering a pair of beautiful, ornate throwing axes. The handles were oak, and the bearded, iron blades were inscribed with an intricate, knotwork design of two battling beasts. Her long hair was elaborately braided to keep it from her face, and Sólveig noticed a small, hag stone had been woven into her braids along with the bead and feather she usually wore. Beside her, on the dock, was an oaken sea chest inscribed with a bindrune.

'There's something different about you, Lady,' Sólveig teased.

'There's no Lady here, Sólveig,' Kadlin responded with a smile. 'For as long as you have me, I am Kadlin Ulfriksdaughter. Nothing more.'

'Then you'd best get used to calling me Captain,' Sólveig replied. She addressed the crew when they were all assembled. 'For the duration of this voyage,' she said, 'this woman is no longer a Völva. She is to be treated no differently than anyone else. If you wish to show her respect, do so by honouring her wishes and accepting this fact. She is Kaldin Ulfriksdaughter and she is here to learn.'

Sólveig expected Kadlin to quickly tire of being treated as 'one of the crew'. In her experience, those with power rarely gave it up for long. To her surprise, the girl seemed to thrive, throwing herself into every task and even making friends aboard ship. She and Vendi became close as sisters, and Sólveig was proud to see her shipmates had taken her instructions to heart.

Kadlin had learned little during her time aboard The Ox. She had no idea how to steer a ship, how to navigate, or even how to raise or fold a sail. She was fascinated by the sun stone used to locate Sól on a cloudy day.

'It feels so good to breathe the sea air again,' Kadlin said on their second day, as she leaned over the hull to watch a school of dolphins.

'Don't lean so far or you'll be breathing sea water,' Kodran cautioned, with a grin. Kadlin laughed, a sound Sólveig had never expected to hear from the dour-faced passenger of their previous voyage. Kodran had been reluctant to accept her as one of the crew, but even he was won over by her enthusiasm and eagerness to learn. She was, Sólveig thought to herself, an entirely different person to the woman who had been carried aboard Sea Serpent just three weeks ago. That woman had been sullen and morose, consumed with grief and anger, and had kept to herself. As Kadlin Ulfriksdaughter, although still grieving, she was bright and cheerful, and full of passion.

It made no sense to attack their own neighbours and countrymen, so they were at sea for ten days before their first raid. During this time Kadlin managed to learn the basics of how to sail a ship and began to pick up the Saxon language from the crew. She asked about the differences in build between the snekkja and her father's knarr and seemed intrigued by the design. Each night, when they put ashore to eat and sleep, Sólveig trained her in how to use an axe. Foremost, she taught her several grips so that the weapons could be wielded without being easily knocked from her grasp. Then they moved on to defensive moves, how to use the bearded edge to drag down an opponent's shield, and finally Sólveig taught her how to attack.

Kadlin was a keen student and wasn't discouraged by mistakes. Instead, she took them as a personal challenge, and determined to do better each time. She was fit enough, but lacking in stamina, and hadn't yet developed the appropriate muscles. Sólveig set her physical tasks every morning, and it wasn't long before Kadlin had the lean, hard body of a warrior.

Initially, they put her ashore before mounting a raid and returned for her later. Sólveig instructed her to use this time to train with her weapons and Kadlin soon became proficient at wielding the two together, although her aim still needed work when throwing them.

'There is no time to think when you're fighting for your life,' Sólveig told her. 'Instinct takes over, and you simply react. That's why it's so important to practise, and practise, and practise. Your body may be ready, but your mind is not. You need to train until your instincts are always right, and you don't need to think. It must become a reflex.'

Kadlin made up for her lack of participation in the raids by assuming the duty of cooking for the crew. She was always able to find some wild herb to add flavour to the dishes, and often – when they returned to the inlet or cove where they had left her – they found she had already trapped rabbits, birds or fish and begun to cook the meal.

They were on their return journey, more than a month after leaving Ingisbruk, before Sólveig felt Kadlin was ready to join a raid. She discussed it with Kodran, her second in command, before speaking to the girl.

'If you say she is ready then she is ready,' Kodran shrugged. 'I trust your judgement on her skill. But how do we know she won't lose her breakfast when it comes to the kill?'

'How do we know that of anyone,' Sólveig asked. 'There's no way to prepare her for this. She has the skills. It's up to her to decide if she has the courage to use them.'

Kadlin was strangely muted when Sólveig told her she would be joining the next raid. She had expected excitement, or nervousness, but not silence. It worried her. 'What's the problem,' she asked. 'I thought this is what you wanted. What you've been training for.'

'This is different,' Kadlin replied. 'When I'm training, I see Asbjorn. I see his face, and think of what he did, and I take that rage out on the target. But these people... they've done nothing to me.'

'They're Franks,' Sólveig said sternly. 'They've done plenty. Every man and woman aboard Sea Serpent has a story like yours, and the Franks are responsible. Ask your friend, Olvir.'

'What about Olvir,' Kadlin asked, frowning. Sólveig sighed and shook her head.

'It's not my story to tell,' she said, 'but you should ask him one day. Everyone has their own Asbjorn, Kadlin. Everyone.'

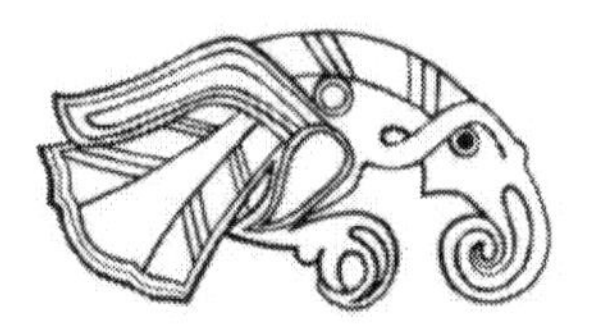

KADLIN

Kadlin was woken by Vendi in the early hours of the morning while it was still dark. The faintest glimmer of light could be seen on the horizon, but the birds were already filling the air with song. Vendi put a finger to her lips. *Quiet.*

They had spent the night at an inlet a short distance south of a coastal monastery. Sólveig was sure they would find much silver and gold there and meet little resistance. The plan was to row Sea Serpent up the coast under cover of darkness and attack while the monks were at morning prayers. Better to wait for them to gather in one place voluntarily than waste time and effort rounding them up.

The crew packed up quickly and quietly and slid the ship

silently into the sea. They used the oars to row Sea Serpent closer, allowing the snekkja to hug the land rather than sailing further out to catch the wind. Three weeks ago, this short time spent rowing would have had Kadlin's body screaming in pain. Now, though, she felt the muscles of her back, stomach, legs and arms working together, and found the task a simple one.

The sun was a white gold blaze and had just crested the skyline by the time they beached the ship on the shore. They followed Sólveig and Kodran, scrambling up a low bank that offered a view of the monastery gates. The faint, melodic sound of chanted prayers could be heard coming from the stone building.

The hairs pricked on the nape of Kadlin's neck. She was overwhelmed by a sense of dread and a feeling that something was very wrong here. She scoured the monastery for signs of danger but saw nothing amiss. And yet...

'We need to leave,' she warned in a whisper.

'Calm your nerves,' Vendi replied, soothingly. 'Stay beside me and Ragnar.'

'No,' Kadlin said, a little louder. 'We need to leave. Now.'

'Find your courage,' Kodran rumbled. He and Sólveig drew their weapons and began to creep forward.

In her mind's eye, Kadlin saw the huge, two headed eagle from the vision she'd had the day Thorvald One Eye was killed. The great, black bird whose shadow had covered the land, who had attacked her while she was a falcon, and from whom she had only escaped by plummeting into the ocean. It terrified her! Kadlin grabbed a stick and hastily sketched it on the ground.

'What does this mean,' she asked Vendi, urgently. 'A double-headed eagle. A huge, black bird. What does this mean to you?' Vendi glanced at the image.

'That's the crest of Charlemagne,' she replied.

So much had happened since Kadlin had sought answers from the gods that day. It seemed a lifetime ago that she'd asked Olvir to watch over her while she journeyed to meet them. Now she understood their warning.

'Wait!' Kadlin ran after Sólveig, seizing her by the arm.

'Leave if your courage has failed you,' Kodran hissed, angrily, pulling her away. Instinctively, Kadlin grabbed his wrist, turned her back, and used his own weight and momentum to flip him over and bring him to the ground. It was a move Sólveig had taught her in the very first week and Kodran was not expecting it.

'What the fuck is wrong with you,' he growled, angrily, getting to his feet.

'Charlemagne,' Kadlin gasped, pointing. 'I don't know

why, but this place is defended. If we don't leave now, we will die.' Sólveig shushed them both and gave a signal for everyone to stop, and to be silent. They waited for what seemed like an eternity until the prayers ended. Then, on the air, no longer hidden by the chanting, came the unmistakable nicker of horses. A lot of horses. Sólveig threw a sharp glance at Kodran.

'Soldiers!'

The atmosphere changed, instantly. What had been a stealthy, predatory approach now became a fearful and hasty retreat. They scrambled back toward the beach, racing across the dunes to where Sea Serpent waited. Kadlin tripped, but felt Ragnar's arm around her, lifting her back on her feet.

Behind them, an alarm was raised. Kadlin heard shouts, the crash of the monastery gates being thrown open, followed by the galloping of hooves and the baying of hounds.

'All hands,' Sólveig cried. 'Push!'

They each leant their weight to the ship, pushing Sea Serpent back to the water. After the initial shove, she slid relatively swiftly down the shingles and into the sea. Kodran and Ragnar waded out, continuing to push while the rest of the crew clambered over the side.

Kadlin grabbed an oar and began to row. Getting over the

first few waves was the hardest, but once they cleared the shore and Kodran and Ragnar climbed aboard, they quickened the pace. Kadlin saw a swarm of mounted soldiers flood the beach. The sun was still low in a sapphire sky, and the flaming arrows that flew toward them looked like shooting stars. Most fell with a hiss into the water, but others hit the ship with a terrifying thud, and Sólveig yelled at Kadlin and Inga to ditch their oars and put out the flames. Kadlin couldn't help but think of her father and the crew of The Ox as she crawled around the deck stamping out fires before they could spread.

Kodran cried out as an arrow pierced his leg. He slapped the flames out with his hands and continued to row, gritting his teeth through the pain. Eventually, all had been extinguished, and they were far enough out to sea to be beyond range of the archers. Despite having seen no other ships, Sólveig didn't want to risk the chance that they may be being pursued, so they put further out to sea and hoisted the sail as soon as they were able.

Kadlin examined Kodran's leg. The arrow had nicked the muscle of his calf, but the wound was shallow and slight. The greater damage had been done by the flames, and the skin of his calf and both palms was blistered and burned. If she'd had her herb pouches with her, Kadlin would have been able to give him something for the pain and apply a compress to help the wounds heal. Without them, she felt helpless, and began to regret leaving them behind at the ring fort with her cloak and staff.

'What do you need,' Sólveig asked, crouching beside them.

'I need herbs, and fresh water,' Kadlin replied.

'No,' Kodran saw the look on Sólveig's face and shook his head. 'We can't risk it.' Kadlin knew he was right. They needed to put as much distance as possible between themselves and the monastery. Instead, she cut the burned fabric of his breeks away from his leg and bathed his wounds with salt water regularly throughout the day. Without her herbs, she was risking infection, but the sea salt would speed the healing process and help to limit the amount of scarring.

Sól's chariot was on a downward arc by the time the captain gave the order to set ashore. The crew were hot and tired, having rowed beneath the summer sun for most of the day. Sólveig sent Ragnar in search of fresh water to refill their supplies while she and Inga went hunting. Kadlin and Vendi harvested what herbs they could find, including large quantities of plantain which grew in abundance near the shore. They selected the smaller, fresher leaves, which could not only be cooked as a nutritious addition to a meal, but also helped prevent infection and had exceptional healing and pain-relieving qualities.

Kadlin cleansed Kodran's wounds with fresh water when they returned to the ship and made him a plantain tea for the pain. She bound the burns with leaves from the plant, and he seemed more comfortable once she had done so.

'Thank you, Lady,' he said gratefully. She noted his return to formality.

'Kadlin,' she reminded him. Kodran shook his head.

'You have a gift, Lady, and a calling,' he said, solemnly. 'Don't turn your back on it. You saved our lives today.' His words upset her. He had not intended it, but they had that effect all the same. She had enjoyed being Kadlin Ulfriksdaughter, shipmate, fighter and friend. She knew it was over, though, when Inga returned with a brace of rabbits and refused to let her cook.

'No, Lady,' Inga said, respectfully. 'You have done enough.'

Vendi noticed her dejection and brought her a cup of nettle tea. She sat beside her in silence for a while before asking about her mood.

'Why so low?'

'I have enjoyed this,' Kadlin replied. 'This life. The ocean. Even these.' She touched the axes. It had been a liberating and educational experience and she wasn't ready for it to end.

'Why do you think you need to make a choice,' Vendi asked, curiously.

'I don't,' Kadlin said. 'I have no choice. I never had a

choice. I was deluding myself to think otherwise.'

'We don't always have to be one thing or the other, Lady,' the flame-haired Celt said in her lilting voice. 'Sometimes we're only complete when we are both.'

★

Kodran's wounds were healing well by the time they arrived back at Ingisbruk. He would always bear the scars, but his pain was less, and he had no trouble walking. The raids had gone well, and the crew were happy. A percentage would be due to King Sigfrid, but Sólveig put it to a vote, and everyone agreed that the seer deserved an equal share of the profit.

'We would likely all be dead if not for you,' Sólveig said. 'You earned your place on my ship. I'd be happy to have you sail with us again.'

'I would like that,' Kadlin replied, 'but I need to get home.'

'Ah, Asbjorn.' Sólveig grinned. 'I suspect he won't live to see another winter.'

'It's not just him,' Kadlin admitted. 'I miss my family. My grandmother.' So much had happened since she'd left Yrsa, Aud and Jöfrið at Tromø. Her gut said they were still alive, but she had lost her connection with them and that worried her greatly. She wondered if Ingvar was a father yet, and whether she was aunt to a nephew or niece.

'At least you can pay your own way back to Bramsvik now,' Sólveig added, handing Kadlin two saddlebags containing her share of the plunder. 'You don't need to wait for King Sigfrid.' Kadlin took the bags gratefully. It was easily sufficient to buy passage home, with enough left over to replace the ox Yrsa had sacrificed, buy another horse and ensure they had food through the winter.

Before returning to the ring fort, Kadlin asked at the dock regarding traders or fishermen heading to Agder. There was one ship going that way, with another expected in the next few weeks. Kadlin spoke with the captain of the vessel and arranged to leave with them in two days. She left him with a hefty deposit and his assurance that a space would be saved for her.

'I'll miss you, Lady,' Vendi said. She was surprised when Kadlin hugged her, but not nearly as surprised as Ragnar when she hugged him. The big man froze as if expecting retribution from the gods at any moment. There were tears on Kadlin's cheeks when she let him go. Much as she yearned to return to the routine of her old life, she would miss the companionship of her friends.

Solveig and Kodran took the tribute to King Sigfrid, giving permission for the crew to find their families. Inga was eager to see Gretter again. He should have recovered from his encounter with the boar by now, and six weeks apart had been too much for her.

'Will you eat with us tonight,' Vendi asked, as she and Ragnar walked Kadlin to her hov. 'I'm sure Niklaus will want to see you.'

'He'll be very interested to hear what you saw at the monastery,' Ragnar added. Kadlin was exhausted, and wanted nothing more than to cleanse the sea salt from her skin and go to bed, but she'd had a while to think things over during her time aboard Sea Serpent and realised that she owed Olvir an apology. Her behaviour toward him had been unfair and had undoubtedly caused him extra pain. She wanted to make things right between them if she could.

'I will be there,' she agreed, 'but first I must sleep.'

Lisetta seemed happy to see her and commented on the difference in Kadlin's physique. She fetched a pitcher of water, a bowl and cloth, and prepared a drink while her mistress washed. Kadlin had only just sat down when there came a loud knocking at the door. She was alarmed when Vendi entered looking distressed.

'They've gone,' Vendi said, barely holding back tears.

'Who has gone?' Kadlin motioned for Lisetta to pour a cup of ale for her guest. 'Sit down. Tell me what's happened.'

'The Raven's Kin,' Vendi said, taking a seat. 'They've

gone. Sigfrid sent them back to Saxony soon after we sailed. I thought the gods cautioned against it? Nik told us you cast the runes and were told we should wait until after winter.'

'That's true,' Kadlin confirmed. 'I was very clear with the king about that.'

'We're going after them,' Vendi told her, sniffing. 'Ragnar and Inga are sorting some horses and we'll leave at first light. I wanted to let you know, and to say goodbye. Safe journey home, Lady. I will miss you.'

Kadlin was furious after her friend had gone. How could King Sigfrid be so foolish? She was pleased she had opted not to join Sólveig and Kodran when they delivered the king's percentage. If she had heard this news from him, she doubted she would have been able to stay quiet. Lisetta fixed her a light supper, but Kadlin found she had no appetite. She retired early to bed that evening, and her dreams were restless.

She was back in the meadow where she had met Freya. The ground was still littered with frost-covered corpses. A battlefield of white, made more sinister by the silence. This time, though, she recognised their faces. Niklaus, Cuneglas, Maida, Vendi, Ragnar... they were all here. All the Raven's Kin. None had survived.

Kadlin ran to the oak tree at the centre of the meadow. The lone warrior was sat beneath it, as before, features frozen in death. Kadlin dropped to her knees and wept as she looked at Olvir.

★

The sun had not yet risen when Kadlin left the hov the following morn. There was a chill to the air despite the season, and she wore her blue cloak over her tunic and leather vest. She carried her staff in one hand, and had the saddlebags slung over her shoulder.

Vendi, Ragnar and Inga were preparing to leave when she found them.

'We'll be needing another horse,' she said.

Printed in Great Britain
by Amazon